SWORDS IN EXILE: THE RAKEHELLY ADVENTURES
OF CLEVE AND D'ENTREVILLE, VOLUME 2

Kingdom Come

BY MARTIN MCCALL

*Henry Rides the Danger Trail: The Complete
Tales of Sheriff Henry, Volume 3*

BY W.C. TUTTLE

Z is for Zombie

BY THEODORE ROSCOE

*The Bait and the Trap: The Complete
Adventures of Tizzo, Volume 2*

BY MAX BRAND

Minions of Mars

BY WILLIAM GRAY BEYER

*Men With No Master: The Complete
Adventures of Robin the Bombardier*

BY ROY DE S. HORN

The Torch

BY JACK BECHDOLT

*King of Chaos and Other Adventures:
The Johnston McCulley Omnibus*

BY JOHNSTON MCCULLEY

The Blind Spot

BY AUSTIN HALL & HOMER EON FLINT

SWORDS IN EXILE

THE RAKEHELLY ADVENTURES OF CLEVE AND D'ENTREVILLE, VOLUME 2

MURRAY R. MONTGOMERY

ILLUSTRATED BY

V.E. PYLES & STANLEY MAXWELL

STEEGER BOOKS • 2019

PUBLISHING HISTORY

"Blades of Intrigue" originally appeared in the December 7, 1940 issue of *Argosy* magazine (Vol. 304, No. 1). Copyright © 1940 by The Frank A. Munsey Company. Copyright renewed © 1968 and assigned to Steeger Properties, LLC. All rights reserved.

"Swords in Exile" originally appeared in the July 26, August 2, 9, 16, 23, and 30, 1941 issues of *Argosy* magazine (Vol. 309, No. 4–Vol. 310, No. 3). Copyright © 1941 by The Frank A. Munsey Company. Copyright renewed © 1968 and assigned to Steeger Properties, LLC. All rights reserved.

"About the Author" originally appeared in the August 2, 1941 issue of *Argosy* magazine (Vol. 309, No. 5). Copyright © 1941 by The Frank A. Munsey Company. Copyright renewed © 1968 and assigned to Steeger Properties, LLC. All rights reserved.

Visit steegerbooks.com for more books like this.

TABLE OF CONTENTS

BLADES OF INTRIGUE

Yes, rakehellies, 'tis a quiet corner of France. For quick poison and the silent knife best serve a traitor's dark design

CHAPTER I

TOO EASY TO BE SAFE

CAPITAINE PHILIPPE CORDEAU had no liking for Cleve and d'Entreville, but he could not permit them to get themselves killed. After all, they were officers in the Cardinal's Guard, and he its *commandant.*

Consequently, the moment he heard the news he went to the tavern known as Les Trois Chiens and found them at their favorite table, ringed by plates and tankards. D'Entreville was reading one of his poems; Cleve, covertly flirting with a blond barmaid. The grog-room was deserted except for three troopers of the King's Horse.

Cordeau pulled up a chair and sat down. He said: "I have heard talk concerning the Girard brothers, *messieurs.* I want to know if you're going through with it?"

D'Entreville looked annoyed. He was a tall man garbed rakishly in maroon; thigh-high riding boots and a black cape. He had thin, even, lips; hair like rippled pitch, and an aristo-cratic hawkish nose. He was gallant looking, well bred. And a devil for trouble.

He lowered the manuscript he had been reading, hitched his basket-hilt rapier closer to his side and smoothed the crispness of his clipped mustache.

"We're going through with it," he agreed shortly. "The Girards warned us to stay clear of Hôtel de Rohan; called us cheats and braggarts, and all by note. It will be interesting to see if they'll say it to our faces."

1

Driven back, the fellow hurried a candlestick at Cleve,
while d'Entreville was busy in the next room

Cordeau jerked angrily at the bristle of his black spade-beard. He had expected that sort of an answer from Guy d'Entreville. But, he knew something about this affair that neither of these two rakehellies realized.

"Mark this, *messieurs,*" he said. "The Girards are excellent swordsmen. Not only that, they enjoy the full patronage of le Duc d'Orleans, the King's brother. Rumor has it that their blades will be poisoned. This duel is a trap, *messieurs,* and as your superior officer, I forbid you to go to the Hôtel de Rohan!"

Cleve pulled an impudently tilted nose out of an ale tankard. Cleve was the unpredictable one. He had a deceptive nonchalance, a casual manner, which was offset by sudden merry-mad outbursts. He was of slighter build than d'Entreville; two inches shorter; clean-shaven and chestnut-haired.

"Faith, Cordeau," he remarked mildly. "You have authority only during business hours remember?"

Cordeau cursed, but there was nothing he could do. Somewhere in the city a clock tolled twelve slowly. D'Entreville listened to it and nodded. Then, he folded the poem-manuscript into his sash and stood up.

"Thank you anyway, *mon capitaine*," he said, "but if we stay away from Hôtel de Rohan, every bravo in Paris will question our courage."

He pulled his broad-brimmed hat tightly over one ear, adjusted his sword-belt and loosened the blade in its sheath. Cordeau watched him sourly.

"*Pecaire!* Don't thank me, you young fool. *Monseigneur le Cardinal* told me to warn you."

Cleve chuckled, pushed aside his tankard and stood up. He

took the rapier on the bench beside him and belted it on. He did it carefully. "I didn't actually think you were concerned over our health," he told Cordeau and looked at his companion. "All set, Kitten?"

D'Entreville's dark eyes flashed. The sobriquet The Cardinal's Kitten had been pinned on him months before, because of his youth and his ability to scratch adversaries first with verse and then with his sword. But to him, it sounded derisive. He loathed it.

"Sangodemi! Don't call me Kitten," he snapped and went to the door. "Come on!"

They reached the center of the street, paused for a moment, then turned to the right and commenced walking.

UNDER HIS tan d'Entreville looked pale. To go up against two excellent swordsmen was one thing—to go up against two poisoned blades, another. One small cut and the business was over. His face was waxen, but his eyes were smoldering angrily.

Beside him Richard Cleve moved deliberately, placing one boot carefully before the other. He held his head rigid, seeming to stare straight down the middle of the street. But he wasn't missing anything. His brown eyes held a chill alertness that belied his amiable smile. As he walked his gauntleted fingers brushed the hilt of his sword. Merely brushed it.

The street was almost a hundred rods long. It was comparatively deserted. The people used to traversing it had heard about the duel and were giving it a wide berth. Tense, bated, silence pervaded, broken only by the gritty scrape of their footsteps.

The Girards might choose to appear at any point, but logically they'd wait until they found out how far Cleve and d'Entreville would dare. Nevertheless, the two rakehellies weren't taking chances. They came on slowly, one step at a time; shoulder to shoulder, plumes rippling slightly, swordhilts twinkling in the sun.

Hôtel de Rohan was halfway down—fifty rods or so from

the door-sill of Les Trois Chiens, but it took them ten minutes to reach it. And then they met the Girards.

The Girards were twins who even dressed alike. They wore goatees beneath spiked mustaches and possessed the coldest black eyes Cleve and d'Entreville had even seen. Their swords were bared, held aslant across their boots.

"Did you not receive our note, *messieurs?*" one of them asked.

Cleve grinned. He pinched his nose slightly at the tip and cuffed back his hat-brim. "Why yes, among other things," he said. "Understand you lads like to play safe."

"What do you mean?"

Cleve's fingers curled about the brightness of his hilt. He had been doing a lot of thinking since Cordeau's appearance. He realized that half of the powerful anti-Richelieu clique at Court wanted d'Entreville and himself out of the way. Especially, le Duc d'Orleans. Cleve and d'Entreville had been thorns in that worthy's side for a quite a while. It would be like him to equip the Girards with poison-smeared blades. But this affair had gone too far for him to back down now. It had to be settled.

"You play safe with poisoned steel," he said.

The Girards' swords came up. Quite clearly, the brothers were startled. "*Sandiou!* You swine, we'll—"

Cleve drew. His eyes darted to d'Entreville and then to the Girards. Guy would follow his lead. They had that intuitive coördination of men whose friendship had been born of action. He laughed and a lie sprang readily to his lips.

"Well," he said, "we desired that this meeting be on an equal footing—so we've poisoned our blades also. Now come on, you snakes, and taste it!"

But after that the Girards wanted no part of the duel. They fled howling.

LATER, CARDINAL RICHELIEU, sitting in the sober confines of his palace library, eyed the two cavaliers before him and frowned. Cordeau had brought them in, abetted by a pistol and squad of ten husky guardsmen.

"Not satisfied by making the brothers Girard fly," the Cardinal said coldly, "you two rakehellies had to pursue them through the crowded salon of Hôtel de Rohan, catch them in the garden and cast them into a fountain before the very eyes of their friends. *Messieurs,* you have managed to create a scandalous display of roguery, discourtesy and conduct unbecoming to gentlemen of my Guard!"

He paused, out of breath. His fine pallor was flushed, giving his delicately chiseled features a sharper, more vital cast. The ornate clock on the mantle behind his desk chimed one.

"But that isn't the chief reason for my displeasure," he resumed. "Such conduct is common with rascals such as yourselves. When *monsieur le capitaine* told you about the trickery and warned you to stay away from the *hôtel,* why didn't you obey?"

"A point of honor, *monseigneur,*" d'Entreville said.

The Cardinal sighed. He relaxed against the red plush of his chair and considered them wearily.

First there was Guy, le Comte d'Entreville. An impulsive young fool, hasty to act and quick to regret, but possessing an innate conscientiousness which made him trustworthy and loyal.

Then there was Lord Richard Cleve, the easy-mannered Englishman who had been exiled from his native land because of his fondness for speaking the truth at the wrong time—especially since the truth had concerned the King's favorite and a missing ten thousand pounds in tax-money.

He and d'Entreville made a Devil's pair. They argued violently with each other when not engaged in arguing with a common enemy. But they got things done, although at times Richelieu was inclined to wonder whether this virtue wasn't outweighed by their tremendous capacity for nuisance.

"A point of honor, eh?" he said to Guy. *"Ma foi!* With half the assassins in Paris being hired to kill you, you expose yourself because of honor. Brainy, *monsieur!* Extremely so!" He leaned forward. "Mark this, *messieurs.* Although, you be utter villains I'll not have you murdered by the powerful nobles who oppose me. Beneath your streak of wildness lies the courage and resourcefulness that shall some day make you true servants of France!"

He stood up, a slim, dynamic figure in a trailing red robe. With fingers interlaced, he began to pace thoughtfully.

"Monsieur le Duc d'Orleans hates you for wrecking his coup at Beaucaire. Vendome loathes you for exposing his plot against me. Prince Conde has neither forgiven or forgotten Grenoble. *Ma foi!* Do you realize that this is the fifth attempt to dispose of you in as many days, *messieurs?*"

Cleve shifted and smiled slightly. "I wouldn't vouch for our popularity in certain circles, *monseigneur,*" he said.

RICHELIEU DIDN'T speak for a moment. On the oak-paneled wall beside him was a huge map of Royal France. Certain sections of it were shaded—estates and provinces of noblemen who maintained the feudal right to levy private taxes, to raise personal armies, and to threaten secession should the Crown displease them. In short, the territories that must be won over or subdued before France could become a strong nation, free at last of its medievalism and united under one leader—the King.

It was to this end that Richelieu had been working. But the nobles did not take easily to being stripped of their power. They hated him and were constantly brewing intrigues to dispose of him.

But at the immediate moment, Richelieu wasn't concerned with their plotting. His dark eyes swept down the length of the map and came to rest on a small shaded section nestling on the Spanish Border beside the Bay of Biscay. The marquisate of Oloron in the province of Bearn.

"Well, *messieurs,*" he said looking up, "I can protect you from the political power of your enemies—but not from their assassins. Therefore, I am sending you from Paris for awhile."

D'Entreville flushed indignantly. *"Pecaire, monseigneur,"* he exclaimed. "I'll not run from my foes!"

The Cardinal's dark eyes chilled him. "You shall do as I say, *monsieur le comte,"* he replied. "Let that suffice."

Beside the Frenchman, Cleve chuckled. He said obliquely: "See."

"Quiet," Guy returned softly.

The Cardinal returned to the desk and sat down. His lean, tapering fingers shuffled dextrously through the litter of documents.

"The old Marquis d'Oloron has at last agreed to coöperate with me," he said absently. "For years I've been attempting to procure that senile rebel's permission to garrison his estates with King's troops. He's on a border pass, you know. A danger spot. I'd have made him coöperate ere this, had he been in any other section. But those provinces in the south are veritable powder-kegs. If I make one false move they'll plunge France into another civil war."

His fingers finally found a large document, and he scanned it briefly. *"Mais oui.* Here's the agreement. A fort to be built on the border pass facing Spain in return for a royal grant of five thousand livres." He looked up, a grim smile on his face. *"Monsieur le marquis* needs money. Isn't it strange how a man's oft-declared sentiments soften when poverty leers in his direction?

"D'Oloron fought to place Henri IV on the throne back in 1594, and because of it, he has ever maintained that the King rules for the nobles and not *vice versa.* A stubborn, autocratic old fire-eater, but he has agreed at last to aid me in uniting France and that is all that is important."

The Cardinal flipped two more documents out of a drawer. He signed them quickly and stamped them with the seal of state.

"Your commissions, *messieurs,"* he said handing them to the cavaliers. "You are to proceed to Bearn and Oloron immediately. *Monsieur le marquis* is expecting you. When he has signed the agreement, you are to select a site for the fortress and then return to Paris with your report. That is all. You have precisely one hour in which to quit Paris. And remember, *messieurs,* avoid mischief. This mission is important to the unification of France."

Outside in the corridor, Guy stared first at the impressive looking commission, and then at Cleve. *"Corbac!* Short, easy and to the point, eh?" he said.

Cleve frowned thoughtfully. "Too easy," he said after a pause. "Yes, too cursed easy for my peace of mind!"

CHAPTER II

ONE BOTTLE MEANS DISASTER

BUT THE EVENTS of the next five days didn't bear out the Englishman's pessimism. They were warm autumnal days and the rolling French countryside was brilliant, peaceful within the reds, greens and yellow of harvest time.

Outside Blois Guy's horse shied violently at a scarecrow. In Perigueux Cleve became involved with a merchant because he had speared apples from the stall with his sword. But as neither of these incidents could be considered truly exciting, their trip southward was peaceful, serene—in fact, drab.

Cleve didn't like it. Inaction made him feel uneasy.

"Up at dawn," he mused. "Ride till dusk. Dust in your throat, your hair and your eyes, and nothing but the monotony of peaceful landscapes." He looked up and sighed. "Damme, Kitten, when His Eminence called the south the powder-keg of France, he must have been referring to face powder."

Guy smiled slightly. As a rule, he was the impetuous member of the two, and to have the usually indifferent Cleve rail at their fortunes made him complacent.

"Don't call me Kitten," he reproved mildly, reaching for another slab of fresh-baked bread. "And be easy. Our host claims that we are but an hour's ride from the end of our journey."

They were seated in the grog-room of a wayside tavern. It was high noon and the vertical sun washed the surrounding hills and mountains with pale yellow. On the table between them lay the remains of a once-succulent leg of mutton.

"Good," Cleve said. He crossed one travel-grimed boot over the other and stared out of the window. In the distance the white caps of the Pyrenees rose like mammoth waves of stone.

He eyed them thoughtfully. "Faith, at first sight, the mountains in this part of the country are beautiful. But after riding through them for a day and half, their beauty palls. Château d'Oloron is in the next valley, eh?"

"*Oui.* We'll be there by two at the latest."

Cleve sighed. He dipped his nose into the depths of his tankard for a long satisfying draught. At least, the wine was violent in this part of the country. It packed the kick of an overloaded musket and relieved his boredom considerably.

When he lowered the vessel, five men had entered the tavern. Five hard-faced, deliberate men, who sat with quiet alertness and ordered nothing. When the paunchy innkeeper approached, they asked one inaudible question, then sent him arrogantly away. The innkeeper withdrew, casting worried glances at Cleve and d'Entreville.

Three more riders trooped in. They moved with the preoccupation of men who had a specific position to occupy—namely a small table beside the rear door. They didn't speak to the five at the front—merely nodded.

CLEVE'S EYES began to glint with interest. There was something wrong here. For a remote tavern, so many customers at the noon hour was highly unusual. There had to be a reason for their presence.

The English cavalier recognized the reason at a glance. A trap was being laid. Every one of the eight newcomers was alert, expectant. Cleve stared at d'Entreville and saw that the Frenchman, too, had figured out what was happening.

"One of the local lads is in for a nasty session," he said.

Guy nodded. "Apparently. Perchance we had best quit this place. After all, we're outsiders. This is none of our affair."

Cleve shook his head emphatically. "Uh-uh! If something *does* occur in this land of hills and ennui, I desire to see it. Besides, our presence will assure a fair fight."

D'Entreville knew what he was thinking and attempted to veto it. "Now see here, *mon ami, Monseigneur le Cardinal* told us to stay free of trouble."

Cleve said: "I heard him, but I'm staying anyway. I dislike buckos who run around setting traps, and if these eight bravos plan to jump upon one man, I'm purchasing an interest in the game." He grinned wryly. "Cleve—knight errant."

D'Entreville grinned too. "Well," he said resignedly, "At least, I can always say I spoke for duty. And now that it's settled, another bottle wouldn't be amiss while waiting." He caught the staring landlord with a gesture. *"Hola.* Fetch another bottle, *mon ami.* And quickly."

The white-faced proprietor skirted the silent trio sitting by the rear door and disappeared into the kitchen. He reappeared almost immediately bearing a dusty black bottle and walking at a nervous half-trot. When one of the trio grabbed his arm, he emitted an involuntary yelp of terror and froze, trembling.

"I'll take that bottle, *mon petit,*" said the man. "Give it to me."

He was a huge fellow, dressed in blue velvet, gray boots and a swirling cape. The little innkeeper stared fearfully up into his grinning face.

"But, Monsieur Vorey. This wine is for those gentlemen over there. They are couriers on the King's business."

Vorey's grin died. His eyes grew flinty. He wasn't a man to be crossed. "I know it," he rasped. "Now give me the bottle before I break you in two. It isn't healthy for King's couriers to drink during a mission."

ON THE other side of the room Cleve frowned. "So he knew our identity," he muttered. "Damme! Now that is very interesting."

D'Entreville didn't hear him. The French rakehelly's lean features had gone white at Vorey's insulting tone and manner. He stood up suddenly and walked stiff-legged across the grog-room. The five men at the front door leaned forward. Vorey had snatched the bottle from the innkeeper's flaccid fingers by this time. Guy stared at the hulking fellow coldly.

"I believe I ordered that *sac, monsieur,*" he said. "I'll trouble you to hand it over."

Vorey turned deliberately and placed the bottle on the table behind him. Then he faced Guy again.

"*Pecaire.* No trouble, my fine-feathered Parisian, for I am not handing it over. *Comprenez?*"

"Then I'll trouble myself, *monsieur!*"

The cavalier reached for the table-top. Vorey jerked him back. "No you don't, *cochon!* I'm keeping that bottle!"

Flecks of fire began to dance in Guy's eyes. At the front door the five men stood up. Their gloved fingers were resting on their swordhilts. Cleve looked at them, sized up the situation, and cursed. A trap had been set true enough. A trap for Guy and himself! He didn't bother asking the reason for it. Things began to happen too swiftly.

D'Entreville's blade leaped out just in time to parry Vorey's sudden and treacherous thrust. But Cleve wasn't watching. By the door the five whipped out their swords and began to converge on him. Hemmed by the wall and the edge of his table, Cleve felt the chill of helplessness. But he remained seated, apparently cool. The five drew nearer.

"You gentlemen care to join me, eh?"

The five hesitated, confused by the casual attitude. Cleve grinned. His heart was still attempting to burst through his chest, but the pause had delivered the game into his hands. He suddenly knew what he was going to do. Attack was his only defense.

"No?" He tensed imperceptibly. "Then I'll join you!"

CHAPTER III

SCRATCH, KITTEN

HIS ARMS SNAKED under the table, scooped it up like a shield. The quintet, bunched before him, half-raised their blades—but too late. The heavy oak surface bowled into them with the Englishman's sinewy hundred and sixty pounds behind it. They went down in a swearing, grunting mass with the table atop them. Cleve pounced on it for good measure and glanced about wildly.

"Hey, Kitten. Are you having trouble?"

In the corner d'Entreville parried the blades of Vorey and the two men who had joined him, and laughed.

"*Corbac!* I'm not losing!"

Cleve laughed. Three men had been pinned under the table. A fourth lay panting, the wind knocked out of him. The fifth was beginning to rise, blade in hand, anxious to murder some one. Cleve's boot caught the fellow neatly on the point of the jaw and he lost interest in murder.

But the battle couldn't last. Eight men against two, in an open area, were impossible odds. Especially since the eight were proficient with steel. D'Entreville had a cut on his thigh and another in his shoulder. Minor wounds, but they indicated that these men knew their trade, for d'Entreville was presumed to be the best blade in the Guard. He stared across the sword-sheen at Vorey.

"*Sandiou!* Two cuts for a deep one, *monsieur,*" he gasped and lunged.

Vorey tried to scream. But the ragged hole in his throat choked the sound. He reeled back, bumping against the arms of his companions, and slumped to the floor, dying.

D'Entreville leaped away. His adversaries were too involved

with Vorey's corpse to pursue. He glimpsed the English rake-helly whirling toward the steps leading to the second floor.

Then a pistol went off in his ear and his cheek felt the lick of powder-flame. He pivoted. A man was standing beside him—too close for effective blade-work. The fellow was gaping fool-ishly at the pistol that had missed at such close range. Guy rammed a swordhilt into his face, hurled an upturned bench, and beat Cleve to the foot of the stairs by two steps.

They held the narrow pass for fifteen minutes. But the press of seven blades tired them. And there was that wretch who dropped back occasionally to hurl bottles and pieces of pottery. They retreated slowly.

At the top landing, d'Entreville bagged another. The fellow forgot to parry and received, as a reminder, twelve inches of Toledo steel through the stomach. His body sprawled into the arms of his comrades and set them staggering back down the stairs. Cleve gripped Guy's arm during the intermission.

"Hold the fort, Kitten. Be right back."

HE DARTED into the corridor behind them and returned as the six assassins started another rush up the steps. He bore a heavy brass musket with a horn-muzzle and an awkward wheel arrangement at the breech. An old-fashioned wheel-lock of the blunderbuss type.

"Come closer, lads!" he mocked. "I'll wager this will do for all of you in one discharge!"

But the six killers weren't in a wagering mood. One look at Cleve's murderous old weapon and they fell over each other getting out of the way. Nor did they pause at the foot of the stairs. They'd had enough. The wrecked grog-room resounded with the pound of their feet as they bolted across it and out the door.

Guy listened to the diminishing pound of their horses' hoofs and sheathed his blade. He nodded toward the blunderbuss.

"*Sangodemi!* Where in the devil's name did you find that relic?"

"Over the hearth in one of the rooms," the other chuckled. "My original intent was to fetch logs for hurling purposes. The rooms in this inn have fireplaces, you know. But, when I saw Betsy—" He grinned and threw the musket aside. "Faith! 'Tis a good thing our friends didn't call my bluff. That damned firearm is dismally empty."

D'Entreville started to laugh. *"Ventre saint gris,* Cleve, we've had the luck of—" And then the laughter died in his throat.

Outside, horsemen were drumming into the courtyard. Cleve's eyebrow jerked up quizzically and he retrieved the blunderbuss.

"Faith! Did you say luck, Kitten?"

The Frenchman's blade whispered from its sheath. He didn't know why those bravos had attacked, but if they were returning for another try, he was ready. "Best fetch those fire-logs," he muttered.

It wasn't necessary. The trio of riders entering the room below were not members of the assassin band. One was richly garbed in a black and gold doublet studded with seed-pearls, gray hat, soft blue plume, and a wide sash of white satin. His companions wore russet surcoats with a heraldic device emblazoned on them. The nobleman lifted his gaze to the top of the staircase.

"Ah, *mes amis,"* he said. "I feared that I was too late."

D'Entreville sheated his steel. "Too late for what?"

"Too late to save you from the plot on your lives, of course. You are the couriers from Paris, are you not?"

"That's right." Cleve cradled the blunderbuss and led the way down the stairs. A faint frown of inquiry creased his forehead. "You appear to know much of us, my friend. You'll pardon me I'm sure, but who the devil are you?"

THE OTHER laughed. It was a pleasant and disarming laugh. The very sound of it seemed to lessen the tension left by the battle. "Permit me, messieurs, I am le Vicomte de Brissac. These," he indicated his companions, "are Henri and Jean, my secretaries."

The speaker was blond and blue-eyed; he had a firm chin, high cheekbones and thin, sensitive lips. There was a feline grace about the way he handled himself. He looked to be a man who could acquit himself equally well on the field of war or in midst of a brilliant social group. Guy liked him.

"I am honored, *monsieur*," he said. Then he frowned. Seeping from beneath the silken cords of de Brissac's cape-clasp was a thin line of crimson. *"Mordi! Monsieur le vicomte,"* Guy exclaimed. "You're wounded!"

De Brissac jerked the collar of his cape quickly over the stain. He smiled wryly. "We encountered your friends en route here," he explained. "Through my own stupidity, I was nipped in the shoulder. A minor wound, let me assure you. It bleeds but a trifle. I feel no discomfort."

Cleve nodded. "Were I you, I'd have it taken care of as soon as possible," he advised. "And incidentally, concerning the playful lads who—"

"Mais oui," said the other quickly. "The assassins. Well, *monsieur*, they were sent to stop you. I learned of it quite by accident." He frowned. "A Spanish plot. The Spanish have crammed this part of the country with agents. We are so near the border, you see. When they learned that you were coming down from Paris to consolidate Oloron and to erect a fort at the head of the pass, they plotted to nip the enterprise in the bud by disposing of you."

"Nice idea. Yet how did they know?"

"The family d'Oloron has a fondness for gossip." Here de Brissac smiled ruefully. "Especially Gaston, *le marquis'* son, *messieurs*. Myself? I knew you were coming because it was upon my council that le Marquis d'Oloron communicated with Richelieu in the first place.

"You must be a close friend," Guy observed dryly.

"Close? *Mais oui.* Yesterday, *monsieur*, the date for my marriage to *le marquis'* daughter was set. Yes. I am a very close friend. Congratulate me." The *vicomte* sighed happily and then shook himself free of the reverie. "But *peste!* I waste time. Come. I will escort you to *le château* where *monsieur le marquis* is waiting."

He led the way into the court. But as Cleve quit the tavern, he paused to look back at the shambles of battle. The wreckage, the two stiffening bodies, the shattered glassware bore mute testimony to the deep undercurrents of this apparently peaceful land.

The Englishman frowned. Spain—powerful, avaricious Spain—had entered the lists of treachery. He considered the implications thoughtfully and sighed.

"What the devil. I merely forgot that gunpowder looks harmless. Faith! Maybe Richelieu was right about the powder-keg, after all."

CHAPTER IV

THE RED CHÂTEAU

CHÂTEAU D'OLORON LAY like a mile-stone of time on an abrupt hillock, footed by a rustic village and the swift waters of the river Gave. Past its gray battlements, its high towers and shooting slits, the bloody pageantry of nearly three centuries had surged. Centuries of violence, rebellion and war.

But the years had softened the castle's grimness. Where once the soldiers of England's Black Prince had pitched tents, there was now a flowering garden. The earthen abutments left by the beseiging army of Pedro de Castile were now verdant terraces. Vines intertwined the raised portcullis. Château Rouge—the Red Castle, as men had called it—no longer looked its name. It had grown peaceful, picturesque.

Framed by the glistening Pyrenees in the background and the beforested green of lower hills to east and west, it presented a scene of serenity to the little cavalcade of five who trotted toward it. But the scene was deceptive. Rebellion, hot pride and the warrior spirit had been bred into the Olorons for generations. It still existed. The English cavalier realized that the moment he stared into the dark eyes of Marie d'Oloron, the marquis' only daughter.

The girl met them at the heraldic stone pillars that marked the estate proper. She appeared suddenly from a copse of wood, riding a spirited Arabian, and dressed daringly in men's clothes.

"Bonjour, mes chevaliers," she greeted them. "Welcome to Château d'Oloron."

De Brissac made an effort to smile. His wound was distressing him more than he let on and Guy had been eyeing him anxiously since ten minutes out of the tavern.

"Marie," de Brissac said, "allow me to present Monsieur le Comte d'Entreville and M'Lord Richard Cleve. They are the King's couriers whom your father has been expecting."

Suddenly the light of pleasant inquiry died in the girl's eyes. Her manner became frigid, distant.

"La! Charles. So the Red Cardinal has sent his hirelings to us already?"

The smile that had been curving d'Entreville's lips grew stiff. He found himself flushing uncomfortably. But not so Cleve. If anything the Englishman's grin broadened and he swept his plumed hat off with a bow.

"Quite right, *mademoiselle*. As a hireling, to a hireling-to-be, I trust we are still welcome."

THE GIRL was truly beautiful. Her anger only heightened her fine coloring, emphasizing the contrast with the dark froth of hair. Her features were delicate, her chin pointed and her small mouth warm and full. But now her white teeth were biting her lower lip.

"I'll thank you to spare me your humor, *monsieur*," she snapped. "Your appearance at our château is a thing which my father has been fighting for years. We of Oloron have been independent of the King too long for us to sell out to him without resentment, and I'll not be hypocritical. During your stay here, please do not confuse official hospitality with friendship. Is that clear?"

Cleve nodded, laughter dancing in his eyes. "Painfully clear, *mademoiselle*. Officially you like us; unofficially you consider us nasty boys." He sighed. "Let's become official. Mayhap you'll be a nicer person."

"The finesse of an orang-outang," d'Entreville assured him in a whisper. He regarded the girl. "Pardon this lout, *mademoiselle*. The English have no manners anyway."

Marie froze him with a stare. "Really? When I desire information, *monsieur le comte*, I shall request it."

Cleve shook his head reprovingly, pointed a gloved forefinger at Guy and whittled it with the other. A small smile curved Marie's lips for a moment, but she erased it.

De Brissac moved forward. He was pale. "Marie—I—I believe it best if—" His voice faltered and he reeled slightly, clutching the saddle.

Only Cleve and the secretaries, Henri and Jean, prevented his falling. The girl, seeing the streak of crimson on her fiance's doublet, gave a startled cry. De Brissac regained himself and looked up, smiling waxenly.

" 'Tis but a pin-prick, *cherie*. A small sword-wound that I barely feel. When we reach the château I shall feel better for a flask of brandy and the services of your father's physician, Doctor Jaca. The ride has tired me."

Marie turned savagely on Cleve and d'Entreville. "You might have seen to it that he rode a coach instead of a horse, *messieurs!*" Then she went to the vicomte and slipped a slender arm under his shoulder. "Jean—Henri. Ride ahead and prepare Jaca. If he isn't about, search until he is found. And make haste! These brave men of the Cardinal have almost allowed your master to die from loss of blood!"

Guy sighed. *"Pecaire!* But isn't she lovely, Cleve?"

Cleve grinned wryly. "Like vinegar. But I must admit that I have never seen vinegar in a prettier bottle."

DOCTOR JACA was a paunchy, full-faced, little man with a comic pomposity; he wore a goatee and a brace of fierce black mustachios. He took immediate charge of the wounded man, carting him off to a second-floor chamber with Marie d'Oloron following anxiously in the wake. Cleve and d'Entreville were left quite abruptly in the oak-paneled main hall of the château, facing a horse-faced individual named Lussac.

Lussac was the château's majordomo. A tall, spare person, dressed in a livery of gold-trimmed blue that made his watery eyes appear milky in contrast, and his dry lips purplish-white.

In thickly accented Bearnese he said: *"Monsieur le marquis* is not in at present, *messieurs.* He is riding. His son, Monsieur Gaston, is riding with him. Even *madame, monsieur le Marquis'* sister, is riding—but in her coach, of course."

Cleve's eyes had been roving over the huge medieval hall, but he turned as Lussac terminated his discourse.

"Apparently, this house enjoys to ride," he observed dryly. He stared at the spurs on Lussac's boots, and smiled. "Even the servants."

Lussac nodded. "I usually accompany *le marquis'* sister on her journey to take the air, *monsieur.* Today I forgot your arrival until I had ridden almost a league. I trust you will forgive my serving you in spurs, *messieurs.* May I fetch some brandy for your refreshment?"

"Sangodemi," Guy laughed. "Brandy is brandy whether served spurred or barefoot. Fetch it quickly, *mon ami."*

But as Lussac turned to go, Cleve deterred him. "Tell me, Lussac. This Doctor Jaca—Spanish, isn't he?"

"Oui, monsieur. From Burgos."

"I see." Cleve inclined his head significantly in d'Entreville's direction and dismissed the man. But again the majordomo failed to leave. As he crossed the hall, a sharp cry stopped him. A slim young fellow in green burst into the room. He was bareheaded. His cape was slipped half off his shoulders and his boots were saddle-stained and dusty.

"Lussac! *Mon Dieu!* Lussac! Fetch Doctor Jaca! There has been a accident. My father lies senseless at Falcon Pass. He lies at the foot, broken but still breathing. I feared to move him."

The speaker looked to be around eighteen. Now his face was disturbed, twisted with worry, but even so, it was a sensitive face, finely chiseled, almost effeminate. His large brown eyes took no notice of Cleve and d'Entreville. But the two cavaliers took note of him. It was heir first glimpse of Gaston, the *marquis'* son.

Suddenly Cleve cursed. "Damme! Come Kitten. Let's get out of here!"

HE MOVED quickly. He swept a quill and an ink-pot from a nearby stand and gripped Guy by the arm. The French rake-helly followed passively enough until they were outside. Then he jerked free. "*Sandiou!* Release me, you English lout!"

Cleve vaulted into a saddle. "Lively, Kitten. To horse!" He summoned a bewildered groom with a crook of his finger.

Guy climbed into a saddle. "*Corbac!* Have you gone mad?"

"No. But d'Oloron is lying at the foot of some local Pass. Probably dying. If we intend getting his signature on Richelieu's agreement, we'll have to ride like blazes." The speaker turned to the groom now standing beside the horse. "Do you know where Falcon Pass is, my man?"

"*Mais oui, monsieur.*"

"Then fetch a mount and lead us to it. Damme! Shake the lead from your legs. Get moving!"

Ten minutes hard riding brought them to the base of a mountain where several peasants were clotted in the crease of a ragged ravine. Ordering the groom to remain and care for the horses, the two cavaliers swung down and forced their way through the press.

"Too late, *messieurs.* Le Marquis d'Oloron is dead."

The body lay sprawled across a clumsy wedge formed by two huge boulders. The legs were twisted grotesquely; the head bent at a sharp angle. But even in death there was a sort of magnificence about le Marquis d'Oloron. D'Entreville doffed his hat and bent over the still figure.

"Broken neck," he adjudged and arose frowning.

Two or three rods away was the battered body of the horse d'Oloron had been riding. It, too, had a broken neck. The French rakehelly cursed softly. He had seen death in many forms, but it moved him nevertheless.

"Well, Cleve?"

"Damme! Not so well."

Cleve stared up the cliff-face to the summit from which d'Oloron had fallen. Then he returned to the corpse.

"It's quite obvious," d'Entreville said. "The old man was riding along the edge of this cliff. His horse slipped, and—" He pointed to the broken figure and shrugged. "I suppose we'll have to get young Gaston's signature on Richelieu's agreement now."

Cleve didn't answer. Somewhere in the back of his brain there stirred a suspicion that all was not as the facts indicated. Then his curiosity focused on a tangible thing—the pistol that *le marquis* held tightly in his dead fist. Cleve bent over and freed it.

"Why?" he asked holding it under d'Entreville's nose.

The Frenchman shook his head. *"Pecaire!* Who knows? Maybe he was hunting rabbits as he plunged over the side."

Cleve chuckled and thrust the weapon into his boot-top after examining it. The pistol had been fired. "Perhaps," he agreed and stared up at the cliff again.

Guy's eyes narrowed. He knew and respected the Englishman's deductive powers, but it was ridiculous to infer that *le marquis'* violent death had been other than accidental.

"Now mark this, Cleve. There is no need for that suspicious expression on your face."

"All right," Cleve assented. He grinned and stared at the other. "But his death *is* rather convenient, don't you think? Let's ride to the top of the cliff and see if he got the rabbit he was shooting at."

Guy closed his eyes and shook his head. "Very well, *mon ami*," he surrendered. "Proceed! Make a fool of yourself."

THERE WAS a rock-strewn path that led from the valley up toward the dent in the mountains. The two cavaliers found it as young Gaston, Jaca and countless members of the château's household rode up to the mouth of the dead man's ravine. Cleve didn't watch them. He was still wondering about the pistol; pondering the reason why a man would draw as he plunged over the side of a cliff.

"*Corbac!* I wonder why he was riding here in the first place," Guy grumbled as he negotiated a difficult turn. "We shouldn't have horses. We should be riding mountain goats!"

Ahead of him, Cleve chuckled. "Where's your sense of sport, Kitten? To a true horseman such as d'Oloron this perilous trail was a challenge to his skill."

Guy cursed. He was fast losing whatever pride he had ever had in his horsemanship. He stared down at the sickening distance and gulped. "*Ventre saint gris!*" he muttered. "Why can't you leave a thing well enough alone, Cleve? Figuratively and literally I'm too near heaven for comfort."

"Why friend, you will never get any closer to heaven," Cleve observed and reined up. The narrow path had suddenly widened sufficiently to allow four horses to advance abreast in comfort. D'Entreville drew alongside Cleve and looked about.

"Mark, *mon ami*. No rabbit."

Cleve grinned, slipped from his saddle and paced gingerly to the edge of the path. Below, pygmy-like in perspective, were the members of the dead nobleman's entourage. They were lifting the cloak-covered body to a litter. Cleve retraced his steps, studying the ground intently.

"By Jupiter! That settles it!" He looked up, a grim smile twisting his lips. "No rabbit, Kitten. We have unearthed traces of snake."

D'Entreville scowled. "The altitude is too rare for riddles," he retorted. "What do you mean?"

"Precisely what I say. A snake has struck today."

Cleve hoisted himself into the saddle and sat for a moment staring thoughtfully ahead. The mountain trail meandered down from where they stood. It threaded irregularly over the rough terrain to disappear into a thick copse of wood a mile away. Beyond that could be seen the trim outlines of the tavern wherein he and Guy had been ambushed. This was a back-trail to the main highway.

"Le Marquis d'Oloron was not killed accidentally," Cleve said. "By my Faith, no! He was murdered! And cleverly, Kitten. Very cleverly."

The French cavalier gaped in astonishment, and then he demanded: *"Oui?* Well, how?"

Cleve pointed a gloved finger at the spot where the marquis had gone over. The ledge was filmed by a layer of moist earth, scuffed by horses' hoofs—two different and distinct sets of horses' hoofs.

"Pushed. Or more accurately, his horse was shoved. The evidence is there in the earth, Kitten. He was not alone."

"Murder!" Guy rolled the word on his tongue. He nodded. *"Sandiou!* Now I see it. The pistol served as your clue. *Le marquis* saw what his riding companion was about and he drew to defend himself. He fired! He missed! The killer's horse crashed into his and he went down to death. *Oui,* I see it!"

Cleve reached out and patted the speaker on the back. "Damme," he chuckled. "Damme. You're improving, Kitten."

Then they turned the horses and returned to the valley.

CHAPTER V

WE BRING YOU GOLD

FOR A DAY the body of the marquis lay in sate. A coverlet of blue, bearing the crest of the house, was draped across it and two liveried retainers stood in solemn attendance, pikes reversed. The peasants, the local tradesmen, the gentry of the neighborhood, filed by slowly, paying the last respects to a man whom they had not loved particularly but whom they all had admired.

And during this time, Cleve and d'Entreville remained aloof, preferring to allow the family the privacy of grief. As a matter of fact, Guy wanted to leave the château to take up residence at the village inn until after the funeral, but Cleve vetoed the suggestion.

"To leave our point of vantage now wouldn't be wise, Kitten. There is a murderer loose. A murderer who knew *le marquis* well enough to go riding with him. No, we had best remain here. I want to watch this household."

Guy wrinkled his nose. He and Cleve had agreed, returning from Falcon Pass, not to mention their discovery. It was to be a game of watchful waiting and casual questioning until a definite basis for action had been established. But the French gallant had already developed suspicions. The murder of the marquis was a family affair.

He frowned slightly as he considered it, and then asked conversationally: "Have you spoken to Gaston, Cleve?"

The Englishman shook his head. "No. But I've heard his tale. His sister spoke for him. He claims not to have been with his father when the—er—accident occurred."

"Folderol!"

Cleve cocked an amused eyebrow at Guy, and pulled himself upright. He had been lying across the canopied bed in their west-wing quarters. The room was large, well-furnished, recently renovated. It overlooked the west terrace of the château. He stood up and sauntered to the latticed window through which the golden wash of the afternoon sun was cascading.

"Why folderol, Kitten?"

"Because he is the only logical person to have done the deed. From what I have gathered, he and his father did not get on well together. They quarreled often and violently. The boy is of a delicate temperament, sensitive and idealistic. His father was a fire-eater, a tyrant. Small wonder that they clashed often."

"Yes, small wonder. But then the old boy quarreled with everyone, it seems. Take Madame la Grande."

"The marquis' sister. *Corbac!* You take her!"

Cleve chuckled. "But she also quarreled with *monsieur le Marquis*, Kitten. Damme. In this affair one must take all things into consideration."

D'ENTREVILLE REGARDED the toes of his boots and shook his head. He was sitting atilt in a chair with his feet on the table. It was a position extremely helpful to thinking. He decided Cleve's statement was superfluous.

The marquis' sister, Madame la Grande, was aged—almost seventy. Though spry, the old dowager was hardly energetic enough to travel over the countryside on horseback, to mount that hazardous trail at Falcon Pass and push her vigorous brother off the cliff.

"Don't tell me you think she did it," he chided.

Cleve sat down on the window. The warmth of the sun on his back filled him with a cat-like languor. He remained for a long moment silent, end then he said: "No. But she might have had it done, Kitten."

"Folderol," was Guy's comment.

"Folderol yourself! Damme! She resented her brother, and not without cause. Apparently, he enjoyed humiliating her as a poor relation. Her husband was le Duc Ravanac and he was killed fighting for Henri de Guise, back in the nineties. He left her a widow and penniless. The marquis took her in, but he never allowed her to forget it."

"So?"

"So, my bright bird, Madame le Grande had a motive, and I can't help remembering that Lussac was riding yesterday. He is devoted to the old woman."

"*Corbac!* Everyone was riding yesterday!" exclaimed Guy

suddenly and dropped his feet to the floor. "Curse you, Cleve. I had this affair solved until you muddled everything with suspicions. Now I don't know who to suspect!

"Spain might have done it to prevent *monsieur le marquis* from signing Richelieu's agreement. Young Gaston had both reason and opportunity; although he claims to have quarreled with his father and left midway in their ride together. But now you spring Lussac on me!" He shrugged. "Bah!"

Cleve grinned and polished his nails on the shoulder of his shirt which was carelessly open at the throat. Since awaking at the crack of ten, he had only managed to don boots and breeches. What investigations he had made had been executed the night previous.

"Ah, but we are not complete, Kitten. Damme! The deeper one delves into this powder-keg, the more one unearths. One of the grooms tells me that Doctor Jaca keeps carrier pigeons in the south bastion. Now that, I think, is very enlightening."

Guy's eyes widened and his jaw muscles knotted tightly. The presence of carrier pigeons seemed very significant to him. Honest people correspond by coach or horse. Spies used the swifter, more secret air lane. He stood up.

"Where are you off to?" Cleve asked.

"To arrest Doctor Jaca. Being an officer in the King's service, I have that authority."

Cleve moved from the window to a chair. The sun had grown uncomfortably hot. "You have the authority," he agreed. "But faith, Kitten, where's your evidence? You can't arrest Jaca because he keeps pigeons, you know."

"*Sangodemi!*" sighed the Frenchman. "For a split sou, I'd bring a regiment up from Pau, and throw the whole marquisate under martial law. Things have come to a pretty pass! First we are ambushed. Then the object of our journey is murdered. Now we have spies. *Mordi!* What next?"

A faint knock sounded on the door. "Tell you in a moment," Cleve laughed and swung it open.

IT WAS Lussac, standing on the threshold, blank of face and bearing a silver tray laden with food. As he moved into the room, a brown ball of fur romped between his spindly shanks and assumed an expectant attitude at the foot of the table. Fifi, Marie d'Oloron's small spaniel.

"Hola, you spoiled little cur," Cleve chuckled. "Don't they feed you in this hostelry?"

Fifi regarded him brightly, tongue lolling and tail a-thump. She didn't move. Lussac, muttering apologies, placed the tray on the table.

"Followed me from the kitchen, *messieurs.* I could not discourage her. Mademoiselle Marie feeds her often from a tray and she thinks that this is for her."

"Leave her be," Cleve told him. He bent down and scratched the dog's silken ears. "What have you brought us, Lussac?"

"Since you have felt it indelicate to intrude upon the family for the midday meal," the tall majordomo said, "Mademoiselle Marie suggested I bring this food to your quarters, *messieurs.* It is meat pie."

D'Entreville's nose twitched appreciatively. The crisp, nut-like aroma made him suddenly and acutely conscious of his hunger.

"Parbleu. I hardly blame Fifi for following."

Lussac's knobby fingers deftly spread the table. There was wine, steaming cakes fresh from the oven, a tureen of onion soup, a pitcher of spring water. He paused suddenly and frowned.

"Ma foi! The stewed fruit. I beg your indulgence, gentlemen. I forgot it. One moment."

He crossed to the door as a drumming knock sounded. The knocker, a lackey from the stables, delivered his message and disappeared. Lussac turned.

"A detachment of soldiers has just arrived from Pau, *messieurs.* They wait in the castle bailey."

D'Entreville reached for his hat. Cleve rubbed his hands together and took a seat by the table. The French rakehelly frowned.

"Come along. This is as much your affair as mine."

The Englishman shook his head. He raised a knife and cut through the golden crust of the meat pie. He lifted a piece of steaming meat and Fifi eyed it anxiously. Cleve grinned.

"Uh-uh. I'm in shirtsleeves. It wouldn't do for an officer and a gentleman to receive new orders in such niggardly dress. Besides, I'm famished."

Guy cursed and crammed his hat tightly over one ear—backward, with the plume dangling comically over one eye. *"Corbac!"* He yanked it off and readjusted it. "If there is a duty to perform, I'm always the man who has to do it!" He stood in the door and pointed a warning finger. "Take no more of that pie than is yours! I'll be right back." He jerked his head at Lussac. "You come with me. I may need you to billet the men."

Cleve laughed and flipped the piece of meat into Fifi's mouth. "I'll save a portion, m'love." He regarded the toothsome spread and added: "Maybe."

IN THE bailey the detachment from Pau stood in rough formation, arms stacked. They were musketeers, and being a Cardinal's Guardsman, Guy took an instinctive dislike to them, but he concealed it. After all they weren't the King's Muske-teers—the Paris regiment with whom the Guard had been feud-ing for nearly ten years.

"Who is in charge here?" he asked.

A beetle-browed sergeant stepped forward, dust-grimed from the fourteen-mile march he had just completed. There was a fold of paper in his glove. He drew it briskly.

"Grinod reporting, *monsieur,* with a detachment of twenty."

Guy nodded absently and took the orders. They had been signed by Richelieu and forwarded by courier to the *comman-dant* at Pau. Due to the increasing tension between the crowns of France and Spain, he and Cleve were to levy two-score labor-ers immediately; begin the construction of a blockhouse on the site they had selected for the new fort, and remunerate le Marquis d'Oloron with a five-hundred-livre bonus for his full coöperation. A chest containing ten thousand was to accompany these orders.

Guy looked up. "You have brought the moneys, Sergeant."

Grinod nodded. He gave a crisp order and the ranks split to reveal a two-wheeled cart. Guy walked over, inspected the iron-studded chest lashed therein, and turned to Lussac.

"I'll have need of your strongroom, *mon ami.* Be so good as to fetch the keys." As Lussac hied himself away, he turned to Grinod. "Sergeant, le Marquis d'Oloron has just been killed—er—accidently. There has been some delay as to the selection of the fort site. However, I want you to begin recruiting labor as soon as possible. We shall begin construction of the blockhouse tomorrow."

Grinod nodded. *"Oui, monsieur."*

"Very well. Dismiss your men and see that they are refreshed. Later Lussac will see as to their billeting."

Then Lussac reappeared with four brawny house lackies. They carried the gold chest into the château and deposited it in the strongroom. With a deft twist, Lussac locked the door and turned the key over to Guy.

"Take care of the men in the bailey, Lussac," the Frenchman said. "I'll be in my quarters completing the repast you served us." He sighed dismally. "If there is any left."

CHAPTER VI

DEATH OF A DOG

IN THE ROOM he found Cleve waiting soberly. The Englishman didn't speak. He closed the door and led the way over to the bed. On the quilted surface lay the body of Fifi. The little spaniel's eyes were glazed and staring. She was quite dead.

Cleve met Guy's silent inquiry with a word: "Poisoned."

"What?"

"That's right. The meat pie. I gave the dog a piece."

D'Entreville's mouth was white. He stared at his companion, then licked his lips.

"Poisoned! *Ventre saint gris,* Cleve! Do you know what it means. Our secret is out. This is—"

A grim smile touched Cleve's features. He had considered the implications while Fifi died in agony. "This is most inconsiderate, Kitten," he said. "By Jupiter! I was hungry!"

There was a moment of silence, and then Guy erupted. *"Sacré nom d'un cochon malade!* I'll run him through! I'll carve his heart out. Poison! A coward's method!"

His sword snaked out, describing a shimmering arc, and he whirled toward the door. Cleve's darting fingers snapped the hem of his cape and hung on. Guy stopped.

"Damme! Where are you off to, Kitten?"

The Frenchman glowered and tried to wrench his cape free of Cleve's grip. "To take care of the poisonous wretch. *Corbac!* He can't do that to me! Let go! Release me!"

"What poisonous wretch, m'lad? Lussac? Marie d'Oloron? The chef?"

Guy paused. "Why—er—." He glowered the more deeply. "Lussac!" he said. *"Oui!* Lussac! I see it all now. He is the murderer."

"How do you know?"

"Well, he was riding yesterday, wasn't he? Just now, he served us poison." He turned to the door once more. But Cleve's hold on the cape dissuaded him abruptly. *"Sangodemi,* Cleve. This is no time for playfulness! Release me, and I'll save the gibbet a customer."

"Relax, Kitten." With a deft motion Cleve took the other's sword away and released the cape. "Now you be a nice little lad. We do not know who tried to give us indigestion, and going-off half-cocked won't help matters. Gad! Suppose you skewer Lussac and it turns out later that he is innocent?"

Some of the storm in Guy's eyes abated. *"Sandiou!* I don't like him anyway," he grunted.

Cleve grinned, sighed and shook his head. "All right, Kitten," he soothed. "Now, here is the wise thing to do—"

D'Entreville scowled. "And that is another thing," he snapped. "How many times do I have to tell you not to call me Kitten? So far I have ignored it, hoping that you'd forget. But—" He paused in mid-speech and stared. "What?"

CLEVE RETURNED the sword and stood arms akimbo in the center of the room. "First, we say nothing about the dog's death," he said. "Crying treachery will only caution our murderous friend. Silence might force his hand. Second, we dispose of Fifi so that she shan't be found."

"Pecaire! Is that all?"

Cleve nodded. "Surely."

"Now see here, *mon ami!* I am growing weary of this sit-and-do-nothing policy. What's to prevent our being murdered in our beds?"

The Englishman shrugged. "Nothing, Kitten. But forewarned is forearmed." He went to the bed, picked up the limp corpse of the spaniel and deposited it in a worn saddlebag hanging from a peg on the far wall. Guy observed him thoughtfully, the fire of his indignation finally gone.

"On second consideration," he said, "I cannot understand the motive. We have not been in this country long enough to make enemies."

Cleve buckled the straps of the saddlebag and brought it over to him. "Faith, our enemies were created before we arrived, Kitten. Marie expressed it neatly. The whole house resents us because of our mission."

"Corbac! They asked for it, did they not?"

"Certainly. That makes it the more bitter pill. Incidentally, what are the new orders?"

Guy told him, concluding: "I had planned for us to ride toward the border this afternoon and select a site."

Cleve handed the saddlebag to him. "You do it, and rid yourself of Fifi in the process." He frowned. "Things must be growing quite tight if they want a blockhouse erected immediately. Perhaps His Eminence fears a treacherous invasion. When work begins tomorrow, we had best use Grinod's men as guards. Spain might try to stop us."

"*Oui*. What are your plans for this afternoon?"

Cleve flipped the Cardinal's agreement out of a drawer in the table. "Young Gaston is nominally the head of the household now," he said. "I intend to have his hand on this paper before something else happens."

Guy's eyes narrowed. "You fear something?"

Cleve shrugged. "Who knows?"

He stood for a full minute after Guy had departed, regarding the wall, considering the meager clues of this affair; asking himself questions and receiving blanks. He felt like a man groping through the dark in the midst of unseen dangers. Finally he shrugged and began to finish dressing.

HE MET Marie d'Oloron in the hallway. Her face was strained, wan-looking. She felt the loss of her father deeply; but as Cleve greeted her he noted that her dark eyes immediately filled with a proud defiance.

"I am in search of your brother, *mademoiselle*," he said.

"Gaston is not in the château, *monsieur*."

He shrugged and turned away. Hesitantly, she detained him. "He went riding, Monsieur Cleve. He is trying to keep himself very busy, in order to forget our father's death. What do you desire of him?"

Cleve stared at her. "Your peace of mind, *mademoiselle*."

She didn't understand that. Her manner became confused. "You mean, *monsieur?*"

"Your brother is now head of the family, *mademoiselle*. If he signs the cardinal's agreement, d'Entreville and myself will be able to quit the castle and free you of the burden of our presence."

The girl flushed, half-ashamed. "Yesterday, I did not mean to—"

A pleasant tenor voice interrupted. "Of course you didn't, Marie. It was that fiery little tongue of yours."

It was de Brissac, arm in sling, a faint smile touching his lips. Marie bit her lip. She was close to tears as she went to him.

"*Merci,* Charles," she murmured. "You have always helped—even in little things." She kissed him lightly on the cheek. "I fear I am tired."

The blond *vicomte* nodded. "Best rest, *cherie.* I shall accommodate M'Lord Cleve." He kissed her gently and led her to a chamber door. "Try to sleep, *ma petite.* 'Tis the best cure for sorrow."

As the door closed behind her, he turned, his handsome face serious. "I desire a word with you, *monsieur.* Privately."

Cleve nodded. "As you wish."

De Brissac led him into a small room near the head of the staircase. Inside were several high-backed chairs surrounding a table upon which was a decanter of brandy and two goblets. Cleve sat down, feeling somehow that he was about to participate in a carefully prearranged scene. He couldn't explain the sensation, but it was there, warning him not to be too credulous.

DE BRISSAC poured two drinks and took a position crosstable. He raised his glass. "Your health, m'Lord."

Cleve smiled slightly and nodded. He had lived in exile for so long that the use of his title sounded strangely alien. He sipped the smooth warmth of the liquor, cupping the goblet thoughtfully in hand.

De Brissac said, "I trust I can rely on your discretion, *monsieur.*"

Cleve looked up. "You can. What's preying on your mind?"

"The welfare and health of Marie d'Oloron and the honor of her house, *monsieur.* The house of which I already feel myself a part." The speaker set down his goblet. "You were searching for Gaston, weren't you?"

"That's right."

"Well, *monsieur*, you'll not find him."

The statement fell in flatly, without warning, and the English cavalier's chestnut head lifted abruptly. He matched the other's suddenness with a single crisp word: "Why?"

"Because he has fled over the Spanish border."

Cleve was becoming used to surprises. His expression did not change, but he was wondering what else de Brissac had to say. Surely the flaxen-haired *vicomte* had not set so elaborate a scene for so simple an announcement.

De Brissac hadn't. He hesitated, gnawing his upper lip, his face revealing his distaste for what he was about to say. He shrugged.

"Gaston has left the country because I sent him, *monsieur*. It was the least I could do. I desire that you understand my position."

"All right. What is it?"

"One of compromise, *monsieur*." The *vicomte* picked up his goblet, drained it and poured himself another. He stared at Cleve and said: "I have been forced to compromise with my sense of duty. In a sense I have abetted treason. But could any man reveal the treachery of a man whose sister he cherishes and plans to marry?"

Cleve regarded him sharply. "Damme! Are you inferring that young Gaston has been dabbling in treason?"

De Brissac inclined his head sadly. "I am, *monsieur*. You see, Gaston was very ambitious. He loathed the role of a rural noble. He desired more prestige and wealth than accompanies the title of marquis. He often spoke of it to me, and I cautioned him about the dangers of his ambition. But he ignored me. If France could not bestow upon him a prouder title and more wealth—he knew of a nation that would!"

The speaker nodded gravely. "I see that you follow me,

monsieur. You are astute. *Oui.* That nation was Spain!" He arose. "For two generations the Spanish have cast longing eyes on this marquisate. It has a wide pass, easily defended by the château. It is admirably situated as a defense post against invasion. The Spanish know it; they know from experience that to attack it is futile. However, there is always bribery. In young Gaston d'Oloron they at last found a receptive ear.

"Gaston was wont to ride over the border, ostensibly to visit friends. That was my first inkling of his treachery. I became curious. Two days ago I sent my man, Henri, to follow him. I thought at that time, that Gaston was merely in love with some dark-eyed *señorita.* Imagine my distress upon learning the truth! Henri overheard a conversation, and after investigation, I discovered the shameful truth.

"It was a duty. I searched Gaston's effects and here is what I found."

DE BRISSAC went to a cabinet, jerked open a drawer and withdrew a sheaf of papers. Documents, letters and maps, addressed to Gaston d'Oloron and signed by Don Luis de Sanibel, Grandee of Spain. Cleve examined them closely as the *vicomte* paced the floor.

"I remonstrated with Gaston, but to no avail. Out of love for his family I held my tongue, hoping that in time he would come to his senses."

The speaker paused and leaned across the table, his tone suddenly soft. "I made the mistake of waiting in silence, *monsieur.* Even as you are waiting now!"

Cleve sat very still. There was heavy implication in those words and he felt uncertain as to how to react. In this game it seemed wise to hold the cards tight and wait for another to lead. He looked up finally and shrugged.

"I fear that I do not understand, de Brissac," he said.

The *vicomte* sat down. His face was tight-drawn. "Let us be brutally frank, *monsieur,*" he advised evenly. "We both know that le Marquis d'Oloron was murdered, don't we?"

Cleve shifted. De Brissac's words were both a question and a statement. The English cavalier teetered back on his chair and stared. "Do we?" he inquired.

"*Oui.* But you still search for the killer—and I know him."

Cleve said, "That's nice," and waited.

De Brissac raised his goblet and drained it. Setting it back upon the table, he regarded the other sagely. "I am not entirely dense, *monsieur,* and when this morning two peasants told me that *monsieur le marquis* had been holding a discharged pistol in his dead fingers, and that you had relieved him of it, to ride to the top of the cliff from which he had fallen, I immediately surmised the answer.

"D'Oloron was too fine a horseman to fall from a trail over which he has ridden since childhood. The fact that he held a discharged pistol proved but one thing: murder!"

"Does seem logical, doesn't it," Cleve observed.

"Precisely. And so, acting upon my intuition and the facts with which I have already presented you, I confronted young Gaston."

Cleve bent forward. "He admitted it?"

"*Sandiou!* He was forced to. He was the last man seen with his father; he had much to gain from the latter's death and his hatred for the marquis was well known. Besides that, as the new Marquis d'Oloron he would have free rein to deal with the Spanish. Therefore this knowledge and his admission left me but one course, *monsieur.*

"I gave him a horse and sent him over the border into Spain. That is why I have requested your discretion, m'Lord. Marie must never know of his perfidy. Keep his treasonous correspondences—I warned Gaston that I would turn them over to you—and, tell *Monseigneur le Cardinal* the true facts of the old marquis' demise."

De Brissac sighed deeply and poured another brandy for himself. "There," he said, draining it. "I have told all. Young Gaston must remain forever in exile, so that the honor of his family will not be tarnished. *Corbac!* Should he dare set foot in France again, he will be arrested for high treason and the murder of his father. Is that not so, *monsieur?*"

Cleve smiled slightly and picked up the documents. "He will have much explaining to do, at any rate," he said folding them carefully and tucking them into his sash. Then he arose. "Thank you, de Brissac. This has helped immeasurably."

CHAPTER VII

LA GRANDE DAME

BUT LATER, WALKING thoughtfully down the corridor, his brow creased skeptically and he muttered: "Or has it? Faith! Who signs Richelieu's agreement now?"

As if in answer a voice said mechanically: "Madame la Grande would like to see you, *monsieur,* in her suit in the east wing."

It was a house lackey. Cleve told him to lead the way and followed, wondering vaguely what the dead marquis' sister wanted.

He did not have long to wait. Madame la Grande was nothing if not direct. "I have summoned you here, *monsieur,*" she said crisply, "to gain a retraction of your monstrous accusation that I murdered my brother."

Cleve licked his lips and ran a finger around the inside of his laced neck-piece. The manner in which secrets became public property in this château was amazing. He could remember telling Guy of his suspicion concerning Madame la Grande, and no one else.

He attempted to be evasive, but the dowager would have none of it. She sat imperiously beside the open window, cane held scepter-like across her skirted knees, regarding him with challenging blue eyes. She must have been beautiful once. Even yet her delicate face was striking. She was not a large woman, and her dark velvet dress, the fashion of another era, made her appear more fragile than she actually was.

"Well, *monsieur?*"

"By my Faith, *madame!* How can you credit me with such infamy?"

"Hmmmph!" She leaned forward on her cane, her brilliant eyes intent on him. "You are a polished liar, *monsieur.*"

Cleve smiled faintly. Madame la Grande, despite her dowager's manner, was rather likable. Nevertheless, he decided to maintain his pose of innocence. "I fear I do not understand, *madame.*"

The dowager sighed. "Oh, you know very well what I mean, *monsieur.* There is little that goes on in this château of which I am not aware. You accused me of having my brother murdered. Do not deny it—apologize, instead!"

Cleve grinned. *"Madame,"* he said abruptly, "you have snoopers in your pay. It has just occurred to me that Lussac entered my quarters with a tray of food shortly after I made that statement."

Some of the sternness left her face. She smiled with her eyes. "Lussac is very dependable, *monsieur.* But you avoid the issue. I am still demanding your apology."

"You have it, *madame.*"

"Bien. And now that it is settled, perhaps you'll explain why you think my brother has been murdered, in the first place."

CLEVE TOLD her, and when he had finished Madame La Grande leaned back against her chair and stared thoughtfully.

"La!" she mused. " 'Tis a black thing, *monsieur.*" Her thin face tightened. "Mark you. I do not mourn my brother's passing overmuch. He was a miser. He took care of me, but grudgingly and took a supreme delight in my humiliation. *Oui.* I am rather glad he is gone. But I did not kill him." Then she looked up. "You believe that, *monsieur.*" It was a command.

Cleve wanted to smile at her imperiousness, but he contained himself. "Yes," he agreed. "But I am positive that some member attached to this house did it, *madame.*"

The dowager rapped emphatically on the floor with her cane. "Then eliminate Lussac and my nephew Gaston immediately. They were with me yesterday when I took my airing."

"Gaston? I understood that he accompanied his father."

Madame La Grande shook her head. "He did not, *monsieur.* He began to, but they had a falling out as usual, and Gaston joined me as my coach passed. As for Lussac, he was with me until we neared the border and then he returned to the château to greet you.

"Obviously he had little time for a murder. Lussac is too timid a man for it anyway. Young Gaston was with me until I was midway on my return home, and then, he left me to ride ahead. A peasant hailed him en route and told him of his father's accident."

Cleve nodded soberly. Apparently Madame le Grande was sincere. If what she said was true, then de Brissac's dramatic tale had to be discarded. Considering all this, Cleve had an urgent desire to turn his back on the whole affair and return to Paris where trouble made no mystery of itself. But no, that was impossible.

Cleve bowed and said: "Thank you, *madame,* I deeply appreciate your assistance. Have I your permission to retire?"

She inclined her head graciously, but as he reached the door she stopped him.

"Young man, if you really want to uncover my brother's assassin, I would investigate Doctor Jaca. He was not in the château until ten minutes before you and le Comte d'Entreville arrived yesterday. You didn't know that, did you?"

Cleve sighed. "No," he admitted reluctantly. "No, *madame,* I didn't."

"Well, it is the truth, *monsieur.* And when you consider it, who would be a more logical suspect? Jaca is Spanish. In fact, I am not certain that he is not an agent of Spain. As you well know, *monsieur,* Spain does not wish Oloron fortified."

Cleve nodded. He quietly closed the door behind him and set off down the corridor. He tried to marshal the facts he had gathered into a composite picture and failed miserably. It angered him. By the time he reached his room, *l'affair d'Oloron* was a jumble of sharp contradictions. He decided to cease worrying about it. Instead he would sit upon his bed, bottle in hand, and get himself pleasantly drunk.

CONTENT WITH this thought, he pushed open the door. As he stepped inside, he heard a startled gasp. It came from the far end of the room by the cabinet in which were kept the various documents connected with the Oloron mission. Cleve stopped, his fingers instinctively darting to the sword at his side. Then his hand fell away from the hilt.

"Doctor Jaca! Damme! Now this is a surprise."

The rotund little man, his face very white, stepped back from the cabinet as though it had grown suddenly hot. He smiled weakly.

"Er—I knocked repeatedly, *señor. Si,* I knocked repeatedly. And when you did not answer, I—er—took the liberty, *señor.*"

Cleve smiled. He kicked shut the door and said: "So I see. Suppose you explain the extent of your liberty."

The fact that Jaca was completely confused was obvious, but he attempted a halfhearted pose of indignation nevertheless. Drawing himself up to his full five feet four, he twirled his mustaches and scowled.

"*Señor!*" he snapped. "*Señor,* I do not like your inference. My mission was entirely innocent."

Cleve continued to smile, but the doctor could not help noting that the English rakehelly's hand had dropped leisurely to his rapier hilt. The indignation faded from Jaca's voice and he began to speak quickly and apprehensively.

"Truly, *señor.* As a matter of fact, I was searching for—er—*Por Dios!* Must you fondle your sword, *señor?*"

Cleve inclined his head. "That's right, m'lad." His eyebrow cocked. "You were searching—" He patted the hilt and smiled cheerfully. "Best make it good."

The doctor moistened his lips. "I was searching for my bullet probe, *señor. Si.* This is the room in which I doctored le Vicomte de Brissac. I mislaid it."

Cleve's sharp eyes studied Jaca's round face. The little man was speaking the truth. "You used a bullet probe on de Brissac yesterday, doctor?" he asked quickly.

"*Si,* a probe. If you will observe the third shelf of that cabinet, *señor,* you will see it lying there."

Cleve saw that the metal probe was on the shelf, true enough. The third shelf. Frowning slightly, he picked it up and fondled it thoughtfully. Then he looked at Jaca and took him gently by the arm.

"I feel certain that you will allow me the use of this implement for a day," he said, ushering him amiably to the door. "And before you leave, remember in the future to gain my permission before you enter this room."

Jaca nodded meekly and stepped into the hall. It was not until Cleve started to close the door that the doctor found his tongue again,

"But, why do you desire a probe, *señor?*"

"I have a bit of probing to do," Cleve replied and shut the door.

He stood in silence for a moment, staring at the medical instrument. Then he cursed softly and placed it on the table. He did it absently and the probe teetered uncertainly and started to slip off the edge. He bent over in an attempt to retrieve it. As he did so, the half-open window shattered explosively and something whizzed past the spot where his head had been but a moment before. The object struck the far wall with thudding impact.

"By Jupiter! That was close!"

Prone on the floor, Cleve stared at the object that had nearly terminated his interest in the world of men. A steel bolt jutted from the wall. It was buried half its length into the wood. Regarding it, Cleve smiled crookedly. It was a quarrel from an ancient arbalest or crossbow and from the angle of its embedded shaft, the shot had been made from a point level with the room. Undoubtedly the wall-walk ten feet from the window outside.

But why a crossbow bolt? Then Cleve had the answer. This unknown enemy was extremely anxious to go about his task in silence. First he had tried poison; then the crossbow.

CHAPTER VIII

WALK WITH US TO PRISON

THE ENGLISHMAN REMAINED on the floor for a full two minutes; and then he cautiously crawled to the near wall and stood up. He fought down the impulse to run to the window and peer out. That was inviting death.

Outside the day was fast dying. He stared at the deep shadows that were moving across the floor, and frowned. This was the second attempt on his life within the past three hours, and although he had been half-prepared for it, the reason for his unseen assailant's attacks still remained a mystery.

He was preparing to approach and draw the window-drapes when the door burst open and a battered figure reeled in. Cleve's blade flashed in a quick arc, to center on the intruder's back.

The man was down, slumped on the floor before the table, half-sobbing. Cleve approached as d'Entreville strode in, slamming the door shut behind him. The Frenchman's face was dark, scowling. He carried a crossbow in one hand, a bared rapier in the other.

"There's your filthy snake, Cleve," he snapped. "I caught him in the act. *Pecaire!* Do you know who he is?"

Cleve rammed his sword back into its sheath and shook his

head. Obviously the fellow was his unseen assailant, but his identity remained undisclosed. Guy placed the crossbow on the table and tapped the man on the shoulder with the tip of his sword.

"Turn over!" he commanded.

The captive obeyed slowly. His face was puffed by a brace of angry red welts; his clothes gritty with dirt. His hat was miss-ing and his black hair veiled one eye and part of the cheek. But Cleve recognized him. It was the man known merely as Henri, de Brissac's swarthy secretary. The fellow caught the savagery in d'Entreville's face and cringed, raising an arm to shield himself.

"I cuffed him around slightly," Guy admitted.

Cleve's lips twisted. "Apparently."

Henri misread that smile and crawled dog-like to the English cavalier's boots. He jabbed a trembling finger at d'Entreville. "He—he sword-whipped me, *monsieur!* And for no reason!"

"For no reason! *Corbac* and *Sangodemi!* So I'm now a liar, eh? Well—" Guy cursed and started after Henri, sword lifted, but Cleve shook his head. The Englishman walked over to the wall where the crossbow bolt was embedded and jerked it free. He turned thoughtfully.

"Tell me about it, Kitten," he said.

D'ENTREVILLE SHRUGGED. Henri started to stand, but the French rakehelly raised the hard toe of his boot warningly and the prisoner subsided.

"*Sandiou.* There is little to tell, Cleve. Returning from my fort-site survey, I noted this creature stealing furtively along the wall-walk toward our window. I became curious and followed—but not soon enough. He was able to discharge the crossbow before I could reach him."

Henri's harsh voice broke the short silence. "My master shall make you pay for this, *messieurs!*"

Cleve nodded soberly, eyes thoughtful. "I think perhaps your master has to be paid for a number of things," he said. He jerked

Henri to his feet; raised him with surprising dexterity by his shirt-front. Yet his voice seemed amiable, almost idle. "Suppose you tell why you desired my death so hungrily, little man?"

"A life for a life, swine! One of you slew my brother. I swore to get you both."

Cleve chuckled cheerfully, but his grip did not lessen and Henri was helpless. "Faith! You father botched it, didn't you? Who was your brother?"

There was hate in Henri's eyes. "Jacques Vorey," he said.

"Vorey! *Parbleu*, Cleve! The ambush at the tavern!"

The English gallant nodded. His expression did not reveal the thought behind his next question. "Damme, now that is interesting, Henri. How long have you and your brother been in le Vicomte de Brissac's service?"

"Three years and a—" Suddenly, Henri's tongue froze as he realized the admission into which he had been tricked. But Cleve had heard enough The assassins at the tavern had not been Spanish agents. He led, half-dragged, the captive across the room and thrust him behind a stout closet door and bolted it firmly.

"Lie near the crack on the floor if you crave fresher air, Henri," he advised cheerfully and turned to Guy. "Come along, Kitten. We have a call to pay on de Brissac with about five of Grinod's soldiers."

Guy followed more out of curiosity than anything else. As they strode down the corridor he peppered Cleve with questions: "What is this about anyway? *Sangodemi!* What are you calling on de Brissac for? Why the need of soldiers?"

Cleve eyed him and smiled. "It's considered customary to have guards in attendance when you make an arrest," he observed. "And damme, when so important an arrest comes up, I'm a stickler for form."

"Arrest de Brissac! *Mordi!* What for?"

They were in the bailey of the château and Cleve stopped. "For the murder of the old marquis," he said slowly.

Guy gripped him tightly by the shoulder and pulled him closer. *"Pecaire!* Let me smell your breath, Cleve. You've been drinking!"

"Should have thought of that," the Englishman remarked and smiled. "Mark me, Kitten. I may be wrong, but I don't think so. Remember the wound the *vicomte* received yesterday—the so-called sword wound which Doctor Jaca treated?"

Guy couldn't comprehend the reason for the question, but he nodded anyway. *"Oui,"* he said. "What has that got to do with it?"

"A good deal. You don't use a bullet probe to treat a sword wound, Kitten."

"Parbleu, of course you don't."

"Well, Doctor Jaca did. He admitted it not an hour ago and showed me the probe to prove it."

D'Entreville frowned. He mulled the information over in his mind but he still couldn't see what Cleve was pointing out. He looked up, his lean features a trifle darkened by impatience. "All right, wise-man, cease talking in riddles. What does it mean?"

"It means that d'Oloron did not miss when he fired that pistol, to my way of thinking," Cleve told him calmly. "Not only that—Henri just admitted that his brother was in de Brissac's service, which proves that de Brissac isn't quite as fond of us as he'd have us believe. Furthermore, we have both agreed that the murderer knew the old marquis well and that—"

Guy's face was flushed. *"Sangodemi!"* he snapped. "You needn't draw me pictures, lout! Do you think me an imbecile?"

Cleve chuckled. "Rather not answer that question, Kitten," he responded and turned. "Come on."

THEY FOUND the *vicomte* in the library. Marie d'Oloron was with him. Staring at them through the crack in the door, d'Entreville began to have doubts. Somehow the smooth, pleasant-mannered noble did not seem like a murderer—or, for that matter, act like one. He turned to Cleve and the five musketeers they had brought with them.

"*Peste!* Perchance we are making a mistake, Cleve."

The Englishman nodded agreeably. "All right. We'll leave the men out here and go in and talk with him."

That decided d'Entreville. He shook his head and kicked open the door. "No good, *mon ami.* He might escape."

De Brissac half-rose as the seven streamed into the library. A look of startled indignation was on his face, but it changed to amazement at Guy's first crisp words.

"Don't move, de Brissac! You are under arrest in the King's name. Submit peacefully or suffer the consequence."

Marie d'Oloron's eyes were wide. She stood up suddenly, white-faced and furious. "*Monsieur le comte!*" she snapped. "You go too far with your prank! Take yourself and your men away immediately and leave this house."

"In good time, *mademoiselle,*" Guy returned. "Let me assure you that this is no prank." He stared hard at de Brissac. "Present your blade, *monsieur.*"

The *vicomte* had recovered much of his poise. A faintly amused smile played across his lips as he surrendered his sword. Cleve found himself commending the man's self-possession.

"I have no desire to prevent you gentlemen from making fools of yourselves," de Brissac said coldly. "However, I trust you don't intend carrying this any further."

Guy flushed beneath that sarcasm. "We intend carrying it all the way to the gibbet," he said.

"Really? And of what am I accused?"

"Tell him," Guy said to Cleve.

THE ENGLISH cavalier nodded. He glanced at Marie standing stiffly against the wall. Her face was pale from anger and bewilderment. He found it suddenly difficult to deliver the blunt accusation forming on his tongue. Marie did not know that her father had been murdered. To learn that now and to learn that the man she loved was the murderer, would be unbearable. Cleve could not bring himself to such cruelty. He shrugged and indicated de Brissac's shoulder.

"You are merely being arrested, m'lad, for harboring a sword wound that needed a pistol ball taken from it. Understand?"

At that, the *vicomte's* smile became fixed. A startled, almost worried, expression came into his eyes, but it faded. He inclined his head.

"I comprehend, *monsieur.* And as I have said, you are very astute." He shrugged. "*Pecaire!* Much more astute than I gave you credit for. I should have seen to it. But I am not perturbed."

D'Entreville mentally applauded the way Cleve had handled the situation. He glanced at Marie and found her openly confused by the seemingly senseless conversation. She was beginning to grow angry. Guy wanted to be done with the business as smoothly as possible and that wouldn't be possible if Marie interfered.

"Allons," he said. "Let's be on our way."

Marie stepped forward. "But—this is incredible!"

"It's the King's business, *mademoiselle,*" Guy replied. "Do not hinder it."

"Monsieur—" Eyes flashing, Marie began an angry retort; then suddenly, biting her lower lip, she turned her back on them. Cleve said, "Let's go, m'lad."

They marched de Brissac down into the bowels of the castle and locked him in a cell. He didn't talk—apparently amiable about the business and unworried—but his blue eyes were coldly calculating as they closed the door and bade him a pleasant evening. Outside Guy frowned.

"Sangodemi! Is that all? Don't we question him? Force the truth from him, or something?"

Cleve tossed the key into the air, caught it and tucked it into his sash. He shook his head.

"No. Having adjudged M. de Brissac, I doubt that the Devil himself could make him talk. Silence and time fight for him, Kitten. This arrest is the initial step, but without concrete proof it is liable to become embarrassing. We cannot hold him long without actual evidence. If such isn't immediately forthcoming, we'll have a cursed amount of explaining to do—false arrest of a peer of the realm, you know. Our friend realizes that. He'll not say a word."

"*Mordi!* Then why did you arrest him? Placing our heads in the lion's mouth, Cleve. That's what you've accomplished! What are we going to do?"

Cleve raked a strand of hair out of his eyes and grinned. "Simple," he said easily. "We prove his guilt before morning. We'll start on Henri."

CHAPTER IX

TRAITOR'S HOUSE

ON THE WAY back to the room Guy pieced together the evidence against de Brissac and didn't like the picture it made. Too flimsy! Cleve must be mad.

Even if the wound in the *vicomte's* shoulder had been made by a bullet, it did not necessarily follow that de Brissac had killed d'Oloron. Nor did the fact that his men, and not Spanish agents, had attacked them at the inn, prove very much. Guy sighed. He was as much involved in this as Cleve, and so he could not retreat.

"*Parbleu!* I hope you know what you're doing," he told the Englishman as he opened the door and entered. "Frankly I feel we've made a blunder."

Cleve chuckled and his answer wasn't very reassuring. "We *are* basing our actions on fearfully thin ice, Kitten. But, if the worse comes, the Spanish border is but a league away. We can make it easily ahead of pursuit."

"Now I feel better," Guy said sourly. "Come on, let's to work."

Henri was sitting on a pile of clothes in the far corner of the closet, glowering at nothing. They had decided beforehand what to do and they didn't waste time. The captive was seized and lashed, none too tenderly, to a heavy chair. He protested sullenly at first, and then quite vehemently as d'Entreville deftly strapped a pistol to the back of another chair and placed it opposite him. The cavaliers ignored his protests.

The trigger of the pistol was tied down; then a long candle was crushed; its wick extracted and inserted into the flint-hole and left to dangle. Henri's eyes bulged in terror as he recognized the purpose of these preparations. Cleve eyed him.

"And now, m'lad. You are going to tell us a few things."

Henri lifted his gaze from the pistol and cursed darkly. *"Corbac!* I will not speak! Do your worst. I remain silent!"

Cleve nodded. He sat on the edge of the table, one leg swinging leisurely. "Faith, if we do our worst you will remain silent, true enough." He bent forward. "We know that your master had us attacked at the tavern. We want to know why he suddenly appeared as the rescuer?"

"I don't know," said Henri.

"Damme! You are going to play the dunce, eh? Very well, my bucko. We'll skip that question and the others and break this session down to a single interrogation. Young Gaston d'Oloron has disappeared. He went riding this morning and hasn't been heard from since. From things that your master has told me, I feel that he knows where he is. In fact, I think you also know where Gaston is, my friend. Tell me!"

Henri's dark face was set. Cleve repeated the question: "Where is Gaston?" And still the prisoner remained adamant. With a sigh, the Englishman nodded to d'Entreville. The Frenchman struck a light and touched it to the naked wick dangling from the pistol.

HENRI STARTED as the flame gnawed upward toward the flint-hole and the powder. Possibly a minute would pass before the weapon would fire a ball into his chest. A minute of torture.

His eyes flew to the impassive faces of his captors and then back to that rising flame. Sweat began to bead his forehead. He tried to lean out and away from the ugly black maw of the pistol. His bonds held him rigid, helpless. He stared fascinated, knowing that he was watching death in that flame.

Guy's voice broke the silence. He held thumb and forefinger to the wick five inches above the flame.

"I merely have to slide my fingers down to put it out, Henri," he said softly. "A sudden jerk and you live. Where is Gaston?"

The prisoner was gasping now; his face was working with terror. The flame continued to creep. He licked his lips.

"Le bon dieu! You will murder me!"

"Damme, laddie, you're dying now. Where is Gaston?"

And then Henri broke. He couldn't stand any more. "I'll tell. I'll tell. Put it out! Put it out! Gaston is at de Brissac's manor house." He was screaming it now. "At de Briss—Aaaah!"

The flame had struck a particularly inflammable stretch. In an instant it had leaped and climbed into the flint-hole. Nothing happened—but Henri didn't know that. Henri had fainted.

Cleve stared at d'Entreville over the slumped figure, his lips twisted grimly. He shook his head.

"Faith, Kitten! Out like a light. I'll wager he thought the pistol loaded."

Guy nodded. "It's possible, Cleve," he assented. "It's quite possible, and I wonder why. We did not tell him so, did we?"

DE BRISSAC'S manor lay six miles to the north, near Pau. It had been erected in the Renaissance after the original castle had been razed during the reign of Louis XI. It was a rambling structure, ivy-covered and well kept.

By the time Cleve and d'Entreville arrived at the rough stone-wall that enclosed the grounds, the moon had come out. The house was thrown into a somber scheme of silver and shadow.

Tethering their horses in a leafy thicket, the two rakehellies advanced stealthily. De Brissac's home, they discovered, was shaped roughly in the form of an L. Wide latticed windows faced out upon dark formal gardens. Two had light streaming from them. Above was a gently sloped roof that broke near the eaves into a series of overhanging gables. As Cleve approached one of the casements, Guy melted into the moonlight toward the stables. He joined the English cavalier a moment later with the whispered information that there were only two horses in the stalls.

"Excellent," Cleve murmured and pointed through the window. "There, I believe, are the owners."

The room into which they stared was richly furnished. The *vicomte's* other secretary, known simply as Jean, was sitting with his boots on the table, sampling a goblet of wine and reading a book held open on his lap. Another man, this fellow short-limbed and swarthy, appeared carrying a tray of food. He said something to Jean and the secretary put aside his book, drew a keyring from his sash and went to the door opposite the window. He opened it and the tray-bearer entered. Guy's fingers gripped hard on Cleve's shoulder.

"Pecaire! I'll wager ten to one that Gaston is in that room, Cleve."

The Englishman shook his head. "I won't take it, Kitten. I think you are right."

Suddenly from the front of the house there came the clatter of horses' hoofs and the rumble of a heavy coach. The two rake-hellies sank deep into the shrubbery surrounding the window and waited tensely. Cleve kept one eye on the room. At the sound of the newcomers, Jean and his companion reappeared from behind the door. Jean locked it and followed the other toward the front of the house. Cleve straightened.

"Now's our chance," he whispered. "Come on."

He pressed gently with his palm and the window swung inward. It took but a moment for them to enter the room, but it was going to take a good while longer for them to open the locked door. Cleve's eyes flew wildly around the room in search of some lock-opener. He caught sight of the ruby brooch which held the flowing plumes of d'Entreville's gray hat.

"This will do nicely, thanks," he said and whisked it from the Frenchman's head.

"*Sandiou!*" wailed Guy. "That brooch cost five livres. Why not yours?"

Cleve unhinged the gemmed clasp and returned the hat to its owner. "Mine cost six," he replied.

"*Peste!*"

The brooch did not make a very good lockpick and two tense minutes passed while Cleve feverishly probed the keyhole. From the front of the house came the sound of many voices. Voices with thick Spanish accents. Possibly six of them.

Then Guy whispered from his position by the hall door. "Drop it, *mon ami!* Some one is coming!"

CLEVE NODDED, folded the brooch in his palm and glided over beside his companion. Only one man was coming down the hall. Guy sighed in relief. Beside him, on a wall shelf, was a globular bottle. He picked it up, flexed it thoughtfully, and waited.

The sound of footsteps increased; and then Jean entered. He took two steps into the room before Guy nailed him with a well-timed blow. Cleve caught the limp figure before it reached the floor.

"Neatly done, Kitten. We're in luck. He has the key."

While Guy bound his victim with the silken tie-backs of the portieres, Cleve unlocked the prison door and entered a small chamber that held the trussed person of young Gaston d'Oloron. He was lashed to a chair in front of a table. The food tray was there steaming in the light of a bottle-based candle. Gaston had a gag over his mouth and his arms were tied behind his back. Jean and the other man hadn't had time to untie him for the meal.

"*Les cochons!*" Gaston muttered as Cleve slipped the gag. "For five hours I have been here! *Corbac!* And why?" He looked up. "You are the Paris couriers, aren't you?"

"One of them," Cleve admitted. Guy appeared, dragging senseless Jean into the room. "That is the other. Repulsive, is he not?"

Gaston stared. "Huh?"

"Never mind." Cleve grinned and untied the remaining ropes. "Come here, Kitten. We'll substitute your friend for Gaston. 'Twould be best to gag him and face him away from the door."

It was a business that took but three minutes, and then the three withdrew from the room, locking the door after them. But they had no time to loiter. Even as Cleve turned the key, the sound of many feet could be heard clattering down the hall from the front of the house.

"Back out the window," Guy said. *"Allons.* Quickly."

"One moment," Gaston muttered. "I have some business to settle with de Brissac!"

"Settle it later, m'lad," Cleve grunted and boosted him over he sill after d'Entreville, "You'll find him in your château's dungeon anyway. I placed him there for the murder of your father."

"What!"

"Sacré nom!" muttered Guy. "Silence!" He eyed Cleve as the Englishman squatted in the shrubbery beside him. "Why did you tell him that when we've no time to explain?"

"You claim de Brissac murdered my father?" Gaston asked.

"That's right, laddie. 'Tis one of the reasons you were being held. Now hold your tongue."

They had made it just in time. As Cleve turned and pulled the window closed to a crack, a half-dozen men sauntered into the room. The three sank low against the side of the building, concealing themselves in the shadows and bushes outside the window. With his eye held level with the sill the English cavalier frowned.

The foremost of the six was a richly garbed man of military

carriage with silver-streaked hair and a high-bridged beak of a nose.

"*Mordi!* Don Luis de Sanibel," Gaston whispered.

But Cleve was staring in amazement at the two men immediately behind the Spaniard. Two whom he least expected to see here. Vicomte Charles de Brissac and paunchy little Doctor Jaca!

CHAPTER X

SWORDS OUT FOR RICHELIEU

"*SANGODEMI!*" EXCLAIMED GUY. "Do you see what I see, *mon ami?*" Cleve nodded briefly and held up his hand for silence. The men in the room were talking. De Brissac's unexpected appearance wasn't so much of a mystery when one considered it. Marie had freed him.

The *vicomte* said: "My dear de Sanibel, now is the time for action. Quick action. For if Spain desires Oloron as badly as claimed, then Spain must aid me in taking it."

The ornate Spanish nobleman took a seat beside the table and regarded the speaker with enigmatic black eyes. "Suppose *señor,*" he replied, "suppose you outline briefly your activities since our last conversation."

De Brissac nodded and sat down opposite him. Of the six men in the room, four wore the russet surcoats of the *vicomte.* The other two served the Spaniard. De Brissac hung a limp arm over the back of his chair and relaxed.

"As you know, *monsieur,*" he said, "I have been playing a deep game. Clever, if I may say so. And one in which no suspicion could have been thrown on me."

"But I understand suspicion has been thrown on you, *señor,*" de Sanibel interrupted. "I understand that those two Cardinalist officers placed you under arrest."

The *vicomte* nodded. "They did. But I'm sure they acted purely upon intuition. However, we shall begin at the beginning.

"Let us consider the situation as it was three days ago. The old Marquis d'Oloron was still alive and threatening to interfere with my marriage to his daughter. But more dangerous was his decision to allow Richelieu the privilege of fortifying the border pass.

"Already the couriers bearing the agreement were on their way for his signature. They were due the next day. I had to work quickly, *monsieur*, for if the old marquis signed, then the troops of Louis XIII would be in control of the marquisate and my chances of becoming the new Marquis d'Oloron would be gone.

"Obviously, there was but one thing to do. The old marquis must be disposed of. Not only that, his son and heir, young Gaston, also had to be—er—eliminated. I knew that the sudden deaths of the two might cause suspicion. Suspicion of me, *monsieur*, as marriage to Marie would make me the new marquis.

"Richelieu is no fool and if he suspected foul play in regard to the succession, he would fill d'Oloron with the King's troops and have Louis create a peer to his liking. Such a thing would ruin our scheme."

De Sanibel shifted impatiently. *"Por Dios!"* he snapped. "I am acquainted with the situation."

De Brissac shrugged. "I merely seek to refresh your memory, *monsieur*. Realize the delicacy with which I had to proceed."

"I realize it, *señor*. The marquis had to be murdered without suspicion, as did his son. Now proceed."

"Very well." The *vicomte's* eyes were cold. "I killed the old marquis. While eight of my best men lay in ambush for the cardinal's men, I waited on a hillock south of the château. When the marquis appeared for his daily ride, as I knew he would, I joined him pleasantly and suggested that we try our horsemanship on the path leading over Falcon Pass.

"Naturally, the old fool accepted. He was ever a conceited pig about his ability in the saddle, you know. We rode up the mountain side. When we reached the highest spot, I maneuvered my mount between his and the outer lip of the cliff. And then, as I commenced to veer into him, he saw my intent and drew his horsepistol. Too late, of course, to save himself.

"He was already sliding to death as he fired, but his wildly aimed ball caught me in the shoulder. And then he was gone." The speaker smiled grimly. "A riding accident, you see."

A SOBBED curse burst from young Gaston's throat and he started to rise, but Guy jerked him down and held a hard palm over his mouth. Inside, de Sanibel was nodding approvingly.

"Excellently conceived, *amigo.*"

De Brissac didn't smile. It was as though the Spaniard's praise had sharply reminded him of his failure. De Sanibel recognized it.

"But your plan to ambush the two officers of Richelieu's Guard failed, didn't it, *señor!*"

"*Oui.* However, I thought at the time I could make use of the failure. My secretaries, Henri and Jean, awaited me on the other side of Falcon Pass. When we met my men in full flight, I conceived what I then considered an excellent plan. Remember, young Gaston had yet to be put out of the way, and it has always been my belief than a man can trust luck only so far.

"I had been fortunate in the elimination of the old marquis. But Gaston's death too soon on its heels might bring about an investigation. I decided to allow the Crown of France dispose of Gaston for me."

"*Dios!* How?"

"Simple. I appeared before Cleve and d'Entreville as friend and savior. The pistol wound I claimed as a sword-wound received from the men who had just attacked the two of them. It worked beautifully. When they discovered, by the ridiculously simple method of investigating d'Oloron's pistol, that the old man had been murdered, I created a tale to the effect that Gaston had committed it. I told a neat story concerning his treason and proved it by producing forged letters. You understand?"

"*Si.* Clever indeed, *señor.* You put a traitor's noose neatly about that young fool's neck. *Por Dios!* And yet tonight you were arrested."

"*Oui.* And if it had not been for Marie, I would still be languishing in a dirty cell." The speaker looked up. "But for your henchman, *monsieur,* young Gaston might still be wanted for treason and murder."

IN THE background Doctor Jaca's round face grew pale. He quailed. "But, *señor*—I was flustered by that mad Englishman. I did not know you had claimed that a sword had wounded your shoulder. The probe was there. I said—"

De Sanibel frowned. "*Dios!* Of what is he babbling?"

De Brissac said harshly, "Your stupid intermediary, Don Luis. That fat little slug! That blunderer told Cleve that my wound was a pistol wound."

De Sanibel scratched his cheek. "I still do not see—"

"*Sangodemi!* Richard Cleve has the mind of a steel snare. It clamps suddenly upon trifles and makes much of them. The moment he learned that my wound had not been caused by a blade, he put two and two together and glimpsed the truth.

"That is why I was suddenly thrown under arrest. That is why this whole beautiful plot has to be abandoned. Cleve is clever. Given enough time and he'll prove those things which are now only suspicions. I had planned to become master of Oloron by trickery. But now I must use force.

"The moment Cleve speaks his suspicions to Richelieu, I am undone. We must work quickly, *monsieur,* Spain has troops at the border. Lend them to me and I'll take the château before France can stop me. My marriage to Marie will give me some legal claim to the marquisate and we'll dispose of Gaston immediately. Say the word, *monsieur* and Oloron belongs to Spain."

Don Luis de Sanibel stood up. "You are suggesting war, *señor,*" he said. "A thing contrary to our previous agreement. You were to establish yourself as legal Marquis d'Oloron before Spain supported your secession from France."

"*Mordi!* You want the mariquisate?"

"*Si!* But without a war which could not be justified. Become the Marquis d'Oloron on your initiative, *señor*. Spain has promised you the title of duke and a chest of gold to turn the mariquisate over to her, once you have been recognized. She cannot support a frank usurper. She *will* support the legal heir if he should petition to become part of the Spanish Empire. That is the way it must be."

De Brissac rose to his feet. His face was white, determined; the face of a man made suddenly desperate by the press of his ambition. "Very well," he said. "That was our agreement. I'll abide by it. Within the week, *monsieur,* I shall become the legal marquis. Mark me, one week."

De Sanibel smiled and put on his hat. "*Bueno, señor,* and I shall await the occasion with pleasure." Then, with a nod for his attendants to proceed him, he left the room followed shortly by Doctor Jaca.

De Brissac stood scowling into space for a moment; then he turned to the four men remaining. From the front of the house the rattle of coach-wheels announced the departure of the Spaniard. The *vicomte* paid it no heed.

"Rene, Paul. Ride to the village and collect twenty of your fellows. Tonight we rid the earth of the only two men who suspect my secret. Cleve and d'Entreville! With them out of the picture, perchance—"

"Damme! Did somebody mention my name?"

IT WAS Cleve. With a grim chuckle the English rakehelly had stood up and kicked open the window. Behind him rose d'Entreville and young Gaston. For a moment the five in the room presented an amazed, frozen tableau; and then Cleve broke silence.

"I want to thank you, de Brissac. You talked yourself into a traitor's noose just a moment ago. Prior to it, I admit being a trifle hazy as to your method and motives."

"*Sangodemi!*"

De Brissac's uninjured hand darted to his rapier. He retreated behind his retainers. Cleve shook his head. Guy had his blade out and glittering in the light of the candles. For lack of a sword, young Gaston had picked up a garden tile and the expression on his face indicated an urgent desire to use it.

"Put down your blades, gentlemen." Cleve smiled. "You are all under arrest. Monotonous, isn't it, de Brissac? We have nipped you twice in one evening."

"*Sandiou!*" snarled the *vicomte*. "You'll never take me! You won't leave this place alive!" He laughed, almost hysterically. "*Ma foi!* You have played into my hand. Take them, men. Cut them down. All three!"

But the *vicomte's* men did not start it. Young Gaston did. With a wild cry he hurled the heavy garden tile straight at de Brissac's head. The intent was excellent, but Gaston had not seen the sudden forward dash of a sword-flourishing hireling. The fellow took the tile alongside the jaw and sat down abruptly. His sword described a twisting arc through the air. D'Entreville caught it in mid-flight and tossed it hilt-first to Gaston.

"Here, *mon enfant*. Fight like a gentleman!"

Then steel began to ring in earnest. The men whom de Brissac had hired were not amateurs. Cleve started to engage two at a clip, but found it too dangerous and relinquished one to Guy's more nimble blade. Then he began to drive his single adversary toward the front of the house via the hallway, the main hall and the foyer. It was a pretty duel until the fellow broke the rules and commenced hurling things.

"Gad! Two can play that game," Cleve panted. He ducked a twirling candlestick, thrust quickly in *sixte* and scooped a bottle from the debris at his feet. The bottle was headed for the fellow's nose and he lifted his swordarm to fend it off. It was a mistake. Cleve's blade licked deep into the exposed side and the man collapsed like a stringless puppet.

IN THE other room young Gaston found his work cut out for him. He was faced by a cursing adversary; short, bearded and powerful of wrist. The youth had to use every bit of his skill to keep from being skewered. But the fight reached a stalemate. Each man had a strong defense and little inclination to forget it long enough to press a sustained attack.

Meanwhile, Guy faced de Brissac and a hard-eyed bravo with a scar. The *vicomte* was undeniably a superior swordsman. Guy recognized it by the deft manner he employed in attack. But de Brissac's pistol wound hampered him.

The scar-faced man fought from a deep crouch. Guy had been up against that sort of duelist before. Suddenly he bent away from the crouched man, feinting lightly at de Brissac's wounded side. Scar-face straightened. His face held triumph as he lifted his blade for a high downward thrust.

But he was exposed now. Guy came down into a neatly squatting position, swerving as he did so. He put his point into Scar-face's belly, and the man screamed.

Then de Brissac struck. His blade licked into Guy's exposed shoulder. The *vicomte* laughed as he saw the blood.

"Now we are equal, *cochon!* Each with a wound!"

The French rakehelly retreated slightly. But de Brissac wasn't allowing him to recover from the shock of the pain. He charged forward to finish the business. And Guy met him. Met him with a deftly twisting blade that gripped the *vicomte's* rapier hilt and smashed the weapon from his hand. It had happened so quickly that de Brissac stood stunned for a second, staring.

"Surrender, *monsieur,*" Guy gasped.

But de Brissac turned and fled. *"Mordi!* You'll never take me. You'll never take me—"

He paused in the hall. Advancing cheerfully from its other end was Cleve, sword slanted carelessly. Behind the *vicomte* was d'Entreville. The glare of a trapped animal was in de Brissac's eyes. There was a staircase near the middle of the hall wall and he leaped toward it. The two rakehellies converged and pounded up after him.

They reached the second floor in time to see the *vicomte*

fumbling at a window. He whirled at their appearance and fled down the hall toward another set of stairs at the end. Up he climbed and they followed.

"Give it up, de Brissac! You're through."

"Am I?" The *vicomte's* voice laughed harshly from the far end of the attic. Then the roof-trap was flung open and he was climbing through it into the starlit night.

"*Corbac!* He's going over the roof and toward the stables," Guy shouted. "It's a mad chance, but he might make it!"

But de Brissac didn't make it. The roof slates were slimy with the dew of night. He started to climb toward the peak and then one foot slid from under him. Cleve and d'Entreville heard his yell of terror and the scratching, kicking slide of his body toward the eaves. There came a fading scream that ended in a sickening thud. And then silence.

They found him sprawled on the tiles in front of the main door. Gaston came up panting, having finally chased his bearded opponent through a window and into the night. He stopped and stared at the still form.

"Dead?"

Cleve nodded. "Very. Broken neck. He was a clever man, friends. Too damned clever for his own welfare."

Nobody said anything for a moment. But finally Gaston stirred. "*Messieurs,*" he said quietly, "if you will return to Château d'Oloron with me, I shall sign the Cardinal's agreement."

D'Entreville nodded and slid his blade back into his sheath. Something about the abrupt termination of the whole affair affected him deeply. Then he shrugged. "Very well, *monsieur le marquis,*" he said. "Let's go. *Sandiou!* You know I sense a poetic justice here tonight. The old marquis was murdered by a fall. He died of a broken neck, too."

SWORDS IN EXILE

Ho for the Cardinal's men! With sword in hand and peril their companion, Cleve and d'Entreville carry the might of Richelieu into a traitors' paradise

CHAPTER I

THE MASTER OF FRANCE

THE DAY WAS one of blue and gold and the veins of the city—the narrow, twisted Parisian streets—were swollen with life, raucous with the yells of hawkers, the clatter of hoofs and the rumble of wheels. But quiet hung over the Cardinal's palace, the quiet of efficiency, as Sir Harry Winthrop's travel-dusty coach rolled past the headquarters of the guard into the courtyard.

A glittering fountain, pluming spray, centered the expanse of cobbles, while metal hitching-racks, stone stanchioned and topped by leonine heads of bronze, appeared to right and left. In a far corner a squad of the Cardinal's Guards were drilling—drilling smoothly against the handsome façade of the east wing, their crossed surcoats dazzling in the sun, their swordhilts a-gleam.

The coach came to a stop and Sir Harry descended. Ten days ago he had sat opposite the Earl of Strafford at Whitehall to plead vehemently for a French appointment. But; now, pacing down the red-carpeted corridors of the palace, he began to experience his first full elation of relief. Strafford had insisted that he take the Venetian mission. In Venice he wouldn't have to match wits with a man of Richelieu's obvious genius. The thought was comforting.

His guide ushered him ceremoniously through a Gothic archway—an archway portiered in maroon, guarded by resplendent halbardiers—and into a large foyer.

"Make yourself comfortable, *monsieur*. I shall announce your arrival. But it may take a moment. *Monseigneur le Cardinal* is extremely busy."

Sir Harry could understand that. He sat down on a plush-backed chair and placed his hat across his knees. The guide nodded, turned and disappeared through an oak-panelled door. Left alone, Sir Harry fell to a consideration of personal issues; namely, the reason for his presence at Richelieu Palace.

The reason was Richard Cleve. Lord Richard Cleve, a brilliant young fool who had become exiled from England because of a fondness for speaking the truth at the wrong times. The truth in this case had concerned ten thousand pounds which had disappeared into the Duke of Buckingham's pockets instead of into the Royal Treasury.

But now Cleve was to be pardoned and the official document

allowing his return to England was in Sir Harry's possession, signed by Charles I and stamped with the great seal of state.

With a frown, Sir Harry drew it forth and regarded it. He had known Cleve in England and he hadn't approved. For one thing, Cleve was a talent-waster; a man who considered life a game. He had a fine mind, yet he was entirely willing to squander his ability and enjoy himself. To Sir Harry that bordered on the criminal. Winthrop himself had but a single talent—a determination to prevail over an innate lack of competence.

But it had carried him from a merchantman's quarterdeck to knighthood, and if this Venetian mission came off, there was an excellent chance of a peerage. Not bad! He shrugged and returned the document to its place.

He steepled his fingers and stared over their tips at the great clock in the corner. Twenty minutes gone! Did Richelieu consider himself an unapproachable deity that he could keep a representative of Britain waiting?

He felt suddenly and violently urged to go and kick open the door. But he refrained. Another minute crawled away. Then the oaken partition swung inward and his guide reentered the foyer.

"*Monseigneur le Cardinal* will grant you ten minutes, *monsieur.*"

THE CARDINAL'S library was a high-ceilinged room; spacious, yet heavy with carpets and furnishings. Except for patterned shafts of sunlight cast through latticed windows, it lay dim in shadow. At the far end, behind a huge mahogany desk, sat Richelieu, a ribbon of light streaming over one shoulder.

The Cardinal's scarlet robe was brilliant beneath the gold cascade. He was talking in soft tones to a huge monk to whom he gave a heavy folio and dismissed as Sir Harry approached.

The interview began. Cleve's pardon was presented, inspected silently, and returned. Then the Cardinal, frowning slightly, relaxed against his chair.

"Unfortunately, *monsieur,* you are late. Lord Cleve is no longer in my service. It was necessary to discharge him a week ago."

Sir Harry nodded absently. He found himself pondering how

so frail appearing a man could control the destinies of France. Richelieu's thin face was delicately chiseled, aristocratic, almost ethereal; although now, the sunlight reflected from the desk-surface lent it a bright vitality.

Then the import of the Cardinal's statement struck Sir Harry and he frowned. He disliked having his time wasted, much less his patience, and yet his strong sense of duty prevented capitulation without a semblance of effort.

"Perchance Your Eminence has some information concerning Cleve's whereabouts," he suggested.

"I fear not. But I can vouch that he is not in Paris, *monsieur*. That young rakehelly's penchant for trouble usually advertises his presence, and to date my city has been quite peaceful."

There had been dry humor in that statement, but to Sir Harry it only inferred that Richard Cleve hadn't changed. He rolled the pardon into a cylinder and thrust it into his sash.

"I regret this intrusion, Your Eminence," he apologized.

Richelieu's dark eyes glittered with irony for a moment, and then they were enigmatic again. He lifted tapering fingers to the gold medallion on his chest and stood up, not a tall man, but seemingly so because of the sweep of his robe.

"You might try the English ambassador," he suggested.

Sir Harry shook his head. "The English ambassador directed me to you, *monseigneur*." He hesitated. "No. M'Lord Cleve shall have to do without his reprieve for the present. Finding him was not my chief duty anyway."

With a stiff bow, he thanked the prelate for his time and withdrew. Outside he paused. Logically the next move would be to re-visit the English ambassador and have him seek out the exile, but as it would necessitate two hours' delay, he decided against it. He had wasted enough time. Besides, he would repass through Paris next month and could as easily locate Cleve then as now—and with more leisure.

"No by Gad! Cleve may well pay for my inconvenience." And he climbed into the swaying confines of his coach. He leaned from the window and addressed the postillion. "We are leaving Paris, Jacob. Find the road to Troyes. Be off!"

BEHIND IN the library, Richelieu stood thoughtfully by his desk listening as the silver-faced clock on the mantle chimed ten. At length he sat down and stared across the intervening space at Père Joseph, a cassocked figure bending over a small table in the corner.

"And so, Joseph," he said. "Lord Cleve shall remain in my service by virtue of a lie." His fingers traced the brocade of the pen-pad. "I wonder if I have done wisely?"

Joseph closed the folio he had been scanning and stood up. Contrasting sharply with Richelieu, he was a stocky man, full-bellied and bearded. He had eyes of soft brown, deep in his head beneath bushy russet brows. His nose was lumpish. Yet there was a vivaciousness about his ugliness, and a sense of deep intelligence, which made understandable his position as sole confidant to Richelieu. He had little use for Cleve, or for that other young scamp, le Comte d'Entreville.

"As I see it, *monseigneur,*" he replied, "you have relieved England of a peer to give France a rogue!"

The Cardinal smiled thinly at that. "Precisely. But a most resourceful rogue, Joseph. Incidentally you might have Capitaine Cordeau place him under restraint until we are assured that Winthrop has left Paris. It would not do to have him discover that Cleve still serves me."

Père Joseph frowned. "But Cleve is not in Paris, *monseigneur.*"

"Not in—" The Cardinal stiffened. *"Peste!* If that insubordinate scoundrel has—"

"He hasn't, *monseigneur.* He and the other one, d'Entreville, are now in Metz under your orders."

For a moment the Cardinal appeared nonplussed; and then he frowned. "Metz? I gave no such orders, Joseph."

The Capuchin sighed patiently and folded hands over his paunch. "Last week, *monseigneur,* you commanded an Austrian agent, Baron Von Erla, to leave France. A matter of unprovable espionage, if you will remember. To make certain that he obeyed your order, I was told to select two alert Guardsmen as escorts. As the Baron is a clever rogue, I gave him cleverer rogues as guards. Cleve and d'Entreville, *monseigneur.*"

Richelieu remembered it now, but he didn't look pleased. "Did you have to send them both to Metz?"

The monk shrugged. "You have said yourself that one is worthless without the other. I sent both."

"Then recall both. I need Cleve's cunning and d'Entreville's sword."

"Oui, monseigneur."

Joseph left to arrange for a Metz-minded carrier pigeon.

CHAPTER II

NET FOR THE KITTEN

NOW CALAIS IS some two hundred and thirty miles distant from Metz. It borders the sea instead of the Moselle; and on the day in question, it lay somnolent in the noon glare, its harbor a-clutter with shipping so motionless as to seem painted there.

Capitan Laredos, pacing the weather-worn planking of his quarterdeck, cursed the calm with all the fire of his Spanish heart. His vessel, a dainty brig named *Donna Isabella,* sat high— too damned high for a ship due to leave port. But then, she had arrived in the same condition, empty as a result of his ambitious attempt to bring lemons up from Spain. The fruit had been dumped, a mass of putrefaction, into the sea. And now, with a cargo waiting at Cadiz, he was being held by the same sort of tranquility that had allowed his lemons to rot.

He ceased pacing and took a position by the taffrail, to stare askance at the end of the quay.

Threading his way leisurely through the loafers and cluttered ship's gear, came a stranger. A slim-waisted, rakishly clad stranger, who out of deference to the heat, wore a shirt open at the throat and thigh-high Cordovan boots turned down from the calf. The fellow's white-plumed hat was cuffed negligently at a tilt on his chestnut head, and his short, white-crossed military cape was draped carelessly from one broad shoulder. The cape covered the hilt of a long, black-sheathed rapier. He was dashing, gallant spectacle, but to little Miguel Laredos he was a portent of trouble.

THE NEWCOMER was a soldier—apparently an officer in the Cardinal's Guard; and from long experience in all forms of maritime illegality, from smuggling to petty piracy, Miguel Laredos had developed an inherent distrust of officialdom. He started down the break in the poop, intent upon reaching his cabin and seclusion, but he was too late. The newcomer intercepted him.

"One moment, Captain. I would a word with you."

Laredos licked his lips and nodded. *"Si, señor?"*

"I have been told that you are planning to sail for Cadiz tonight, Captain."

"Si. If there is a wind."

The cavalier looked across the harbor and smiled. "Sounds reasonable," he conceded and fumbled in the cuff of his right gauntlet. He produced a rumpled but official looking document, spotted with seals and ribbons. Laredos gulped. This was it—an arrest!

"Dios arriba, señor!" he exploded. "I did not do it! You have the wrong man!"

"Think so?"

Laredos drew up righteously. "I know, *señor!*"

The Guardsman looked up from the document; cocked an eyebrow. "Damme. I don't think you know either. As a matter of fact, this paper is the deportation order for one Baron Von Erla. I have been told to see that he leaves France. He's not a vicious lad really, just naughty. Has a habit of prying, you know—gossipmonger in a political sense. I have been wondering if you would be kind enough to tender him a cabin until you reach Spain—under orders of the French Crown, of course."

"*Si, señor. Si!* But, of course." There was great relief in the captain's voice.

The other caught it and smiled. "Fine. Thought you'd see it that way, m'lad. The baron will be delivered in two hours. And now, good afternoon."

Laredos nodded. He didn't say anything. He found himself trying to place the speaker. Somewhere in the past he had known a man....

And then he caught it. Five years ago, as mate on a small Spanish lugger, he had stood off Portsmouth of a fog-cursed evening, to pick up an English noble going into exile. That nobleman had been—

"*Dios!*" He exclaimed. "Lord Cleve!"

BUT CLEVE was past the end of the gang-plank and strolling along the crowded quay out of ear-shot. He was busy weighing, for the fiftieth time, the practicability of returning immediately to Paris, or idling a week or so along the coast in an impromptu holiday. D'Entreville was against the latter alternative. But then Guy had an unhealthy tendency to be duty-struck, anyway.

The street paralleled the harbor, running south along its edge like a ragged hem-ribbon. It was a conglomeration of noise, fish-stink and listless traffic. Cleve's throat felt cottony and little rivulets of perspiration glistened on his bronzed forehead.

By Jupiter, he decided, a tankard of ale would not go amiss now, and he knew where to get it. He and Guy had put up with their captive at a little inn known as Le Bateau d'Or, and it excelled in full-bodied, nut-brown ale imported from England.

Then rounding the corner, he came upon a small crowd in front of the tavern. A curious, staring crowd, gathered before the tavern's door, pointing and talking excitedly. He frowned, knowing that Le Bateau d'Or was not a place to attract attention. It was small and frequented chiefly by fishermen.

He hitched up his rapier and moved forward as the unmistakable sounds of war assailed his ears. There was hoarse cursing, and the clash of blades. He sighed and collared an urchin.

"What's brewing, laddie?"

The boy squirmed free. "Fight, *monsieur.*"

From the interior of the inn somebody was beginning to yowl curses concerning a slashed nose.

"*Sangodemi!*" a tenor voice shouted. "Perchance next time you'll not be in a heat to thrust that nose into the King's business!"

Cleve nodded. That was d'Entreville. The Frenchman had been left in charge of Von Erla. Something had gone amiss.

THEN SUDDENLY a gentleman appeared in the tavern-door. A lean, fox-faced gentleman with flinty blue eyes, a mustache and blond hair. His pearl-studded green doublet, his wide-brimmed hat and his embroidered cape were worn with a courtier's grace, but the sword-sheath at his side was empty and his laced collar was turned askew. He paused a moment, and then began striding rapidly southward. Cleve shook his head.

"Uh-uh." He intercepted him. "Damme! Fancy bumping into you, Von Erla. Going anywhere in particular?"

The Austrian didn't turn. He stiffened as though doused with cold water. For a moment he seemed prepared to make a break for it, and then he saw the laughing dare in Cleve's eyes and relaxed. A week with the Englishman had proven enlightening and disheartening. The more personable Cleve's manner, the more dangerous he became. Von Erla shrugged.

"No place in particular, my friend."

Cleve nodded understandingly. "I see. Suppose we return to the tavern." He gestured. "After you, *chéri.*"

The baron smiled politely, but only with his lips. His eyes were chill.

The interior of Le Bateau d'Or proved to be in bad shape. Tables overturned, shattered dishes, a dozen pewter tankards scattered on the floor. But the room was silent, apparently empty. Cleve frowned slightly and stared.

Then from behind a toppled table appeared a head. It was the bald, glistening head, the terrified face of Janard, the innkeeper. Cleve regarded him sharply.

Janard was incapable of more than four words. He used them and jerked a pudgy thumb toward the rear. "They went that way."

"Thanks." Cleve turned to Von Erla. "All right, bucko. How did you arrange it?"

The Austrian shrugged. "Last evening at dinner I saw a man whom I had used once in Paris. As we passed his table I slipped him a note promising him ten livres if he'd collect a few friends and rid me of your company."

"Neat," Cleve nodded. "Very neat." He gripped Von Erla's arm. "Let's proceed."

There was a closet near the entrance to the kitchen. He ushered Von Erla into it and rammed home the bolt. He drew his blade and strolled leisurely through the kitchen toward the rear, whistling softly as he walked.

STEPPING OUT into the quay behind the tavern, he came upon a glinting scene of swordplay. Four hirelings were busily attacking a tall, maroon-clad cavalier who met all blades with quick parries and lightning ripostes. Cleve eyed the combat, found a three-legged stool, and sat down.

"Not bad, Kitten. But rather conceited of you to take on four at a time."

The man in maroon countered a thrust in *sixte* and darted a glance at the speaker. He frowned and snapped: *"Sangodemi! Don't sit there, you English lout! Do something! Von Erla staged this for escape. Catch him!"*

Cleve nodded. "I did. He's in the broom closet."

"Huh?" D'Entreville straightened.

"Faith, Guy! Heed your business!"

Cleve leaped to his feet and sent his stool skidding across the dock into the legs of the bravo who had succeeded in flanking d'Entreville. The fellow tried to hurdle, missed and fell flat on his face. Cleve sighed.

"Pure carelessness, Kitten."

Guy d'Entreville's lips tightened. They were thin lips, almost severe. He was dark-eyed, a good two inches taller than Cleve, with hair like rippled pitch, a clipped military spade-beard and an aristocratic nose so high-bridged as to set a hawkish cast to his features. Now he pirouetted to avoid a vicious lunge; countered swiftly to drive the lunger back. He swept aside the jabbing blades of two others with one furious parry. But the fourth man, fast recovering from contact with Cleve's stool, jumped to his feet and his steel licked a cut in d'Entreville's forearm.

At that, Cleve straightened.

A seine was hung for drying at the end of the dock. It slanted like a half tent from a single cable tethered to the tavern wall and running to a high pole at the quay's sea-end. Cleve regarded it thoughtfully, placed the stool directly beneath and climbed atop.

"A trifle left, Kitten," he directed.

D'Entreville wiped the sweat from his forehead and nodded. He showered savage thrusts into the faces of the four bravos, keeping them so engaged that they did not observe the Englishman's intent. They retreated before the sudden fury of his attack. The netting of the seine rippled criss-cross shadows atop their bobbing heads.

Cleve's naked blade swung in a short arc. It bit deeply into the thick cable supporting the seine, jerked free and slashed once more. The line broke, cut neatly at the base, and came piling down—down upon the startled, weaving quartet. There was a crescendo of howls.

"Net profit," he observed, sheathing his steel, "four would-be sharks." He stared. "But, damme! Where's d'Entreville?"

A writhing lump, detached by ten feet from the netted bravos, attracted Cleve's attention. The lump was wriggling furiously and futilely, pausing only to give vent to prodigious oaths. Cleve approached, lifted the edge of the net and chuckled.

"Four sharks and a cat-fish," he corrected. "Climb out, Kitten."

CHAPTER III

FOX IN THE CLOSET

FRIEDERICH CARL, BARON VON ERLA, was not in a good humor. Besides being dark, the broom closet was stuffy, and it was crowded. He jerked the offending stench of a wet mop-head from beneath his chin and sat down.

He had known of Richelieu's deportation order almost immediately. And he hadn't worried. In fact, he had allowed himself to be arrested. Why not? The information he had sought in Paris had been acquired and his next field of operation lay in Savoy. Metz, as a point of egress, had suited his purpose.

But he had reckoned without Cleve and d'Entreville. If only Richelieu had assigned two reputable Guardsmen as his escorts, instead of a pair of impossible rakehellies whose main concern seemed a desire to throw cats into his most carefully conceived plans.

The reason for his presence in Calais was disgraceful. Von Erla could wax as enthusiastic over an *affair d'amour* as the next man, but not when it entailed a breach of discipline, and when it was absurd anyhow. That moonstruck fool d'Entreville....

Guy had met a girl named Mary de Sarasnac at a mask ball in Paris three weeks ago and had straightway become mad. He hadn't seen her since, but at the time she had told him that she lived in Calais; she had given her name and a kiss, and disappeared, leaving Guy with a passionate desire to visit the northwestern part of the country. The baron had learned all this from subsequent conversations between Cleve and the romantic d'Entreville.

Von Erla shifted his seat to wider-based pail which he had gropingly inverted for the purpose. He frowned into the darkness. Because of Mary de Sarasnac, he was now seated in a small broom closet in Calais. Even d'Entreville had not benefited by this outrageous expedition. Apparently, the girl had been playing the coquette, for her address had been a bogus one and d'Entreville had soon learned that no beauty answering the name of Mary de Sarasnac had ever lived in Calais.

Von Erla would remember her name with distaste for as long as he lived. She had wrecked his reputation for efficiency. According to instructions from Vienna, he was supposed to be in Savoy, coercing its fat duke into an Austrian alliance against France. He was supposed to be there now!

HE LIFTED one foot through the dark and placed it carefully against the closet door. He twisted and placed a hand against the wall behind, and then he began to press against the panels.

It didn't work. He lifted his other foot, arched his back and tried again. He held his breath and strained against the black partition. And then somebody opened the door and he shot out of the closet like a cork from a bottle.

"Himmelherrgottkreusmillionen!"

Cleve and d'Entreville were there, flanking him on either side.

"Pecaire!" the Frenchman said. "I'll wager he can't repeat it."

Cleve regarded the prostrate baron, mild reproof in his eyes and said. "Damme! You must haven been in a fearful hurry." Then he turned to d'Entreville. "I'll take that wager."

But Von Erla didn't trust himself to say more than: "I don't propose to serve your perverted humor further, *messieurs*." And climbed to his feet.

Guy turned to Cleve. "He didn't repeat. Pay me."

Cleve brushed an imaginary thread from his sleeve. He looked surprised and pained. "Pay you what? I lose but we set no stakes."

"Peste! I might have known you would default. Of all the—"

"Temper, Kitten," the other reproved with a grin. He took Von Erla by the arm. "Let us leave, Baron. Your coach is without, loaded and waiting."

Von Erla's smile ill-concealed his eagerness. "We are leaving at last for Metz, eh?"

D'Entreville stepped up. He didn't like the Austrian. He took little pains to conceal it, which was typical of him. "We're leaving Calais, true enough. But not for Metz. Since Austria and Spain are in such accord these days, we are sending you to Cadiz."

The baron's smile stiffened. Cadiz! He didn't want to go to Cadiz! It added nearly three weeks to his already strained schedule. Not Cadiz!

"Donner und Blitzen!" he exclaimed. "You cannot do this! You were ordered to place me outside of France at Metz. Gentlemen, I insist that you obey orders."

"Very well," Cleve soothed. "But some other time."

But the bid for harmony was wasted. At the dock, Von Erla was coldly venomous in his objections to embarkation. Guy took it as long as his patience lasted, and then offered the Austrian the alternative of silencing himself, or having it done for him— with the point of a sword. The baron accepted the former, though sullenly, and the last they saw of him was his hard, fox-like features framed in the after-port of his cabin, lips moving in silent curses.

UPON DISPOSAL of the coach, the two gallants stood in the bailey of the royal fort and battled over whether or not they should return at once to Paris. Guy wanted to hasten back immediately. He was having qualms over his flagrant breach of discipline.

But Cleve felt otherwise. "Faith! We've come this far, Kitten. If we are to roast, it may as well be for sheep as for lambs."

Guy frowned. The quiet, reckless philosophy of that statement was characteristic of Cleve. A sort of damned-to-the-consequence attitude, assumed casually and maintained as if its author was ironically amused by his own willingness to invite trouble for the interest of its solution.

"Don't be ridiculous!" Guy snapped. "There'll be no roasting if we return immediately. Richelieu will not be the wiser." He started away. "Come along, *mon ami.*"

"To Paris?"

"Yes."

Cleve turned to an officer idling a few paces away and nodded. The man smiled and stepped forward.

"Your pardon, *messieurs.* I have been given to understand that one of you is le Comte d'Entreville."

Guy paused. "That's right," he said.

The man bowed and produced a fold of paper. "I am Philip Chaumont, *monsieur.* My cousin has entreated me to deliver this note to you."

"Oui? Who is your cousin?"

"Mary de Sarasnac, *monsieur.*"

"Mary de Saras—Parbleu!" The cavalier accepted the envelope with snatching fingers. Tearing it open, he muttered a hurried apology and buried his eyes in the contents.

Cleve stared innocently at the lazily stirring lily-banner over the portcullis, grinned and withdrew a pace with the officer. A slip of paper passed furtively between them.

"Your gambling note for two hundred livres, m'lad."

"Merci. But if you hadn't had such infernal fortune with the dice last night, I never would have considered this. Playing pranks on the Cardinal's Kitten isn't healthy."

CHAPTER IV

TIGHT LITTLE ISLE

AN HOUR FOUND the port of Calais a small lump on the sky-rim behind them. They were riding leisurely southward down the winding shore road leading toward Cap Griz Nez and Boulogne. On one side of them, glinting in the afternoon sun, lay the Straits of Dover, and to their left were the flat, sand-gritted levels of northwestern France. Except for a group of fishermen repairing netting on the beach, the scene was almost desolate.

"Peculiar way to go to Paris," Cleve observed. He spurred alongside so that they rode knee to knee.

D'Entreville didn't answer immediately. He scowled and began to construct an evasion. Capitulation to Cleve's holiday suggestion would be difficult to stomach, and yet it had to be done if her precious note was to be honored.

Finally he said: "I've been considering, *mon ami. Sandiou!* We were becoming jaded in Paris. The summer heat and the stench caused by it from street refuse, the constant brawling and intrigue. Bad for the health, *mon ami. Oui,* very bad. What we need is fresh air, a change of scenery and perhaps—"

Cleve nodded wisely. "Faith! Even the court leaves Paris during the summer, Kitten." He rolled back in the saddle and cuffed his plumed hat aslant over one eye and chuckled. "Now what's the true reason?"

Guy sighed. "Oh well." He shrugged. "Mary de Sarasnac is visiting in Boulogne." Then, more quickly. "Having her so near justifies further detour."

Cleve grinned complacently. "That's the way I thought of it," he said and patted himself on the shoulder.

They followed the shore road for an hour. Then a trim wayside tavern, gay with its red roof and green shutters, appeared in the distance atop a low promontory overlooking the sea. They put up at it and Cleve left to see about fresh horses. Guy headed doorward intent upon ordering their supper.

THE TAVERN'S interior was neat and confined to utilitarian furnishings. Shelves laden with pewter tankards; plates and trays lined the walls. A great stone hearth, wherein a suckling pig was stretched, spitted and sizzling, occupied the furthest end. A small table in a window alcove attracted Guy's attention and he settled himself behind it to wait for the landlord. Then he bethought himself of his letter.

He carefully drew it forth and opened it. There it was! Couched in her own hand. An apology for the trouble she had caused him in a moment of perverse merriment, and an invitation to visit her at her uncle's estate near Boulogne.

He regarded the paper dreamy-eyed, and then grew suspicious. Since when did a woman write from Boulogne on the stationery of the military governor of Calais? How could she?… The answer loomed quickly. She couldn't!

"Something's rotten," he murmured softly, and repeated: "*Corbac!* Something's very rotten!"

He balled the forgery in his fist and started for the door with long strides. He met the stableman entering, and only because the fellow had nimble feet was a violent collision prevented. Guy looked at him.

"Where is that viper? That two faced, double-dealing jackanapes, that lying—"

The stableman was nonplussed. "Viper, *monsieur?* You mean the gentleman with whom you arrived?"

"*Sangodemi!* He's no gentleman, but I came with him true enough. Where is he?"

"Down by the sea-wall, *monsieur.*"

Guy thanked him and strode on. In his mind there was not the slightest doubt that the forgery was Cleve's work. He had been with the English rakehelly too long not to recognize this

species of duplicity. The spirited banter which had always char-
acterized their friendship was all right in its place, but this latest
of Cleve's jokes touched upon a serious, yes, a sacred matter.
Thudding over the turf of the inn's after-yard, he wondered what
he was going to do, and hoped that it was something horrible.

THE GREY sea-wall formed a semi-crescent along the water-
front, punctuated at distinct intervals by twenty-foot appletrees.
It was about sixteen rods in length with the soft cross-chop of
the Straits lapping eagerly at its base.

Seated at the furthermost end, with his booted legs dangling,
was Cleve. He had taken his hat off and his rapier lay across it
on the wall beside him. He was staring intently across the water
toward a thin dark line atop the western horizon. Guy made a
lot of noise stumping up from behind, but Cleve didn't turn.
The Frenchman paused and gnawed his lip, trying to think of
something biting to start with. But he couldn't, and decided to
build up to it gradually.

"They say you can see England from here," he said.

Cleve nodded slowly. "You can. And it seems very near.
Twenty-one miles is near, isn't it?"

Something about his tone caused Guy to stare. He had never
heard Cleve speak that way before. Cleve was ironic, pleasantly
cynical, bantering—never wistful. No matter what his feelings,
he had always kept them bottled tight.

"*Oui*. It is very near," Guy said.

"It's the first sight of England I've had in long time."

Guy shifted uneasily. He suddenly felt that he was seeing
the true stature of his friend for the first time and the feeling
that accompanied it made him uncertain. He wasn't sure that
he wanted to.

"A tight little isle, England," Cleve said slowly after a moment.
"No. Perchance, *smug* would be a better word. Smug in its accep-
tance of a government whose corrupt practices are conveniently
ignored. Revelation of graft amongst the august members of the
royal entourage is simply not tolerated."

He laughed a trifle. He was remembering himself as the young outspoken member of the House of Lords, newly arrived at St. James five years ago. That rash hot-head from Wykeham, crusading for right unwittingly, recklessly, because it seemed sporting; and then being stung by the Royal Master whom he had only striven to serve. It had hurt then, but now the bitterness was gone, replaced by a strange new indifference.

He stared hard at that long smudged line on the sea-rim. He didn't seem conscious of what he said. "Yes. A tight little island, England. But if you've ever seen the soft green of the rolling countryside, the neat little cottages, the proud look in the eyes of the people, you forget the smugness, the—"

Suddenly he stopped, a flush of self-consciousness touching his features. He laughed shortly. "Faith! I should have brought my violin. Shall we go to supper, Kitten?"

Guy nodded. Somehow the earthy emotion of homesickness did not belong to the Richard Cleve whom he knew. But he had seen the truth now. He stared down at the balled letter in his hand, then shrugged and pitched it over the wall into the sea. His eyes swept the horizon and suddenly he frowned.

"*Sandiou,* Cleve! Here comes our Spanish brig with Von Erla aboard."

It was the *Donna Isabella,* true enough; coming from the north with the sagging billows of her sail tugging her slowly down the Channel. There could be no mistake. The yellow-trimmed sides and the sloped poop would identify her anywhere. Cleve smiled.

"I wonder if Von Erla is enjoying the sea? Come along, Kitten. We'll drink him a toast for the De'il of it."

And a few minutes later, as they put the suggestion into action, they little realized what sort of toast was being drunk in the captain's cabin of the *Donna Isabella.*

The baron said: "To Le Havre," emptied his glass and swept a gold-crammed leather sack across the table. "For landing me there at dawn, *capitan*, I pay half now—the rest when our bargain is complete."

In the saffron of the cabin's wall-lanterns, the little Spaniard's face wrinkled with pleasure. "Ah. But this *is* a profitable voyage after all, *señor.*"

"For both of us," Von Erla nodded and stood up. "You make money. And I make my way to Savoy in half the time I had expected. And so, good fortune to us both."

CHAPTER V

THE CARDINAL'S LASH

RICHELIEU'S TONE WAS cutting, with a controlled fury behind it. He sat in the vaulted confines of the palace library and stared at Guy d'Entreville standing quite alone on the other side of the polished desk surface.

Guy shifted from one foot to the other. The Cardinal's calm voice came at him with a bite that was worse than corporal punishment. These soft, deliberate sentences were more painful than a lashing. Guy regretted bitterly the two weeks he and Cleve had stolen and wondered enviously where the Englishman was now.

"Insubordinate men are dangerous," Richelieu was saying. "More dangerous than traitors. You and M. Cleve were ordered to deliver le Baron Von Erla at the City of Metz. Instead, you deport him from Calais; then disappear on one of your rakehelly escapades for half a month. Most commendable, *monsieur le comte.* And, speaking of Cleve, where is that loyal Guardsman now? When I spoke to you last night, I ordered *both* of you to appear before me this morning."

"*Oui, monseigneur,*" Guy agreed. "I have not seen M. Cleve this morning."

Richelieu nodded sarcastically. "I presume that is fortunate. Had you seen him, perchance neither of you would have arrived!"

He fell back in his chair, frowning and absently tugging at the gold medallion on his chest. For a moment the huge library was cloaked in heavy oppressive stillness.

"I have been miraculously patient with you two rogues," the Cardinal said finally. *"Ma foi!* I have been accused of becoming soft. But I have not become soft! In these troubled times, with France filled with nobles who insist upon their outmoded feudal privileges of private armies and personal kingdoms, I need resourceful men. Men who will aid me to build the nation into a great power, united under but one government—the King's. You and Cleve are rascals, *monsieur*—irresponsible, impudent and disobedient. But you have the courage and resource I need. I pay for it with patience. *Comprenez?"*

"Oui, monseigneur."

"Good. I am therefore reducing you to cornets in my Guard with the attendant cut in wage. A light punishment, really, for I *had* considered three months in La Bastille and dismissal. If trouble had not developed in the Duchy of Montferrat, that is what would have happened."

GUY LET the tight breath in his chest ease out relievedly. *Sandiou!* That had been close! He didn't care to dwell on the possibilities. "Trouble in Montferrat, *monseigneur?"* he asked.

Richelieu nodded. He arose and paced slowly to a huge map of France emblazoned upon the rear wall. For an instant a shaft of light from the corner window swept the Cardinal's shadow sharply across the map. Then Richelieu turned.

"Your sword, *monsieur."*

Guy drew his blade and extended it hilt first. The Cardinal took the weapon. He used it as a pointer.

"Montferrat," he said, placing the steel tip on a small section, shaped like an hour glass, that lay squeezed between the Duchies of Savoy and Milan. "Montferrat is a vital buffer-state, *monsieur."*

Buffer-state? Guy regarded the map more closely. The whole

width of the independent Duchy of Savoy separated Montferrat from the French Alpine border in northern Italy. Richelieu
apparently read his thought.

"Perhaps out-post would be a better word, *monsieur*. Montferrat is a vital out-post, and for the mission you are about to
undertake it is imperative that you fully understand why." He
lifted the sword-point. "It is bounded on the north and west by
Savoy; on the east by Milan; on the south by Piedmont. Virtually
an island, *monsieur*. A French island in the center of the alps."

He turned. "I point this out for but one reason. Montferrat is surrounded by enemies, each of whom would like to gain
possession of it. The Duchy of Milan is dominated by Spain
and heavily garrisoned with her troops. Piedmont is dominated
by Austria in the same manner. Needless to say, both Spain
and Austria are allied and anxious to crush France. They would
launch an invasion of Dauphine and south-eastern France in
an instant, if it weren't for our strong protectorate, the Duchy
of Montferrat."

Guy frowned. "But how can a little principality like Montferrat prevent—"

"I shall explain," Richelieu told him crisply and shifted the
sword again. "You will note that no invasion from either Milan
or Piedmont can take place unless the Duchy of Savoy is crossed,
and because of our large garrison in Montferrat, the duke of that
country does not dare permit his territory to be used as a bridge
for an invading army. As long as we hold Montferrat, Savoy must
remain a friend. We have armies on both sides of her, you see."

Guy nodded. "In other words, *monseigneur*, to prevent an
Austro-Spanish invasion from Milan or Piedmont, France must
keep Savoy from forming an alliance with them. And in order
to guarantee Savoy's neutrality, the Duchy of Montferrat must
needs remain in French hands."

THE PRELATE lowered the rapier and turned. He smiled.
"Precisely, *monsieur*," he said. "Montferrat keeps plans of Spanish
aggression in suspense and leaves the cunning Duke of Savoy no

alternative except to be outwardly amiable to the French Crown. Of course, he isn't. If Montferrat were in his hands, he'd be able to threaten France with an Austrian alliance and win for himself inestimable power. But that is neither here nor there. Montferrat is the key to our defense."

"And the trouble?"

"The usual thing!" the Cardinal snapped and paced back to the desk. "Traitors and gold!"

He picked up a sheet of foolscap and examined it savagely. *"Ma foi!* It's more serious than invasion. A treaty with Savoy allows us to ship money over the Susa Road for the maintenance of our garrison in Montferrat, and now thrice within two months the gold-train has been looted! Looted in Montferrat, mind—else I'd know whom to blame. Without pay our troops grow restive, almost mutinous. Desertions are beginning to take place."

Guy nodded. Being a soldier he could understand that. Armies in that day consisted of mercenaries, hastily levied and recognizing no patriotism except that based upon a gold standard. To deprive them of their wages for long meant mutiny.

"Obviously, the duchy is a hot-bed of intrigue," Richelieu continued. "I can read the signs. Not only do the robbers know when to expect our shipments, but the routes, the amount and the number of guards.

"Duke Vincent of Montferrat speaks of treason—treason among his own advisors—unprovable suspicions and apprehensions. Colonel le Viscomte de Boussey, my *commandant* of the garrison, has twice been fired on from ambush. He blames Henri, Duke Vincent's son—but without proof."

He lifted frowning eyes to Guy. "I have already sent men to Montferrat to ascertain the trouble, *monsieur.* They have never returned and the highly organized robberies continue. Another two months of it and Montferrat will fall prey to any power who desires to take her. France cannot afford that. I am still in ignorance of what lurks beneath the surface, but I intend to find out. And immediately!"

"I understand, *monseigneur*," Guy said quietly.

The Cardinal smiled. "I thought you would," he said.

CHAPTER VI

SWORD IN FLIGHT

IT WAS THEN that Richard Cleve walked into the room. Cordeau, rotund *capitaine* of the Guard, waddled after him, protesting vigorously. Cleve had no business bursting into Richelieu's privacy without announcement. *Corbac!* He would suffer for this flagrant breach of Palace etiquette—this deliberate insolence....

Cleve turned. He smiled tightly and said two words in an easy voice: "Keep quiet!"

Cordeau opened his beard-fringed mouth to protest, thought better of it, and obeyed.

From his place by the map, Guy bit his lip. The signs were there: the cold amiability, the leisurely stride, the soft voice. He felt a chill of apprehension as he realized that Cleve was primed for trouble.

Richelieu waited until the English gallant had reached the desk, his thin face mask-like. Then he said flatly: "Quite typical, *monsieur*. Rude, insolent and tardy. Now suppose you explain yourself!"

Cleve tucked the wide brim of his plumed hat beneath one arm and bowed. He was dressed for travel in his favorite costume: stained and worn Cordovan boots that reached to the thighs, black velvet breeches and a gold sash which held the ebon of his silver-slashed doublet close to his waist. He cocked an eyebrow.

"I'll be glad to explain myself, *monseigneur*. But after you have explained yourself."

Guy gulped. *Sangodemi!* A deliberate bait! What was the fool trying to do? Execute himself? He looked quickly at Richelieu to see how the Cardinal was taking it. The Cardinal's face hadn't changed much except to go white. He sat down.

He said icily: *"Monsieur,* perhaps you forget to whom you are speaking."

Something seemed to be prodding Cleve into complete madness. "On the contrary, *monseigneur.*"

The Cardinal started to fondle the medallion on his chest. Guy shifted uneasily. When Richelieu did that he was dangerous.

"I see," the Cardinal said.

"Oh, but I doubt that you do, *monseigneur!*"

Guy couldn't stand by while Cleve literally talked his head off. Men who crossed the Cardinal usually had that happen— after a short trial, of course. The French cavalier swung around the corner of Richelieu's great desk.

"You must pardon Cleve, *monseigneur.* He is still suffering from an old head wound received a year ago in your service. Even this morning he was delirious."

Richelieu regarded him sharply. "I have been given the impression that you did not see Monsieur Cleve this morning, d'Entreville."

"And he didn't," Cleve interposed. He looked at Guy and smiled, but his eyes were hard. "Thanks, Kitten. But this is my affair."

THEN HE returned to the Cardinal. "I had a most interesting breakfast talk with my friend the English ambassador this morning, *monseigneur.* He told me about Sir Harry Winthrop's visit to Paris and the reason for it."

"Am I to assume that is the reason for your tardiness?"

"No," the other denied softly. "No, *monseigneur.* Père Joseph had a bit to do with that. He intercepted me as I arrived. A kindly soul, Joseph." His tones were acid. "He didn't care to have you embarrassed when I asked for my pardon."

Richelieu took a deep breath. "I see," he said.

Whether Cleve recognized the peril of that deep breath, Guy didn't know. The Englishman pinched the end of his nose and continued:

"Excellent, *monseigneur.* Joseph explained how you duped Sir Harry into a belief that I no longer served you. A neatly put explanation too. Something to do with the welfare of France. But, *monseigneur,* when the welfare of France interferes with my—"

Then the fury of Richelieu lashed into words. *"Monsieur!"* he roared. "I've heard enough!" He rose and the thud of his fist upon the desk-top punctuated the command.

But Cleve didn't hold his tongue. Richelieu's loss of control seemed to give him new insolence. "And so have I, *monseigneur.* We are quits! A man who would betray my future for his interests might some day find it to his interests to betray my life. Consider my resignation effective as of today. Once bitten, twice shy you know. Adieu!"

He turned and started toward the door. The Cardinal was waxen white. He lunged across the desk, one finger jabbing toward Cleve's back.

"Cordeau! Arrest that man! If he resists, cut him down!"

"Oui."

Cordeau bit his lip and stepped manfully in front of Cleve. "Er—you are under arrest, *monsieur.*"

He started to draw his blade and succeeded partially. Then he was siting on the floor and Cleve was stepping over him, gently massaging the knuckles that had struck the blow. Richelieu jerked angrily on the silken bell-cord behind his desk. Immediately, the halbardiers outside burst into the library, glinting weapons held ready. Cordeau sat up blinking the library back into focus.

"*Sandiou!* What happened?"

NOBODY HEARD him. Cleve grappled with the nearest of the halbardiers; snatched the fellow's halbard-point in gloved fingers and jerked. The weapon slid free, and its owner grunted in amazement. But his comrade was quicker and backed away to bring his halbard to point.

The English rakehelly had been expecting this. He whirled, the captured halbard locked firmly in his grip, and caught the second guard behind the ear with its swinging butt. The man slumped.

Then the first guard snapped out of his lethargy. He dove recklessly for Cleve's throat. Cleve was acting entirely on impulse. Desperately. He saw the man's arching body, ducked suddenly, butted upward and caught his attacker on the point of the jaw. The man went down and Cleve's head rang. He felt like sitting down himself.

But somehow he managed to turn without falling on his face, his long blade flashing. Cordeau was rubbing his jaw and staring absently into space. The Cardinal glared at Guy.

"You're still in my service, *monsieur.* Do your duty!"

Guy shook himself. None of this seemed real. There was nothing he could do to prevent it. He had stood rooted, held by the spectacle of his friend's suicidal madness. And now Richelieu was telling him to draw!

Impossible! He could not. But it would be even more terrible to betray his pledge of loyalty to the Cardinal. He drew. Drew slowly, reluctantly, while Cleve waited, an uncertain devil's-grin on his lips. Then Guy smiled.

"Oh," he hinted. "So you're going to run, eh Cleve?"

The Englishman got it and chuckled. "All the way to Italy if need be!" He blew Richelieu a kiss and darted through the door.

It brought Cordeau out of his stupor. He arose and his fat fist swept up the silver whistle dangling from a cord around his neck. Guy tensed. One blast on that, and every guard within hearing would bar the fugitive's escape. There was only one thing to do and the French cavalier did it.

HE SHOUTED encouragingly to Richelieu: "I'll fetch him back, *monseigneur!*" then charged straight toward the unsuspecting Cordeau. The ensuing collision was quite solid and satisfactory.

Guy's sinewy frame careened into the fat man's back and they went down. Cordeau lost his whistle and his breath as well; and Guy, sprawled atop him, listened to the diminishing rhythm of Cleve's flight and grinned contentedly. All in all, it had been well executed.

But Richelieu didn't think so. He hadn't been fooled. "You shall pay for that little travesty on duty, *monsieur le comte*," he said coldly. "Now stand up!"

Guy obeyed. Triumph died in him as he realized the consequence of his deed. Behind, Cordeau was trying to stand up, catch breath and curse at the same time. One of the halbardiers began to stir. Richelieu stared.

One of his precepts consisted of a belief in his ability to turn untoward incidents to his advantage. Whatever their crimes, Cleve and d'Entreville were still necessary in Montferrat. Therefore he would have them there. A lesser man would have despaired; Richelieu saw a way.

" 'Twill be unfortunate for France to lose you, *monsieur*," he told d'Entreville. "*Oui.* Despite your roystering way, you have served the crown well."

"*Merci, monseigneur.* Cleve is but homesick and he—"

The Cardinal steepled his fingers. He was frowning. "Spare me your thanks! As a person, I demand that you pay for your crime. But—" He paused. "But fortunately, *monsieur*, fortunately for you, I'm not a person. I am the Minister of France. My judgment must be impersonal, impartial, and devoted to the best interests of the State.

"It is therefore to these interests that I can offer you an alternative, *monsieur*. Bring Lord Richard Cleve back to me under

*Beside that night highway Cleve bent
over the unconscious figure*

arrest, and all charges against you shall be dropped. Otherwise—"The speaker shrugged.

Guy didn't need to think about that one. His reaction was immediate. He said: "Such an alternative is insulting, *monseigneur.*"

"Very well. Both you and Cleve pay the traitor's fee. You to prison; he to death! Of course, had you accepted, I merely intended sending him to Montferrat. But since you haven't accepted, his death is inevitable. I suffer no illusions, d'Entreville. No man, other than yourself can take Richard Cleve alive!"

Guy couldn't keep the edge of triumph out of his voice. "You appear to forget, *monseigneur,* that Cleve has escaped!"

"For the time being," Richelieu agreed and played his trump card. "But I have three thousand carrier-pigeons. Within a day every garrison in France shall be on the alert for your friend—with orders to slay him on sight."

Guy was in agony now. The Cardinal wasn't bluffing. Cleve was a dying man, even as he rode madly after Sir Harry and his permit to go home. Guy hesitated; and then he came to the only decision possible.

"I shall find my friend and place him under arrest immediately, *monseigneur*," he said quietly. "I give my oath!"

CHAPTER VII

DUKES WILL DRINK

SAVOY LAY IN the Rhone Basin amid ice-capped peaks. At the capital, its sovereign lay amid ice-packed compresses. But while the duchy lay serene beneath warm blue skies, the duke lay moaning and cursing beneath a rumpled mass of bed-linen. He felt very sick, the result of a night spent in his cups.

His head ached in thick bulging throbs. A man of fifty had no business to engage in drinking bouts with men half his age. *Por Bacco!* They had been burning garbage in his mouth while he slept. He shifted. The lavish furnishings of his bed-chamber in the Palazzo Madama hurt his eyes. He turned them to the bearded face of Count Zarrini, his beetle-browed prime minister, who stood solicitously at the bedside.

Zarrini looked both disapproving and sympathetic at the same time—no mean feat—and said apologetically: "Baron Von Erla arrived in Turin last evening, Your Highness. He is waiting outside."

Duke Charles Emmanuel glared. He habitually glared at Zarrini. The truth of the matter was that he didn't like Zarrini. Zarrini was a wind-bag and a martinet. But he was efficient, so the duke tolerated him.

"Well, tell Signor Von Erla that I don't want to see anyone," he directed flatly. "I'm indisposed! I'm dying, tell him. *Peste!* Who does he consider himself, pounding on my door at this hour?

"He considers himself the new Austrian ambassador, Your

Highness." Zarrini replied patiently. "Upon seeing his creden-
tials, I consider him the ambassador too. He insists that his
visit is of great importance and apologizes in advance for the
irregularity."

The duke sat up slowly, wincing at the movement. His grey-
streaked mustachios gave him a lop-sided appearance, for one
was erect and bristling, the other adroop. He wore a silken night-
cap with its tassel dangling irritatingly down from beneath the
ice-packs to the bridge of his bulbous nose.

"No peace," he grunted. "I'm dying and this Von Erla insists
upon visiting." He stuck out his tongue and tried to view it. He
only succeeded in appearing cross-eyed and slightly ridiculous.
He tucked it back and sighed.

"You'll see the Baron, Highness?" Zarrini pressed anxiously.
"Remember he is representing the emperor's Court in Vienna.
You can ill-afford to offend Austria, Your Highness."

"Silence!" Charles Emmanuel glared at his aide. He levered
himself into a more comfortable position and groaned as his
head clanged warningly. "Show this Von Erla person in, Zarrini.
Peste! The things I do for Savoy!"

BARON VON ERLA entered, a brilliant figure in green and
gold. He smiled pleasantly, but there was fatigue in the depths
of his eyes. He had entered Turin at dawn in a dust-grimed
coach, springless and hard-seated. He had slept only four hours,
and for two weeks that had been customary. It was Cleve and
d'Entreville's fault. Vividly he had cursed them every jarring
league of the way from le Havre.

After the usual salutations, during which he lied politely
about his health while Charles Emmanuel didn't, he seated
himself beside the bed on a gilt-paneled chair.

"I shall strive to be pertinent to avoid impertinence, Your
Highness," he said, with an eye to the Duke's unhappy state.

"Eh?" the ducal brows shot up. Then he chuckled feebly.
"Pertinent to avoid impertinence. *Si.* Very good." He glared at
his minister. "Why can't you say clever things like that?"

Zarrini shrugged uneasily and said nothing and Von Erla made full use of the pause. The plot he had formulated during his journey across France was simple enough to be practical, and yet not obvious.

"It is about Montferrat, Your Highness," he said.

Charles Emmanuel straightened. It was as though Von Erla had used a magic phrase, changing the duke from a drink-haggard old man into a covetous diplomat. And Von Erla knew why.

Montferrat was the one unfulfilled dream of the duke's life. The dam of his ambition. It was only the vindictiveness of Fate that had robbed him of the Duchy. His grand-daughter, Margaret of Savoy, was the niece of the original duke, with a claim to succession only superseded by Montferrat's present ruler, Duke Vincent. If Vincent hadn't been born, everything would have worked out beautifully. Montferrat would have become Savoy's, through Margaret's accession to its throne. But Fate had decreed otherwise—emphatically.

Margaret's claim was worthless now. Shortly after her second birthday, Duke Vincent had become father to an heir named Henri, who from all reports, had grown into a revoltingly healthy man. Small wonder Charles Emmanuel felt bitter. Mere consideration of Montferrat caused him great discomfort. Its loss robbed him of greatness. And so he was always interested in any plot that might rectify this error of Fate.

"What about Montferrat, Signor Baron?" he asked.

Von Erla shrugged. "Nothing, Highness, except that I can place it in your hands, if you'll promise me an alliance with Austria against France."

HE SAID it in an unpretentious way, as if he were offering the duke a dish of olives, and Charles Emmanuel was taken completely aback. The baron gave him little opportunity to recover.

"Undoubtedly I sound a trifle grandiose, Highness. Permit me to explain. You see, I make the offer not in my official capacity as ambassador, but as a private individual. Frankly, to get your signature upon a treaty with my government would give me inestimable prestige in Vienna. It would give me a greater title and more land. I am prepared to go to any lengths to realize such ambitions."

He smiled tightly. "You see, Highness, I place my cards upon the table, face up. I have in mind a little scheme to place the Duchy of Montferrat in your hands." He tapped the bedspread significantly. "Legally, Your Highness. But before putting it to operation, I desire assurance that you'll sign with Austria against the French after it is done."

Charles Emmanuel rubbed his face. With Montferrat in his control, Richelieu would be unable to harm him should he sign with Austria. Von Erla kept talking.

"At present I want nothing more. After the Duchy has legally become part of Savoy, we can discuss the alliance at greater length. Is it agreed?"

The other eyed him sharply. "What is your plan, *signor?*"

"Begging your patience, Highness. That is my concern. Not even Vienna knows of it. But I am certain of success, else I would never dare broach the question."

"Hmmm." The duke was scowling, thinking deeply. He wished fervently his head would cease aching so much. Von Erla had gone into this business with brutal abruptness, and he needed time to think clearly.

At the moment he couldn't see how one man could accomplish what the combined strength of Spain and Austria had failed to do for six years past; to take the militarily impregnable Montferrat from France. But the duke was an opportunist, and therefore inclined to accept Von Erla's enigmatic proposition, whatever it was. After all, what had he to lose? Von Erla struck him as clever enough to invent a scheme worth the gamble, and if the scheme failed, Savoy couldn't be held accountable. Von Erla was an Austrian.

"Very well, Signor Baron," he said finally. "I gain more than

I lose by giving you my promise; therefore you have it. Grant me Montferrat and I'll become Austria's staunchest ally. But I doubt that any intrigue you may be brewing will be potent enough to succeed."

Von Erla smiled confidently. " 'Tis your privilege, Highness," he said, and as he left, added: "I trust your granddaughter Margaret is enjoying the best of health."

CHAPTER VIII

THE SPIDER FROM AUSTRIA

THE RED LION INN of Turin was a rambling structure, flanked and fronted by hedged gardens and backed by the Dora Riparia River. Von Erla had chosen this unpretentious establishment for his headquarters. As he walked through the door to the deserted grog-room, he was met by Kringelein, his saturnine aide, newly arrived from Vienna. Kringelein, a dark-visaged man of gaunt proportions, was sitting in a corner of the raftered room, his boot-heels on a table, a tankard of wine in his bony fist.

He reported: "There is a lady to see you, Herr Baron," and took his feet down. "I sent her upstairs. She gave the name of Catherine Cordoba."

Von Erla smiled. "Good." He was pleased that Catherine had arrived, for it meant that his plot could now be set in motion. He had written her to come, of course; he had sent his message by a high-priced dispatch rider from Mont Genevre two days ago. But he hadn't expected her for another day.

"Have a bottle of spiced-wine sent up," he told Kringelein. "Then follow."

Kringelein nodded. *Jawohl.* He finished the rest of his wine and stood up, topping his blond superior by a good three inches. Kringelein had worked with Von Erla in the past. "You do not wish to be disturbed, eh, Herr Baron."

Von Erla smiled slightly and walked away.

Catherine was standing by the latticed window of his four room suite at his entrance. She turned, an adorable creature, petite and graceful, with delicate, perfect features. Rippling curls the color of ripened wheat framed her face, and her startlingly blue eyes had a look of charming innocence. But Von Erla had no illusions. Catherine Cordoba was one of the most venomous women with whom he had ever worked. She was an ambitious and quite ruthless adventuress.

He nodded. The sight of her awakened his old bitterness, and he felt the hatred rising in him now. But he controlled it; his face was expressionless as he pulled up a chair for her and took one himself.

"There are matters I would discuss with you, Catherine," he said. "Matters of importance to us both."

CATHERINE SETTLED back and patted absently at her well-groomed coiffure. "Really? You should have come to Montferrat, Friederich. You know where I live."

She had used that tone before. Used it to say: "As an *intrigant*, Friederich, you are a genius. As my lover—a buffoon. Really, darling I—" He shut the rest of it out of his mind. Memory of it now might bring the smoldering bitterness into flame, and he needed complete control of his emotions if he was to set the trap which would make her pay for his suffering three years before. Needless to say, she had used him to better her position as long as she could.

"I did not dare come to Montferrat," he said slowly.

"No?"

Von Erla smiled grimly. "I am not welcome in France. His Eminence the Cardinal saw fit to deport me with assurances that should I return to French soil, my arrest would be immediate. Montferrat is a French protectorate, if you will remember. At the moment, I cannot afford to waste my time in prison."

"You haven't changed," she said dryly, then shrugged. "Well, I am here. What happens?"

He studied her thoughtfully. Then he said crisply: "The chance for which you have waited a lifetime, Catherine. The chance to become a duchess!"

That shook her out of her condescension. Her blue eyes narrowed. She said but a single word, spoken softly: "How?"

"You are with me? You guarantee co-operation?"

"To become a duchess, my darling, I would co-operate with the Devil himself."

Von Erla smiled tight-lipped. "I don't doubt it." He hunched forward. "Within a week, Catherine, a man will appear in Montferrat wearing a sword with three rubies set in the hilt."

"What of it?"

"You will get in touch with him."

"His name?"

"Mazo Gardier. Ever heard of him?"

"No. Who is he?"

Von Erla leaned back. "One of the cleverest assassins in Europe, my dear. A soldier, a professional killer—anything, if the price is right. I met him at a wayside tavern in France and hired him on the spot to—er—dispose of Duke Vincent of Montferrat for me."

Catherine folded her hands in her lap. She regarded him in silence. She wasn't shocked. She was calculating. Finally, she said: "You are playing for high stakes, Friederich. If I'm to engage in political assassination I'll not work for a pittance."

"Naturally. Your reward shall be of the highest. After all, I am counting upon your influence over the duke's son, Henri." He smiled bitterly. "From reports Henri is athirst to marry you."

Catherine shrugged. "Henri's a soft fool; he will do whatever I ask. I have a manor-house, a town suite and two coaches. The only thing that prevents our wedding is his father."

"Excellent. Now returning to Gardier. Remember, you will recognize him by his sword. Three rubies in the hilt. Upon his arrival in Montferrat, make contact with him secretly; acquaint him with the duke's habits and daily routine. If possible, you might steal a palace key-ring for him—"

"Really, Friederich. I'm not an amateur. Let's not waste our time over simple details. What am I to receive for my trouble?"

Von Erla smiled, thinking of the stinging his pride had taken when she had laughed at his love three years before.

"Yes, we mustn't forget your reward, my love." He stared down at her. "But I thought the question answered itself. Gardier will kill Duke Vincent, and with the duke dead, Henri will succeed. As you have just admitted, Duke Vincent is all that prevents your nuptials. Your reward Catherine, is the Duchy of Montferrat. You become its duchess." He shrugged. "Simple?"

She frowned. "No. You do not aid others without first aiding yourself, Friederich. What is it this time?"

He had an answer. "A mere matter of dissolving the present French protectorate over Montferrat. Afterward as duchess, you will allow Austria to assume control."

It was a plausible lie, and she accepted it. Then a knock interrupted them. A lackey appeared with the spiced wine and after dismissing the man, Von Erla poured it into two crystal goblets. He handed one to her.

"To success, my dear," he murmured. "To your new title, Duchesse de Montferrat!"

"I'll drink to that," she said, and her wide eyes regarded him innocently over the rim of the glass.

HE ACCOMPANIED her to her coach, a few minutes later. He bade her a fond goodbye and returned to the room. Kringelein was standing by the window. Von Erla closed the door softly and stood with his back to it.

"Did you hear everything?" he asked.

The big man nodded. He had been posted outside the door during her visit. He always assumed that station whenever his superior engaged in conversations that were of a secretive nature and yet needed an unknown witness. Kringelein's sad horse-face as frowning.

"I heard. I didn't understand it."

The Baron giggled. He crossed to the liquor table and poured himself a drink. "Neither did she. Not the real motive. And that's the beauty of it. She will make an admirable tool to aid my man Gardier—and afterward an adorable widow."

"Widow?" Kringelein went to the cabinet by the door and found a half-empty bottle of brandy. He was tired of wine. He pulled the cork with his teeth and took a swallow. "Oh. After Duke Vincent, comes Henri, eh?"

"Precisely. Gardier has my instructions, and by then she will have acquainted him with the palace, the routines, the secret entrances. She'll trust him, understand?"

"*Ja*. Wheels within wheels, Herr Baron. The duke and his son dead—Margaret of Savoy has the throne."

"And Austria an alliance with Savoy," Von Erla reminded him. "It is to that end we are ever working, Kringelein. Charles Emmanuel will have Montferrat; and Austria will have Savoy, and France will have to eat humble pie." He sat down smiling. "And all that I have to do is to remain here in Turin and enjoy myself."

"Good," said Kringelein and sat down too. He was tired.

CHAPTER IX

HIGHWAYMAN AHEAD

WHEN RICHARD CLEVE charged from Le Palais de Richelieu, to vault into the saddle of his waiting horse, he had expected a chase and had ridden accordingly. He knew nothing of d'Entreville's roughly executed delaying tactics and his only idea was to put as much distance between himself and the Cardinal as possible.

Spurring madly out of the courtyard, he sent pedestrians into terrified flight as he galloped through Paris. The streets became a blur of startled white faces, jammed intersections and bulky carts, ending abruptly at the East Gate to become well-worn country highways.

He hammered onward for a league before realizing the absence of pursuit. It puzzled him somewhat, but he didn't let up. Sir Harry was somewhere ahead in a slow coach, with a fourteen-day handicap. Catching him would take speed and a devil's amount of stamina.

He bent low against the stallion's neck, talking courage into its flattened ear, and streaked like a flame over the green swelling countryside between Paris and Melun. His black cape licked behind him and he reached one hand to tighten its clasp as he frowned into the wind.

Then the tavern known as La Fleur Blanche served him his first definite clue. Changing horses, its proprietor explained at length that an English nobleman had lunched at the tavern two weeks past. " 'Twas a coach and six, *monsieur*. Its postillion told me that they planned to stay the night at Troyes. No, they were not traveling fast, *monsieur*. A good pace, but not fast. Would *monsieur* desire a quick repast to fortify his hours on the road?"

Cleve smiled. "Brandy'll do the trick quicker," he replied. "Fetch a bottle. I'll gulp as I gallop."

Then, Troyes… St. Aube… Chaumont… Langeres. He careened through them all, a sweat-streaked figure pausing for hot soup, a fresh mount, another flask of brandy and then flashing into the night again, down the silvered road that seemed to waver endlessly across France. His body was aching with exhaustion, but his mind remained fresh, and now for the first time he began to understand the pattern of his life these last few years.

It was a senseless pattern. Caught in the bitterness of exile he had followed a reckless rakehelly course, one without purpose. For his early dreams had become meaningless, and there was nothing to replace them. There could be nothing for an exile.

It was not merely Richelieu's duplicity that had caused him to spur hell-for-leather out of Paris. A deeper motive, unrecognized then, had sent him on this frenzied race—this rash defiance of the Cardinal. That same motive had been the reason for all his restlessness, his wild urge to action. In reality he loathed the role of a man without a country—a man without a purpose. He was sick to death of being a useful outsider. He was tired of fighting for foreign causes.

"Risking life and limb for the unification of France!" he muttered. "Damme! What in Hades is France to me?"

What he wanted was roots—roots deep in English soil, with which to grow. Because he was denied that, he had lived restlessly and without aim; and now Sir Harry's arrival in Paris had broken the cynical self-control which he had built up during the long sojourn in exile.

A DEW-DAMPENED wind put its fingers into his doublet and reminded him that it was cold. He took another drink and cast the flask away. The dark country through which he was riding had once been the Duchy of Burgundy—the proud, haughty Burgundy of Charles the Bold, now grown peaceful and submissive to the French crown.

It was hill-studded terrain, well timbered. In places trees arched over the road to convert it into a black tunnel. Cleve cantered cautiously, guided by the moon-shafts leaking through from above. He felt physically grateful for the respite, but his mind chafed at the delay. Faith! He was losing precious time!

Then a ragged S-turn brought him again into the silver translucence of the night. The road ahead was straight. He raised the whip, and then paused. Blotted against the misty white road lay a dark mass. A sprawling mass, which a moment later he recognized to be a horse. A dead horse.

He swung stiffly from the saddle, puzzled by the absence of a rider. Surely the fellow was somewhere near—possibly lying senseless in the roadside brush. By the look of things it had been a nasty spill. The horse had been shot to end its misery.

Then a voice came to him, softly pitched. "Stand where you are, *monsieur*. One move and I—I'll put a ball into you!"

It came from behind, from the side of the road. It didn't sound particularly dangerous so he took a chance and turned quickly. A tongue of flame licked from the shadows, a sharp report— and the trailing part of Cleve's white plume jerked free to float lazily earthward.

"Egad!" It had been close. He immediately assumed that he made too good a target, and dove into the dust and lay limp as death.

"You're not hurt," the voice informed him cheerfully.

He raised his head. "Faith! And 'tis no fault of your's, m'lad." He stood up, drawing. "Now come out of there and I'll give you another chance at me. This time on my terms."

"Drop your sword, *monsieur*. I have another pistol."

Cleve grinned. "Well then, we'll forget my terms," he decided and let the weapon thud to the road.

A SLIM figure, a mere boy, eased cautiously into the moon- light. The barrels of two unwieldy horse-pistols glinted. Cleve eyed them respectfully; wondered which was loaded, which empty; and then decided that it didn't make much difference anyway. They were both trained on him.

He surveyed his ambusher next. The lad was either a page or the scion of some local nobleman, for he was well garbed. He wore the usual accoutrements of travel: high-boots, a long cape and a broad-brimmed hat. Cleve shook his head.

"You don't appear to be the type that makes a living from the highway, laddie. What's the reason for this?"

The youth inclined his hat-brim briefly toward the English- man's horse. The shadow concealed his face. "I need your mount, *monsieur*," he said.

"Oh. Then the attempt on my life was incidental."

"It wasn't an attempt, *monsieur*. Had I desired to hit you, I would have hit you. I am very proficient in the use of firearms."

"I see," Cleve said. In the face of that, there was little else to say. A cocky brat.

"The town of Jussey is but a few leagues away," the boy volunteered. "You should be able to walk there by dawn."

"Your consideration overwhelms me, bucko. What if I object?"

The boy waved one of the pistols. "I still have this, *monsieur*."

"Yes. I was afraid you'd remember it." Cleve sighed and folded his arms. One thing certain, he didn't want to walk if he could prevent it. Time was precious. "Now mark me, lad. There is little need of this. I'll be glad to ride you to Jussey and there you can purchase your own mount. Damme! You can't weigh very much and my horse can carry double."

"*Oui*. But not as fast as it can carry one, *monsieur*. I have a vital need for haste."

The speaker thrust one pistol into his sash and felt cautiously for the bridle. It was going to be difficult to keep one pistol leveled while attempting to mount, and he realized it. After a short fumbling attempt, his voice snapped crisply through the night.

"Go to the side of the road, *monsieur*. Sit there and make no sudden leaps."

Cleve cursed. A fine mess! Still, a pistol and a child was a dangerous combination, so he obeyed. He found an embedded boulder and sat down. He put his hands against the stone and came into contact with the rough surface of a loose rock—a rock the size of a small apple, probably cast there by the wheel-spin of a passing coach. He gripped it thoughtfully and stared at the brat swinging gracefully astride his horse.

"Very well, bucko. Since I can't reason with you—"

The boy, feeling secure now that he was a-saddle and his victim too far away to reach him, thrust the pistol into his sash and waved cheerfully.

"*Au revoir, monsieur*. Thank you for the horse."

"Don't mention it, son!"

The Englishman's arm looped savagely forward. There was

a *clunk* as the rock sped true to its target, followed by a *thud* as the target fell to the ground. Cleve caught the horse before it broke away.

The youngster was out. Out definitely! His plumed hat was off. His head lay framed against the white dust of the highway in a froth of black, moon-glinted hair. A good-looking boy, Cleve thought. Too good looking! The fineness of feature, the delicate arch of the lips under trimly molded nostrils, the amazing sweep of eye-lash, made him beautiful.

"Egad, laddie. You'd make a lovely girl."

Then, because the figure lay so unnaturally still, the English cavalier knelt quickly to feel for the heart-beat. He drew his hand back suddenly.

"Gad's teeth!" he exploded. "You *are* a lovely girl!"

He lifted her to a more comfortable position on a mossy slope. The numerous questions streaming through his mind were temporarily stemmed by his concern. She lay very still, very pale. He began massaging her wrists and then loosened her collar. The fact that she breathed evenly, though softly, was the only indication that she was alive. He frowned. A hat, plus a thick mass of lovely hair, should have been enough to prevent a skull fracture, yet—

Then he heard a faint rippling whisper. He arose, followed the sound and almost fell into an anaemic rivulet coursing through the dark underbrush. He filled his hat with water and returned. And she was waiting—her pistols trained.

"Keep a good distance, *monsieur!*"

Cleve pulled up abruptly and began to call himself names for not disarming her. Then he shrugged. *"Mademoiselle,* I badly need that horse for—"

"So you found me out?"

He grinned. "Yes. And I must aver that you make a delightful boy, *mademoiselle.*"

"Enough!" She began backing slowly toward the stallion. "You shall receive payment for this horse, if you care for it. Send a letter to Mary de Sarasnac, Château de Lesport in the Province of Nivernais and—"

Cleve interrupted. "Egad! You are Mary de Sarasnac?"

She nodded briefly. *"Oui."*

His eyebrows cocked. "Why, then you're the Kitten's light o' love. You're the one we searched the corners of France to—"

But she didn't hear him. She had dug spurs to the horse to gallop away, leaving him staring, mouth twisted in a smile of incredulity, hands still absently gripping the water-filled hat.

"Faith, Mary! You're a woman of parts, true enough. First Calais and now, Nevernais."

Then the frosty blue-grey of the night absorbed her. He stood by the bushes for a long moment asking himself questions and receiving no answer. The only thing definite was the fact that she had taken his horse and left him to trudge the rest of the way to town. A pleasant creature!

"I'd like to wring her neck," he muttered and jammed on his hat. Cold water gushed over his ears and down his collar to knock the breath out of him. He stood very still. "Or drown her," he concluded blackly.

CHAPTER X

THE BRAVO'S BLADE

THE BRIGHT GOLD of morning had washed away night when he finally arrived at the Inn of the Silver Flute on the outskirts of Jussey. The ivy-hung tavern was athrob with activity.

Two coaches stood in its court being trimmed and refurbished. At the side of the building, three groomsmen were saddling horses. A baggage-burdened lackey wavered in and out amongst busy coach-crews, followed by a diminutive postillion in green and white, who bellowed commands to all, with accompanying gestures. After the clammy gray silence of dawn, it was refreshing.

Cleve slid lightly from the tail of the hay-cart which had carried him to town and stood regarding the scene contentedly. He had walked two leagues before the cart had picked him up. He waved adieu to the taciturn peas-ant-wagoner and entered the yard. He needed a drink—a large drink, and then perhaps a few hours sleep.

The tavern's interior was quiet enough, though somewhat crowded. Travelers in France were invariably uncommunicative in morning and over-communicative at night. Hangovers, he decided, for they drank prodigiously after a day's jarring in an effort to wash away the discomfort of the trip.

Then he found an unobtrusive table beside the fireplace and sat down. It seemed years since he had last relaxed. The dancing flames in the hearth warmed him. He reveled in the soothing murmurings of the low-raftered room. Finally, one of the house-lackies drew near and bowed.

"Your pleasure, *monsieur?*"

"Hot buttered rum, m'lad. Plenty of it. Later, a room."

The servant hesitated. It was a mysterious order, undoubtedly expensive, and the order-giver did not look prosperous—dirty boots, rumpled doublet, battered, feather-drooping hat. The man inclined his snout.

"Hot buttered rum, *monsieur?*"

Cleve frowned slightly and nodded. He had learned the recipe from a friend who had traveled in the American Colonies and anticipation of that brew had been adding spring to his gait during the dawn.

"Hot buttered rum," he reiterated firmly and looked sarcastic. "You *have* rum, haven't you?"

"*Oui.* English Jamaica, *monsieur.*"

"Good. A bottle, a slab of butter, a lemon and some honey." The lackey started away. Cleve stopped him. "Then two pewter tankards. One filled with hot water." He tapped the table. "And hurry!"

AS THE lackey left, the proprietor of the Silver Flute approached. He had been standing by the sideboard.

"*Monsieur,* did you arrive on foot?"

Cleve nodded.

The landlord smiled professionally. "Your comrade told us to expect you, *monsieur.*"

Cleve's voice didn't betray his surprise, although it flooded his brain. "My comrade?"

"*Oui.* That young man who brought your saddle bags to our establishment," said the inn-keeper. "The handsome youth. We have placed the luggage in your room, *monsieur.* I trust that you enjoyed your morning's walk. Your comrade told us how you enjoy such things. A healthful eccentricity, *monsieur.*"

"A questionable eccentricity," Cleve corrected. He frowned. "Is my—er—comrade about? I'd like to thank the little—"

The inn-keeper shrugged. "*Mais non, monsieur.* He rode off."

"I was afraid of that. Well, *monsieur le maitre,* perchance you can aid me on another score. Did an Englishman in a coach and six pass through, let us say, a week and a half ago?"

"He did, *monsieur.* In fact he stayed the night. Sir Harry Winthrop. A very important personage, *monsieur.*"

"*Very,*" agreed Cleve dryly and brightened as he saw his lackey threading toward him.

Now, if one hot buttered rum can ease the fatigue of a busy day, then two can restore the energy of a twenty-four-hour ride, so Cleve made three. He was finishing his fourth, when a newcomer to the grog-room attracted his attention. It wasn't the man himself, but the way everyone sidled to one side as he strode slowly into the place.

THE MAN was quite tall, with dark hair and obsidian eyes. He carried himself arrogantly with his gloved fingers touching the hilt of his long rapier. That rapier caught Cleve's eye.

Three bright rubies were set in its haft. They glinted in the sun streaming through the windows, seeming alive in their brilliance. It was a beautiful sword, the sort a connoisseur of fine craftsmanship might carry—or an expert duelist. Observing the newcomer, Cleve decided on the latter.

The fellow looked dangerous. He stood in the center of the room, staring coldly from face to face, as the conversational hum stuttered and faded. His thin lips were straight beneath a hooked nose and a dark waxed mustache. His flinty features were expressionless, deadly. Here was a killer if ever Cleve saw one, and he was looking for somebody. The Englishman decided to tend to his own business. He took another drink. Hot buttered rum was making a new man of him.

Then the bravo spoke in a tone that was flat, colorless: "Which one of you gentlemen walked into town?"

Cleve frowned. Now here was a peculiar question, for he had walked into town. But what had that to do with a man he had never seen before? Nothing, he decided. Nevertheless, he was interested and he placed his tankard carefully upon the table and waited for someone to speak. One minute passed. No one said anything.

"Well?" the speaker challenged. "Who came afoot? Speak up, curse you! I found the horse, a dun-colored mare, three leagues down the road."

Cleve shifted. With a sensation of distinct detachment he suddenly realized that the call was for Mary de Sarasnac. The horse she had left dead upon the highway had been a mare, and dun colored. But that wasn't what caused the English gallant to sit up. It was his active, almost feline, curiosity. In the past it had been the cause of more trouble than he cared to remember, but he forgot that now; it suddenly became vital that he know why this fellow was after her.

"I walked into town, *monsieur*," he said. "That was my horse."

The man's gaze settled on him. Those eyes made Cleve suddenly wary. His cursed curiosity had dropped him into trouble again. If he was a judge of men, trouble was about to be served on a sword-point. The stranger's face was expressionless, but the very blankness of it was a warning. Cleve had met ice-blooded professionals before.

"Well?"

The man started toward him deliberately. "Thought you were younger," he said. His ruby-hilted sword suddenly glinted. "Say your prayers. Your ears are too long. I have trailed you since yester evening just to shorten them."

Still Cleve didn't stand up. Events did race in this country! He was frankly nonplussed. He sat at the table, elbows planted, steaming tankard posed midway to his lips, wondering. True, he had anticipated difficulties, yet not this quickly.

"Faith! Put up your blade. There is no reason for us to fight."

The stranger's voice had no tone to it. "It won't be a fight, lout. Here take—"

BUT CLEVE acted first. A split second before the speaker's steel licked for his throat, he hurled the contents of his tankard into the man's face. A sudden brightening of those flinty eyes had been his warning. Cleve rolled out of his chair as the sword-tip gashed a furrow across its back. The man leaped away, cursing; wiping the sting of hot buttered rum from his eyes.

Cleve came up with his sword out, still confused. "Damme! I've never met a man with such kindly impulses. Now hold it! We ought to talk this over."

"My purpose is to keep you from talking anything over, trickster!"

Cleve just missed being skewered by the accompanying lunge. The steel licked under his chin; severed his cape-clasp as he jerked himself away from it. He decided right then to cease appeasement. This fellow was out to get him!

"All right, bucko! We'll play it your way!"

The grog-room was clear of patrons. At the first exchange everyone had sought less turbulent surroundings. The innkeeper and half his staff stood in the doorway, fearful of the inevitable wreckage costs, but otherwise resigned. Expensive brawls were something to be born—like the weather and taxes.

Cleve eyed the empty room appreciatively over the sheen of the bravo's blade. He needed space. There was a wall to his left and a glowing hearth behind. Every time he bobbed to parry a deep thrust, his sword-arm jarred solidly into the mantle.

"Don't suppose you'd retreat a bit so that I can get out of here," he suggested amiably.

The man cursed and lunged viciously at his throat. The English rakehelly caught it in *quarte* and bent it aside. He sighed. "No. I didn't think you would."

Then he suddenly unleashed a flurry of thrusts, designed to put his opponent on the defensive. It succeeded. The fellow wasn't alarmed, but he was too smart to attempt standing up to them. He retreated slowly, and Cleve's breath gave out by the time they reached the center of the room. The strength the rum had lent was false and beginning to fade.

"I think you're acting foolish," he gasped and grinned tiredly. "But 'tis your funeral." A thrust in *tierce* nearly pinned him and he gulped. "Egad! I *hope* its your funeral!"

The killer was pressing. He met Cleve's feeble attack with a *riposte* in *seconde* and touched off a hornet-like offensive that almost ended the struggle there.

But Cleve dipped away, pirouetting and bobbing like a dancing-master. His opponent closed in. His blade licked hungrily for the throat, the belly, the heart. There was chill confidence in his manner.

CLEVE KNEW the seriousness of his position. At this pace he could last possibly ten minutes before the exhausting ride from Paris would tell on him. The devil's grin on his lips deepened. He wouldn't wait! He'd cram ten minutes energy into one.

"Here we go!"

He took a trio of jabs on his blade and lunged wildly. The point of the bravo's blade ran a scratch from forearm to elbow, but it wasn't important. The offensive was stopped. The sheer unexpected recklessness of that long thrust had thrown calculations into confusion, especially since Cleve's steel had flashed brightly but three inches from the man's nose. The fellow fell back, off balance, cursing.

Cleve didn't permit him to recover. He pursued crazily, forcing the man across the room with a fierce shower of feints, jabs and lunges. His blade had twenty tips appearing from all directions as split-second intervals. Every trick he had ever learned was thrown into the play.

But it didn't work. The other man was good. He retreated without running and met everything Cleve could offer.

Then he brought up against the oak-paneled wall and the impact knocked his cool defense momentarily askew. There was an opening! Cleve drove for it. His opponent ducked. Cleve's blade sang viciously over his head and rammed two inches of its length into the paneling.

The man jerked erect once more. There was a snap, as the steel broke beneath the leverage, and Cleve stood staring hopelessly at half his sword. The remainder, a two-foot spike of glinting steel, jutted from the wall.

"And now, eavesdropper," grunted the bravo, "you are undone!"

He measured the English gallant for the *coup de grace,* but Cleve had a better idea. He hurled the useless rapier at the man and charged, his fist rising from the hip. It connected and the man rocked back on his heels; stumbled in groggy retreat to recover balance. He failed. He thudded against the wall and gasps burst from his lips. His sword clattered to the floor and his legs went limp. But he didn't fall. He sagged there on the wall like a side of beef with two inches of Cleve's broken sword protruding from his chest.

THE WORLD went still and time seemed to freeze. But at last Cleve began to recover from his exhaustion, drawing long, ragged breaths.

"Wheew!"

"*Sacré nom, monsieur!* But with your hands! Your bare fists!"

It was the landlord. Cleve stared at him, still breathing brokenly.

"They call it box-fighting in England," he said.

People were pouring into the room. Somebody gave him a tankard full of cognac and he drank of it deeply. Another person brought his broken sword. He held it thoughtfully. The blade had been purchased only a month before and because the armorer was famous for craftsmanship and fine steel, Cleve hadn't bothered testing it. But now, staring at the break, he could see where the metal was defective.

"Ten livres wasted." He shrugged and put the sword on the table. "Damme, landlord, what's all this ado? These people behave as though I had just won a major war."

The inn-keeper was excited. "But in a sense you have, *monsieur. Oui!* A major war! *Sandiou!* Do you not realize whom you have bested?"

"I'm too weary for riddles, my friend."

"Why, *monsieur,* you have just slain one of the best blades in France! One of the most notorious duellists ever to draw a sword—Mazo Gardier!"

Cleve eyed him blankly. "Never heard of him," he said and frowned. The basic question of the whole affair was still with him. Obviously, Mary de Sarasnac had overheard something— something vital enough to warrant her death. But what? Cleve shook his head. With Mazo Gardier pinned to the wall like a wilted corsage, it seemed that he'd never know. Then the action of the proprietor brought him out of his reverie.

"Since you have ended the sway of a bully, *monsieur,*" the man was saying, "and since you have broken your blade in the doing, it is but fair that you appropriate your late opponent's beauti- ful rapier." He pressed Gardier's ruby-hilted sword into Cleve's hands. "To the victor belong the spoils, *monsieur.*"

Cleve felt a momentary lift in his lethargy. He stared at the gemmed sword, feeling the perfection of it, its splendid balance.

Here was a weapon that would never betray him. He fondled it reverently for a moment before hanging it from his studded baldric.

Then he said: "Now, mine host, lead the way to my room and if anyone else asks…" He smiled wearily. "Tell him I arrived in three coaches, a cart and a chariot!"

CHAPTER XI

YOUR RESPECTFUL PRISONER

AT TEN IN the morning a week later, Señor Juan Enrico Luis Maria Castro sat at the bay-window of his suite in the Red Tassel Tavern in Montferrat. He pondered breakfast. In his case, the word pondered was apt. He was the sort who pondered everything—every conscious act of his life.

Right now he was reflecting that his failure to wreck the coach of Sir Harry Winthrop three days ago had so disorganized his digestion as to cause a definite loss of appetite. Sir Harry should have been killed; his papers stolen. Instead, Sir Harry had been thrown clear of the boulder-bashed coach and was recovering now in the palace of Duke Vincent, while his papers were undoubtedly hidden safely in his room.

This morning, as yesterday, Castro didn't feel capable of consuming his usual six eggs, steak and two cups of chocolate, so again he had to rearrange things.

"One steak and only four eggs," he told Beppo his valet. "One cup of chocolate."

Beppo looked nonplussed—not a difficult task for him—and held up four fingers inquiringly. Castro nodded. Beppo scratched his bald pate and shrugged. Beppo was a mute. He allowed his simian features an expression of concern and quit the room.

With breakfast out of the way, Castro turned attention to

the scene outside the window. Because of it, he had chosen this particular suite. The tavern crowned a knoll some twenty paces from the Susa Road outside Casale in Montferrat, and from his point of vantage he could see both ends—the heavy gate at the town wall and the highway's abrupt termination a mile away. It dipped sharply up and over a sloping hillock. The view also included a section of the front court near the inn's entrance, a steep-swelling stretch of grazing land, and finally the not too distant peaks of the Alps, gleaming white and saffron in the sunlight.

Castro was particularly fond of this window. Being a veritable paunch of a man, and of consequence much opposed to the rigors his profession imposed on him, he found the view happily advantageous to both business and bodily ease.

Strictly speaking, he was a spy. Of course he preferred not to regard himself as such, but rather as an honorable *agent provocateur* in the service of His Most Catholic Majesty, Philip IV of Spain. At present Castro was located in the Duchy of Montferrat for the purpose of turning such sundry incidents as might arise into advantages for his country.

It was not a difficult task. Montferrat was in an uncertain temper. Its soldiery was sullen; its populace worried, and its ruling house disunited. It was fertile soil for a man whose peculiar talents had nearly plunged France into a civil war a year before.

Besides, Castro didn't look like a spy. He appeared more like a complacent merchant. There was something innocuous about his olive, moon-shaped countenance; its button nose and small, amiable mouth lent an air of bovine good nature to the man. He wore a deceptively vapid grin when plotting some villainy, and after its completion, one of sleepy innocence. At the immediate moment, he was looking inoffensively stupid. This indicated concern—deep concern over the appearance of a solitary horseman in the courtyard below.

HE HAD been watching the man since dismissing Beppo, and at first he hadn't paid the fellow much heed. Travelers cantering down the road from the west were not unusual. Castro's examination had been cursory, then attentive, finally apprehensive.

The rider was a tall man, booted and spurred, wearing a short maroon cape upon which was emblazoned the hooped-cross insignia of the Cardinal's Guard. As he drew nearer, the Spanish *intrigant* recognized him as Guy le Comte d'Entreville, called the Kitten, unanimously considered a quick-bladed hellion, and not the least averse to wrecking the dreams of such gentlemen who sought to conspire against France. Watching him approach, Castro was uneasy. He had never met d'Entreville, but in France he had seen him and heard of him from most reliable confreres.

He licked his lips and sighed. With one devil in Montferrat, the other couldn't be far afield. Where was Cleve? He glanced past d'Entreville, up the road, and felt immeasurably better when he found it empty. Perchance, d'Entreville was merely passing. Perhaps there was nothing in Montferrat to attract his attentions—no mission for him to perform.

But then Castro shook his head. He suddenly remembered the night before. At the time his sleep-drugged brain hadn't placed much importance on the incident, but shortly after retirement he had been awakened. A rider had thundered into the inn's courtyard to butt-whipp the door, loudly demanding admission. As the tavern entrance was directly below his bedchamber, Castro had heard everything. The rider had not been permitted to stay, the Red Tassel being full, but he had asked several questions before riding away. Castro had been incensed over the disturbance.

"Señor Guda," he had barked as the inn-keeper plodded back a few minutes later. "Señor Guda! What was the meaning of that outrage?"

"A mad traveler, *signor.* To judge from his accent, a crazy Englishman. I sent him off. I'm sorry, *signor.*"

"Hmmmph!" Castro had grunted.

But now, with Guy d'Entreville standing below, that episode

took on a new significance. That crazy Englishman had been Lord Richard Cleve. And with Cleve and d'Entreville both in Montferrat, something definitely was about to break.

Castro began to smile vacantly—the sign of plotting. With those two roisterers at hand, plans had to be altered; a certain person warned. He brushed aside the litter of crockery and reached for a quill, and wrote three quick lines. He sealed the note in an envelope and called Beppo.

"You know where to deliver this, Beppo," he stated, holding the note under the mute's nose.

Beppo took the note and nodded enthusiastically. He knew. He had delivered others like it before. The note was unaddressed.

GUY D'ENTREVILLE didn't linger at the Red Tassel. A short conversation with the inn-keeper, a beaker of fresh milk while his horse was being watered, and he was en route to Casale with the meager information that a cavalier answering his description had swept past the inn scarcely eight hours before.

"*Mordi!* It's been that way since leaving Paris! And I've been losing! At Troyes, three hours; at Chaumont, four. And now 'tis eight! *Pecaire!* Cleve must ride a Pegasus."

He eyed the approaching town with something akin to defiance. If it did not contain a certain mad Englishman, then to the devil with the whole affair! The pursuit had left him feeling as if clubbed. No man was worth that—not even Cleve. Besides, the English rakehelly was almost clear of French jurisdiction, and there was a modicum of comfort in the thought.

Guy would not admit it to himself, but he had followed Cleve out of France and into Savoy, first, to prove that he could outride him—second, to wish the mad fool Godspeed. But now, if he caught him in Montferrat, his duty was to arrest the Englishman. He had given Richelieu his word and Montferrat was French soil. He pulled his dust-crusted felt hat down over one eye, hitched up his rapier and clucked at his horse.

"*Allons,* Ferdinand. More quickly."

The streets of Casale were clogged. It was market day and

the rural gentry were carting produce to the square for sale. He guided his mount carefully between the overladen wagons and drew up before a group of idlers talking on the corner.

"Perchance one of you gentlemen can direct me to a respectable hostlery."

"Straight ahead, *signor*. The Inn of the Golden Crowns."

D'Entreville thanked the man and rode on. He found the inn, a neat rectangular building with a low stone wall separating its court from the street. He dismounted stiffly and turned his horse over to an adenoidal groomsman. Then he entered the grog-room.

Richard Cleve was in a large room on the second floor rear. He was sleeping. Guy was told this, and at once he climbed the tavern's wide central staircase and burst in upon the somnolent gallant.

"*Corbac!* The end of the chase. *Hola, mon ami!*"

CLEVE DIDN'T wake, and eyeing him Guy suddenly felt less exultant. He realized now that an arrest had to be made. He bit his lip, closed the door and stood irresolutely in front of it.

The chamber Cleve had rented was bare-boarded, sparsely furnished and stuffy. Guy stood staring at the littered trail of garments from the door to the great four-posted bed whereon the Englishman sprawled. He frowned. A man sleeping for long in this veritable oven would come out with a headache.

Finally he went to the latticed casement, swung open its panels and turned from it with fresh, cool air washing the nape of his neck. *Pardieu!* That was better!

But he was still in an unhappy and undecided state of mind. *Ventre Saint Gris!* To arrest one's comrade took courage. Courage of the sort the ancient Spartans used to boast. And although Guy's sense of discipline was strong, it had not yet reached a Lacedaemonian fervor.

He tugged absently at the lobe of his ear, smoothed the crispness of his clipped mustache. The soft luxury of the bed tempted him, reminding him painfully of his own complete weariness.

Peste! Cleve was no man to cope with when one was exhausted and slow-witted. Immediately action was out of the question. The sensible course would be too catch forty winks.

But his decision was not reached without a vague sense of guilt, and as he stripped himself of his cape, draping it over the back of the desk-chair in the corner, he began to fret as to whether postponement of Cleve's arrest was in strict keeping with his vow to Richelieu. Then he noticed the writing desk— the paper, quill and inkpot thereon—and found a compromise.

When Guy crawled into bed five minutes later, the door had been locked, the key hidden, and a laconic announcement pinned to the wall with the point of a poniard.

> *Cleve,*
> *Consideration of your fatigue has caused me to execute my pain-*
> *ful duty in this manner.*
> *You are under arrest!*
> *Respectfully,*
> *d'Entreville*

CHAPTER XII

ARROWS FROM NOWHERE

SLEEP WAS SOFT and velvet black. It was a screen, cloaking him from thought and soothing the dull ache of fatigue, then wearing thin as faint saffron light seeped through. This light grew, dissolving sleep, clearing his mind. Then quite suddenly he was awake.

Guy blinked. The saffron glow was still in his eyes. It flooded the room with a wavering light, and raising his head he saw that it emanated from a bottle-based candle atop the writing desk in the corner. Outside it was dark. He could see part of the star-sprinkled sky edged above the black peak of the roof opposite his window.

"A black good morning to you, *mon ami.*"

He massaged his face, yawned luxuriously and then sat up to stretch. In the process he discovered that the bed-surface beside him was quite vacant. But he completed flexing his shoulders before the import of this struck him; and then he gaped. *Sango-demi!* Where was Cleve?

He felt the sting of mortification, for he had asked for this. Springing from the bed, he wondered how long he had slept and how much of a lead Cleve had on him; and then his gaze focussed upon the note he had written and he cursed softly. Cleve had added a scrawled postscript.

> *P.S.*
> *Kitten,*
> *Consideration of your fatigue has caused the execution of my escape in this manner.*
> *Having business at the palace, I find literary fetters inconvenient. I shall return anon. Wait for me.*
> *Your respectful prisoner,*
>
> *Cleve*
>
> *P.P.S.*
> *Where the devil did you come from?*

While Guy glared at this, its author was striding jauntily down the dark, twisted thoroughfares of Casale, smiling slightly as he pictured the Frenchman's eruptive reaction, and wondering vaguely as to how serious Sir Harry Winthrop's hurts were.

Cleve had found out about the "accident" that morning. He had come pounding into the courtyard of the Golden Crowns to ask its swarthy proprietor news of Sir Harry. He had been turned over to a battered little man named Jacob, who was Sir Harry's postillion.

Sir Harry was not dead. He was staying at the palace of Duke Vincent where he had been carried after his coach had been wrecked rounding a sharp bend in the Susa Road. Sir Harry had suffered a broken leg and sundry lacerations.

" 'Twas a boulder, sir." Jacob informed Cleve. "A great thunderin' boulder. It came down from the top of a steep hill, and before I could halt the coach, it struck us amidships. A most rare sort of mishap, sir. Suspicious."

Cleve had been all for riding to the palace then, but Jacob had deterred him. It was gray dawn.

" 'Twill avail ye naught, sir. 'Tis too early. Besides, the past mornings have been set aside for Sir Harry's full rest, and the duke's physician won't countenance visitors."

Cleve grinned at that. "Damme! I need rest myself, so I'll take the time to get some now. Good evening, or morning, Jacob, whichever the case may be."

HE HADN'T intended to sleep solidly for fifteen hours. Considering it now, however, he decided that it was good. As his boots crunched on the gravel surface of the street, he felt alive again for the first time in days.

He flexed his fingers. They were still stiff from clutching the sill-ledges, wall-cracks and trellis stays that had marked his recent descent from the bed-chamber. Then he pulled the collar of his cape tighter about his throat and increased his pace.

It wasn't late—eight o'clock—but the night was surprisingly chill. The nip of it sent tiny shivers through him. Yellowed windows of a nearby tavern enticed him with their promise of warming brew and a glowing hearth. He shook off the temptation and pressed on.

The street was a narrow, rambling affair that brought him suddenly around one corner and into the cobbled expanse of Casale's market square. Contrasting sharply with the murk of the darker thoroughfares, the place was bright—aflicker with great orange torches and bonfires. A crowd stood in its center, surrounding a rough wooden platform upon which a trio of tumblers cavorted. Cleve was threading his way through the spectators when the first warning reached him.

"Way for Count Henri's men! Make way!"

He skirted the stall of an apple-vendor, little regarding the cry.

It came from the outer fringes of the crowd. And then it rang again, this time louder and accompanied by the clatter of hoofs.

"Split, rabble! Give way for the count's riders!"

The gathering split apart. Cleve suddenly found himself alone, facing the charging cavalcade—the green-clad, closely knit troop which had struck into the square like a bow-ball. Then somebody jerked him out of the horses' path and he turned and found a big friar standing at his elbow.

"Stand not irresolute, son, when you hear that cry."

The riders pounded past, laughing and cursing as they rode, madly drunk. Cleve carefully slanted his hatbrim and stared after them.

"Damme! In a hurry, aren't they?" He turned to his rescuer and smiled. "Thank you. Another moment and I'd have been mingling with the cobbles."

The friar shrugged. "I have done it before."

Cleve rubbed his shoulder where the speaker had gripped it and nodded. "I don't doubt it. You have a professional's touch. But tell me, is it customary for the local blades to ride down pedestrians, or has this Count Henri a special concession in the business?"

The friar regarded him. "You must be a stranger in Montferrat."

"Yes. Definitely."

"Then you have not heard of Henri. He is the son of Duke Vincent you know, though utterly unlike him. Duke Vincent is a sincere well-loved ruler. Henri is a roistering young puppy. But perchance I speak harshly. Henri is not a vicious man actually, but a weak-willed youth with evil companions. It is his brawling, blaspheming friends who are causing his downfall. This I know from conversations with his padre."

Cleve looked around. The crowd was collecting itself, muttering imprecations and sending black glares after the vanished horsemen. He smiled wryly.

"I doubt that you could convince these people of that," he said.

The friar nodded sagely. "True. The people are beginning to murmur. Only respect for their duke prevents their speaking. But many fear the day that Henri ascends the throne. There are black days in store for Montferrat, my friend. And the intrigues of the Spanish and the Austrians are not the least of it." The speaker sighed. "Henri is going to be an unpopular ruler, I fear."

Cleve's smile deepened. "Well. He hasn't given me a reason to disagree with your prediction." Then he thanked the friar again and continued his way.

THE PALACE of Duke Vincent crouched like a grim gray beast atop a sloping hill overlooking the town. To Cleve's way of thinking, it little resembled a palace at all. Palaces were lavish affairs, spired and balconied and set in terraced gardens to enhance their magnificence. This building was stern, forbidding.

The edifice was set firmly in the north-east corner of the town's wall. Its four squat bastions were equipped with arrow-slots, adaptable for muskets. The gate Cleve was nearing appeared strong enough, but it served merely as the first obstacle to an invader. It was set in a high stone redoubt, preceded by a torch-lit fosse of twenty yards, and backed by the palace's main wall into which was cut another portcullis.

He eyed the two breast-plated halbardiers on duty; then hitched up his ruby-hilted blade and marched across the fosse. One of the guards turned and spoke softly into the shadows of the gate. An officer appeared, resplendent in gem-studded doublet, red sash and plumed hat.

"Your business, *monsieur?*"

Cleve arched an eyebrow. The fellow's tone was insolent. He didn't care for it, but felt disinclined to take issue now. "Why, to get in of course." He smiled. "I desire to visit Sir Harry Winthrop."

The officer didn't say anything. He inspected Cleve carefully, eying his battered hat, his travel-stained boots, in particular his sword. Then he turned and held up five fingers. One of the halbardiers disappeared into the gate.

"Do you possess a pass permitting you to see the duke's guest, *monsieur?*"

"My name will prove all the pass I need. Tell Sir Harry that Lord Richard Cleve will shortly visit him."

The officer pursed his lips. They were small lips, arched neatly beneath his pointed mustachios. He smiled distantly. "Indeed? You have the appearance of a nobleman, *monsieur.*" The sarcasm in his eyes brightened visibly. "Incognito, of course."

"Of course." Cleve's fingers settled lightly on the hilt of his rapier. He noted that the halbardier had returned bringing with him five friends. He resumed easily: "And now that we have settled my identity, suppose you escort me to Sir Harry's apartments."

The officer paused. He inclined his head toward the newcomers and they closed in. "I shall be happy to escort you, monsieur—" He reached for his hilt. "But to the deepest dungeon in the palace! Seize him!"

CLEVE BOUNDED back. He had sensed this, though he knew no reason for it. His sword glittered in a silvery arc, but he hadn't realized that they were behind him too. A pike prodded against the small of his back and he froze. The officer bowed his blade lightly and laughed.

"Netted!"

Halbard-points girdled him, a solid ring of steel. He stood immobile, sword still poised, awaiting the next move. Finally he sighed and let the weapon fall to his side. What the devil was up, anyway? He regarded his captors narrowly and smiled wryly.

The officer paced up to him like a parading peacock. "We have been warned of you, Gardier," he said. "Only this morning we received the word. Going to dispose of the duke, eh?"

Now Cleve had a reputation of imperturbability in the face of surprise, but this statement caused him to stare in amazement.

"Me?"

The officer smirked. He nodded. *"Oui.* And feigning innocence will do you little good. Candidly, *monsieur*, it was ill-advised of you to appear wearing that ruby-hilted blade so obviously. It identifies you. Beneath the torchlight the gems shine quite brilliantly."

By now Cleve had composed himself. He decided that he'd had enough. "One moment, bucko. I have no designs on the life of Duke Vincent. There has been a mistake—"

"It was yours, *monsieur*, by showing your face here."

The English rakehelly regarded the steel-points surrounding him and took a deep breath. "I'm inclined to agree with you. But that does not alter the fact that—"

The officer snapped his fingers and held out his hand. "Your blade, Gardier!"

Cleve's grip tightened on the hilt. "You're not precisely a fool, laddie," he said easily. "But the difference isn't enough to quibble about. I'm not this Mazo Gardier. I killed him and this blade is—"

"Your sword, *monsieur!*"

BUT HERE the argument was terminated abruptly. The officer's plumed hat suddenly leaped sideways from his master's head. It zipped past the nose of a gaping guard and grounded itself a few feet beyond. There was a red-feathered arrow in it.

"Shades of William Tell!"

Cleve slowly shook his head. He was becoming incapable of surprise. So much so, that an archer in the seventeenth century seemed completely plausible. Then he turned his attention to the rear and discovered three figures on the edge of the fosse, each fingering a drawn bow with an arrow knotched.

"The next shaft kills the man who makes a move," the smallest of the three promised. "Drop your weapon! And you, Gardier, stand away from those fools."

Cleve obeyed by approaching the trio as halbard staffs rattled on the cobblestones. He noticed that all three men wore long

*Cleve swung around in the coach, holding
his blade against the girl's breast*

capes; that their clothing was cut for riding and that it did not seem in the best repair.

The smallest appeared to be the leader. He was a beady-eyed individual, smooth-featured and bandy-legged. He looked youthful, until one noticed the hardness about his mouth.

The officer's angry voice grated through the silence.

"This but draws the noose tighter about your neck, Antone!"

The little bowman chuckled. It was a bubbling reckless chuckle. "You must first catch me, my friend."

Cleve smiled. He could appreciate the archer's nerve. Besides, his name made a nice alliteration. Antone—Antone the Archer. The English gallant tapped him lightly on the shoulder.

"For what am I indebted, bucko?"

"For being a greater rogue than I," Antone replied. He produced a dirty fold of paper. "Here. This is for you Gardier. *Sapristi!* I've trailed you all the way from the Golden Crowns to deliver it. Take it and be gone. I can't hold these lovelies at bay forever."

Cleve tapped the paper on his fingernail and frowned. So far, the night's adventure meant nothing. It was a puzzle crammed with questions and he didn't know any of the answers. Antone kept talking, but to his compatriots.

"Retreat slowly, my friends. Do not hesitate to loose a shaft at the first suspicious move. We shall split and meet in our accustomed place in the hills." He suddenly seemed to notice that Cleve hadn't left. "*Sapristi!* Are you still with us? Be gone! We haven't risked our necks just to have you recaptured."

Cleve wanted to ask several questions, but upon the other's words he decided to shelve them. The primary consideration was to get out of here.

" 'Tis your party, lad," he said and slapped the little archer lightly on the shoulder. "Thanks." Then he turned and dog-trotted into the night.

CHAPTER XIII

KITTEN, BE COOL

GUY WAS WAITING for Cleve when he returned; waiting with an injured scowl on his lean features and a bottle half-raised to his lips. He was seated behind a dinner-laden table in their room at the Golden Crowns, facing the door. He was completely dressed except for boots and his doublet. He put the bottle down.

"I presume this is the way you honor your arrest!" he grated. "*Sangodemi!* I might have known I could not trust you!"

Cleve closed the door. He felt hot. He was still panting slightly from a hurried circuit of Casale's back streets. Shortly after he had left Antone, an alarm had blared from the palace to send vigilant riders careening through the town. He had had several tight moments.

Antone the Archer, it seemed, was definitely a wanted man. A highwayman; a cunning rogue; a killer who used the bow because of its silence. Cleve learned that even to be suspected of knowing him had caused more than one person to submit to the efficiency of the local headsman.

The Englishman strode to the table and balanced himself on its edge. Guy's characteristic greeting had melted the tenseness in him. He reached leisurely across the lunch, selected a tid-bit from the other's plate and grinned.

"Cheese again, Kitten?" He popped the tiny triangle into his mouth. "Have a pleasant nap?"

Guy kicked back his chair and stood up. He was angry, but it was merely surface rage. During Cleve's absence, he had been thinking. He knew now, despite his word to Richelieu, that it wasn't within his will to be able to arrest his friend. But he'd be cursed if he'd admit it! *Sandiou!* He'd run a bluff first!

"Now mark me, Cleve. You are under arrest. *Corbac!* I do not like this, but it is a fact!"

The English rakehelly smiled amiably, scaled his hat to the bed and slid from the table-top into a chair. He poured himself a goblet of wine before speaking. And then all he said was: "All right, Kitten. But without dramatics."

"*Pardieu!* Cease using that title! I'm serious. My orders are to bring you back to Paris to stand trial for high treason."

"Treason?" Cleve looked innocent. "What did I do?"

"You know well enough. You drew a blade in Richelieu's presence, defied his commands and fled with my aid."

"Ah. With your aid, eh? So you're in this too?"

"*Oui.*"

"And to get out of it, you must turn me over."

"*Sacré nom!*" Guy's fist crashed heavily on the table. The impact sent dishes bouncing and Cleve rescued a bottle from spilling by snatching it with a sweep of his hand. He wagged a finger at Guy, but d'Entreville continued, face flaming:

"*Ventre saint gris!* I might have expected that! *Sangodemi!* Of all the ungrateful, short-witted louts—I ride for days without sleep; go without food and comfort merely to save you from being slaughtered. The Cardinal was about to send carrier pigeons ahead with orders to show you no mercy, to cut you down without warning, to treat you like a mad—a mad—"

"Dog," Cleve supplied and sampled the bottle.

"*Oui!* And then you accuse me of the most heinous motive ever a man could own! *Corbac!* I should call you out!"

"Damme. This is rotten wine!" said Cleve.

He lifted the bottle up to the light—and suddenly it flew apart in his hands, spraying him with wine and bits of shattered glass. A musket's report snapped into the room. It came from the opened window. And d'Entreville, standing to one side, suddenly dove for the floor.

"*Sangodemi!* Down, Cleve! That was a musket-ball!"

THE ENGLISHMAN placed the base of the shattered bottle carefully on the table. His fingers did not tremble. After all, the mysterious marksman *had* missed. Then he arose, went to the window, closed it and drew the shades. He stood there on one side of it, smiling grimly and drying his hand with a kerchief.

"Lovely country, Montferrat," he said.

Guy stood up. He walked over to the wall where the ball was embedded and touched it lightly with his forefinger. The metal was still warm. He turned, frowning.

"*Corbac!* I don't understand it. We're strangers in this town. Why should someone wish our deaths?"

"I fear that ball was meant for me, Kitten," Cleve told him calmly. He returned to the table and drew his blade. "During the course of this night, I have escaped being run down by a hair's breadth. And then when I appeared at the palace gate, I was nearly arrested by a young popinjay who claimed that I was the notorious bravo Mazo Gardier." He stared at the sword in his hand. "This used to belong to Gardier. Perchance it's the reason for everything."

"How did you procure it, *mon ami?*"

Cleve shrugged. "Gardier exchanged it for a spade in Hades. But that isn't important. The fellow apparently had a mission in this duchy—the pleasant business of murdering Duke Vincent."

"Mordi!"

"Yes. And Gardier's confederates are very much in evidence also." The Englishman chuckled. "In fact, three of them rescued me from the clutches of the Duke's guards."

"But that does not explain the musket-shot, *mon ami.* Surely, the duke's guards would not ambush you. An arrest and a public execution is more politic."

Cleve returned the sword to its scabbard. "I know it." He nodded. "That is what makes this affair so damned interesting. Perchance I have a bitter competitor who is vying with me for the honor of murder." He smiled without mirth. "One thing certain, Gardier's mission had a fearful amount of publicity. Somebody knew his intent and spread the word with—" Suddenly he frowned. He was thinking of Mary de Sarasnac and of Gardier's pursuit of her. Was she in Montferrat?

BUT D'ENTREVILLE didn't notice Cleve's silence. The Frenchman was frowning in deep thought. He knew why Cleve had gone to the Palace. Sir Harry's postillion, a little man named Jacob, had knocked on the door shortly after Guy had started to dress. Upon hearing that Winthrop had been delayed in Casale, the French gallant had easily deduced Cleve's intent. He had taken it for granted that Cleve would succeed.

But now Cleve had returned. He had returned without seeing Sir Harry, embroiled in intrigue, and Guy was deciding to make the most of it. He had definitely committed himself to attempt a solution of Montferrat's mysteries, but he knew he needed Cleve's nimble, logical mind. To assure himself of Cleve's aid he was prepared to go to any lengths. *Pecaire!* It was a duty.

France stood to lose much in Montferrat. Furthermore, he could solve the duchy's difficulties, Richelieu's anger would be forgotten. Guy knew that the Cardinal would never forgive him for abetting Cleve's escape or for failing to make the arrest, unless this problem of Montferrat was solved triumphantly. He felt immensely satisfied with himself for regarding the situation with such practical eyes.

"*Sandiou.* You have stumbled into one of the very intrigues that *Monseigneur le Cardinal* had planned for our attention, Cleve. For the past two months the gold train, bearing wages to the garrison here, has been waylaid. Not the least of it, there have been several attempts on the life of Colonel de Boussey, the *commandant. Pecaire!* This duchy is rank with plotting."

Cleve sat down. "This duchy is rank without it, Kitten. I'm not interested. As soon as I receive that pardon, it is Richard Cleve for England."

"But not through France," retorted Guy. "A price is on your head there. To reach home you must sail from Venice and around Gibraltar. Triple the time."

"Faith. I need sea-air."

Guy was nonplussed. He was being eminently logical and it wasn't working. He attempted another tack.

"Mark me, I'm interested in the welfare of France but if I return to Paris without you, I return to La Bastille. There is a personal issue in this, *mon ami.*"

Cleve chuckled. "Egad! Then I fear I shall have to take you with me. You'll like England, Kitten."

"*Pecaire!* You stubborn fool! In the past we have bought the Cardinal's patience with a triumph for him. Settle this Montferrat difficulty and all charges will be dropped. You already have a point of leverage in being mistaken for one of the conspirators."

Cleve shook his head. "It's debatable. I cannot continue to resemble Mazo Gardier for long just because of my sword." He nodded brightly in Guy's direction. "But why don't you solve this riddle yourself? Richelieu will love you again and you can go home."

The French rakehelly's volatile temper began to assert itself. *"Corbac!* I suppose you deem me incapable of slitting open this mystery without your aid."

"Well—" Cleve temporized and grinned.

Guy's lips went tight. *"Sangodemi!"* he erupted. "I was attempting to ease your situation, braggart—not my own. You have been thirsting to arrive in England with all possible dispatch. *Bien.* I was going to aid you to cross France unmolested. But now you can go to—"

Cleve crossed one booted leg over the other and relaxed against the back of his chair. "Ah now, temper, Kitten," he cautioned. "Be uncivil and in England I'll not give you an allowance, a pension or anything."

"You'll give me nothing!" Guy stormed.

"Such bitterness. But I'll lay it to your youth and inexperience. Should you need my sterling advice, old comrade, do not hesitate to ask for it. But soon, of course, because I'll be en route to Venice in a day or so."

Guy started pacing in sharp exasperated circles. *"Ventre saint gris!* The conceit of the lout! The unmitigated conceit!" He spun savagely. "Mark me! I shall solve this affair in half the time it would have taken had I allowed you to encumber me. Four days are all I need. Merely four—"

THERE CAME a knock at the door—A brisk, authoritative rap. The two cavaliers promptly forgot their quarrel and stared. Neither moved, so the knock repeated itself. Cleve deftly covered the hilt of his rapier with the cuff of his gauntlet.

" 'Tis your investigation, Kitten. Perchance that is one of Mazo Gardier's playmates. Answer it."

But the man knocking proved to be a resplendent figure of military carriage; he was standing stiffly before the door, flanked by two soldiers in red-edged surcoats.

"Good evening, *messieurs*," he said stepping easily into the chamber. "I am Colonel le Vicomte de Boussey, Commandant of His Majesty's Arms in Montferrat. I had expected you to report to me upon arrival, but since the nature of your business is delicate, I report to you."

The speaker was a veritable bear of a man. A smiling blond giant. Yet he moved with the fluid grace of a cat and his gray eyes were very keen and shrewd. His great frame was well padded, but there was no suggestion of softness about him. He was meticulously dressed. Cleve thought his choice of a white doublet a trifle flamboyant but only because it seemed to exaggerate the bigness of the man. One thing certain, de Boussey was no milk-mannered courtier. He bowed swiftly, then seized Guy's hand in a firm grip.

"Undoubtedly you are M. d'Entreville, *monsieur*," he boomed. "I am glad to welcome you. When informed that you were being sent here, a weight was lifted from my mind. I'm a soldier and inept at the subtler problems of state."

Then he turned to Cleve, ham-like palm extended. "Lord Cleve, I presume. The other of *Monseigneur le Cardinal's* twin devils." He laughed. "*Corbac!* You do not appear as shrewdly mad as your reputation would have you, *monsieur.*"

"Fortunately," Cleve replied and furtively flexed his fingers, which had been nearly paralyzed by de Boussey's viselike grip. He kept his gauntlet firmly over the hilt of his sword. No sense in inviting trouble. He frowned slightly.

Somehow de Boussey's bluff good spirits didn't sit right. They seemed vaguely counterfeit. He didn't know why he should have this suspicion, but it was there and he fell to mulling it over. In the first place, how did the colonel know that he and d'Entreville were in Casale? It was an interesting point. He and Guy had arrived separately, at different hours and without advance notice.

Meanwhile de Boussey had turned to one of his men. "René," he commanded. "Have wine sent up. The best, *comprenez*. Then

see to it that we are not disturbed. These gentlemen and I wish
to confer."

CHAPTER XIV

MADEMOISELLE HORSE-THIEF

THE THREE OF them sat around the table for nearly an hour.
De Boussey and Guy did most of the talking, while Cleve lolled
indifferently in his chair, drank wine and listened. He didn't ask
a single question. He learned a lot.

The lootings of the wage-wagons were becoming serious.
Officially, de Boussey admitted desertions. A few—not many.
But the truth of the matter was that the French garrison was
reduced to one third its original strength by such losses, and the
thing was like a spreading disease.

Finally Cleve paced to the window. He pulled the shades
aside, opened it. He stood there with the hum of their conversation in his ears, wondering if he'd ever be free of his fascination
for the unknown. He knew that it constantly betrayed him, yet
already his insatiable curiosity was coming awake.

This Montferrat problem was alluring. He tried to ignore the
half-formed conclusions in his brain concerning it. But they
were there, beckoning him, tickling his imagination.

Determinedly he dug thumbs into his sash. No! With his
homecoming at stake he did not dare risk becoming enmeshed
in intrigue. Conspiracies were like threads. By drawing out one,
you became snarled with many. Then, standing there, he realized
that his thumb had touched a crumpled piece of paper—the
note Antone had passed to him. He had placed it in his sash
while running through the streets. Slowly he slid it free, stared
at it an instant, cursed softly and opened it. It was quite cryptic.

*House twelve, the market-square, at twelve. Knock two long,
three short.*

There was no signature. He tore it carefully into bits and sprinkled them out of the window. Then he turned and regained his place at the table. He poured himself another goblet of wine.

"The next shipment of gold is due next week," the colonel was saying. "*Mordi!* It must arrive. Candidly, *Monsieur le comte,* I have a theory. It has been established that our local bandit, a clever knave known as Antone the Archer, has been recruiting men. Before these robberies his Band was composed of but a handful. Now it exceeds two-score rogues."

"I see," Guy nodded. His dark eyes were grave, thoughtful. He frowned slightly. "But surely an ignorant highwayman could not know when to strike with such consistency, *Monsieur le vicomte.* Each gold-train has been cloaked in secrecy as to the time of arrival and the number of guards carried. To my mind, Antone may be a tool. True, he may be the raider, but since the lootings are conducted with such accuracy, it would appear that a traitor lurks somewhere in a high place,"

DE BOUSSEY'S rich laughter rolled through the room. He slapped the table as though highly pleased. "Precisely, *monsieur!* I must compliment your astuteness. Of course, Antone could not do it alone. But who is the rogue's compatriot?"

"That," Guy said slowly, "remains to be seen. Perchance after I confer with His Highness, Duke Vincent, I shall have more information to progress on."

De Boussey nodded. "Undoubtedly. It was for that purpose, among other things, that I came tonight. The duke desires that you and M. Cleve establish yourselves at the palace the better to observe conditions. Had he known of your arrival sooner, he would have insisted that you do so immediately. But as it is now, he regrets being unable to interview you tonight. Poor health, you know. He retires early.

"But even so, *Monsieur le comte,* there is one—er—suspect whom naturally he will not mention in his interview. His son, Henri de Casale. I myself do not enjoy mentioning this, but I feel it my duty. Observe Henri closely, *monsieur*, and remember that he will succeed his father."

Cleve frowned slightly and thoughtfully drained the last of his wine. Outside in the town, the great clock in the market-square tolled the quarter-hour solemnly. Cleve stood up, smiling wryly at them and at himself for what he had decided to do.

"I feel the need of clean night air, gentlemen. I feel assured that you will continue discussing your problem as though I were here."

D'Entreville wanted him to stay, but was too stubborn to admit it. Cleve nodded pleasantly and left.

He walked slowly through the dark streets, gloved fingers curled to his hilt, thoughtful but wary. Casale was not unlike other towns of the times. Its streets were patrolled indifferently by a careless watch and the lone pedestrian at night took his life in his hands by merely passing through them.

But eventually he arrived in the now deserted market-square, feeling relieved at the peace of the city and excited by the prospect of what he was tempting Fate to do.

"Cleve, you're a fool. A nosey, snooping, fool!"

HE FOUND number twelve on the opposite side of the square from where he had entered and after wasting precious minutes in its discovery, he stood at length in the stygian shadow of its overhung second story. It was a fairly big building, pretentious. The lanterns of the watch bobbed across the mall and he waited until they had passed before turning to knock twice upon the door, and then thrice in quick succession. The door swung inward. The market clock took up a monotonous toll of twelve.

"Monsieur Gardier?"

Cleve's grip relaxed on the hilt of his blade. It was a girl's voice, soft, very young. He had been fearful that a man would answer—a man who knew Gardier.

"Of course," he replied.

"Inside, *monsieur*. We must introduce ourselves."

Cleve grinned. Faith, his luck was holding beautifully. She did not know the real Gardier. He accepted the soft fingers that groped for his arm and followed them as they pulled him inside.

The little foyer in which he stood was dark, but not so dark as the night outside. A heavy velvet drape shut out the light from another room, but the small bright cracks from the borders gave a faint illumination. The faint perfume of her reached his nostrils.

"You are most punctual, *monsieur,*" she said.

"In my profession, *mademoiselle,* punctuality is wisdom."

The draperies were brushed aside, and they were in the adjacent room. He discovered that she was adorable; entirely unlike the hardened adventuress he had expected. The innocent loveliness of her face… the exquisite symmetry of a perfect form. It was hard to believe that she could have need for a hired killer.

"Have you completed ogling me, *monsieur?*"

He grinned. "Merely returning your compliment, *mademoiselle.*"

She laughed and indicated an ornate Venetian chair next to the wall. "La, *monsieur,* apparently your wit is as nimble as your blade."

Cleve sat down, drawing his sword across his lap so that the rubies in the hilt glinted alive beneath the candlelight. She regarded the jewels with frank covetousness.

"Perhaps after this affair you might offer me one as a remembrance, *monsieur.*"

"Perhaps." He cocked an eyebrow. "If you make it worth the remembrance."

She flushed at that, a light of anger came into her eyes. "We had best come to the gist of our business, *monsieur,*" she decided. "Since one of my servants observed your arrival this morning, I have arranged a complete—er—playlet for you to act."

"Your servant? Is Antone a servant of yours, *mademoiselle?*"

She inclined her head. "At times I find uses for him. I saved him from the block a year ago."

"Ah. Then he does not work for the same government as do we."

She did not react to this subtle probe for information. "Antone is my agent," she replied.

"As am I now, *mademoiselle.*" He said it with great gravity, but there was a devil dancing in his eye.

SHE REGARDED him stiffly. "For a man of ice, Gardier, you display a remarkable warmth. But we have little time for chit-chat. I will explain what you are to do, and then you must leave. If Henri—"

"Ah. Henri is it? The jealous husband."

"Henri," she explained with some heat, "is secretly my affi-anced. He is the duke's son. I am expecting him soon for a late supper and should he discover your presence here, the baron's whole scheme will be dangerously unbalanced."

CLEVE SETTLED back to consider this bit of information. His purpose had been to learn the background, the surrounding figures, of this conspiracy, but her belief in his complete knowl-edge of the affair had thwarted him so far.

Now, however, discovery of her relationship to the duke's son gave him a clue. Egad! The woman intended to become the Duchesse de Montferrat. It was irrefutable in the face of her statements. She had not claimed Henri as her lover—but as her affianced.

And Henri obviously knew nothing of the plot, else how could his discovery of Gardier's presence unbalance the picture? The intrigue did not belong entirely to her either. It was not a two party plot. She hadn't hired Gardier—she did not know Gardier. It was the baron's plot. But who in the devil was the baron? Cleve frowned; and then her words jerked him out of his conjectures.

"Tomorrow, *monsieur,* you will arrive at this house as my brother from Mantua. Today I was supposed to receive a letter announcing your arrival. You will be expected. You will take quarters under this roof."

"I see." He nodded. "As your brother I shall have egress into most court circles." He smiled as he considered Gardier would have smiled under the circumstances. "Eventually, I shall accompany His Highness, Duke Vincent on a hunting foray and there shall be an accident, a fatal accident to the fine old gentleman."

She bit her lip. "I care little as to your method, *monsieur*. I merely furnish the opportunities." She went to the mantel and took a sheaf of papers from it. Returning, she handed them to him. "Study these references. I have built a complete family history in them so that we may converse before anyone concerning our bogus parents. Remember that your name is Emile. Emile Cordoba."

He stood up. "And yours?"

She frowned. "Catherine Cordoba, of course."

He nodded, smiling. "Of course."

Then she took him lightly by the arm. "And now, Monsieur Gardier, until tomorrow goodbye."

CHAPTER XV

ROGUES' PALACE

THE NEXT MORNING was mist-laden with a noiseless drizzle sifting through, and as the coach Colonel de Boussey had furnished rumbled sullenly toward the palace, Cleve carefully drew the weather-drapes and heightened the collar of his cape. He slanted his broad-brimmed hat low over his eyes. Beside him, d'Entreville observed the action frowningly.

"Pecaire! It isn't that damp," he complained.

Cleve chuckled. "No. But 'twill be a cursed amount damper in the palace dungeon, should that popinjay at the gate recognize me."

But at the gate the popinjay did not recognize him. The popinjay was too concerned over the effect of rain upon his vestments to hinder the great coach for more than a cursory inspection. Cleve grinned. Despite its discomfort, bad weather had virtues.

The coach rolled across the inner bailey of the palace yard and up to the stone dias of the grand entrance. It creaked to a halt.

De Boussey and a spidery little fop, bedecked in rose and saffron with diamond buckles on his velvet slippers, awaited in the shelter of the gothic arch. They started to descend, but a sudden squall drove them back. Liveried lackeys swirled around them, to open the coach door and to porter such meager baggage as the two rakehellies possessed.

"Messieurs," the huge colonel said, as they mounted the stone steps, "I desire you to meet le Sieur de Maupin, steward to His Highness the Duke. Monsieur de Maupin is commanded by His Highness to assure your comfort, and to escort you to the audience chamber."

"Our honor, *monsieur,*" Guy said politely.

De Maupin simpered. In the heavy silk of his clocked hose, his legs were decorative but spindly. He flicked a vermillion kerchief from his satin sash, brushed it lightly across his thin nose and bowed with a flourish. A whiff of perfume floated from him.

Cleve and d'Entreville eyed each other briefly, shook their heads. They detested the breed. Then they flicked gauntlets across their noses, simpered becomingly and bowed in return. De Boussey caught the play and nearly gagged attempting to choke down a great guffaw.

"I—ah—I shall leave you in le Sieur de Maupin's care, *messieurs,*" he told them quickly. "I must fulfill an appointment."

He turned away.

"Now if I could think of a similar excuse," Cleve remarked blandly and shrugged.

But the exchange was lost on the fop. As de Boussey stumped

off across the courtyard, de Maupin gestured airily toward the doorway and minced lightly through it, the wood of his high red heels snapping crisply on the tile. "If *messieurs* will do me the honor of accompaniment—"

"But certainly, *monsieur*," agreed d'Entreville, "We are content to follow you—at a safe distance, of course. Come along, Cleve. I desire to know if it's alive."

"Faith! That makes two of us," Cleve answered.

But this time, the effeminate dandy caught the gist. He sniffed. "Well, really, gentlemen!" And started away.

Cleve nudged his friend ahead. "You first, Kitten. And don't lose sight of it. It knows where we're going."

THEIR MINCING guide ushered them down a high-walled corridor, past a line of stiff-visaged pikemen and into the palace's grand foyer. It was a large room, oval in shape and rimmed midway to its ceiling by a gallery with a marble balustrade. A deep blue carpet covered the floor. Directly opposite the archway through which they had entered was a great sweeping staircase. This interior commanded admiration.

De Maupin swished his way diagonally across the room; paused to throw wide a pair of convergent doors, and turned.

"The audience chamber, *messieurs*," he announced primly. "Be so good as to wait inside and His Highness shall be with you directly."

Cleve patted d'Entreville encouragingly on the shoulder. "We part for the nonce, Kitten. Go there and wait. 'Twill offer you time and seclusion to sharpen the questions you intend asking the duke."

Guy frowned. "What of you?"

"I have other business." Cleve inclined his grin in de Maupin's direction. "Will you be so good as to escort me to Sir Harry Winthrop, *cherie?*"

The palace steward sighed. "Oh very well, *monsieur*. But I must confess it's vexatious. You might have mentioned it sooner."

He pranced off, tugging peevishly at the gold medallion chain looped around his thin neck. "This way, *monsieur*." The chain broke, unnoticed by him, and slid to the carpet.

Guy picked it up. "It has lost its leash," he said and then scowled. "Had I suspected your motive for coming to the palace, I'd have spiked it, Cleve. I thought you had decided to aid me."

The other chuckled. "Come now, why else should I be here? Besides, you're too big for spitefulness, Kitten. And consider—" He held up four fingers, "I'm giving you the four days you say are needed."

He took the chain and strode off after de Maupin, grinning. D'Entreville glared in his wake. "Clown!" The Frenchman then whirled, stumped into the richness of the audience chamber, and slammed himself into a chair. There were times when he regretted knowing Cleve.

MEANWHILE THE English cavalier was offering de Maupin the medallion. They were mounting the staircase. The little fop warmed toward him considerably, and by the time they reached the top he was gushing volubly.

"Undoubtedly you consider me a short-spoken brute, *monsieur*," he said. "But I have been greatly put upon these past days. Affairs of the palace, you know. I fear it has soured my otherwise sweet humor. 'Tis guests, *monsieur*. *Ma foi!* Never have I encountered so many guests!"

They were pacing along the circular gallery now. De Maupin continued: "First the daughter of Charles Emmanuel, Margaret of Savoy, chooses to—er—visit His Highness, ostensibly for her health. And then—"

Cleve frowned. "Margaret of Savoy is in the palace?"

"*Certainment*. And confidentially, *monsieur*—up to no good. She has a personal guard, a brute named Enrico. Totally uncouth, *monsieur*. Ever sneaking about and listening."

Cleve made a mental note to advise Guy about Margaret and her companion. "Did she bring many retainers?"

"Not many, *monsieur*. Four ladies, a coach-crew and that

Enrico person. But Margaret of Savoy is merely the beginning. Also staying with us is Signor Orlando, the close comrade of the duke's son. A most dangerous churl if you ask me, *monsieur*. Ever dueling, drinking and cursing. Some say he was once a notorious highwayman. Then yester-morning, *monsieur*, the duke's ward arrived. Arrived in a scandalous manner, *monsieur*. Unthinkable for a lady of her breeding."

"Drunk?" Cleve hazarded as they turned down a long hallway leading through the palace's north wing.

"But no!" De Maupin looked sincerely shocked. "Heaven forbid! But 'twas nearly as bad, *monsieur*." He stopped talking and gestured daintily with a rolling wrist to a doorway on the right.

"My destination?" Cleve ventured.

"Precisely. Knock and Sir Harry's man will answer. It never fails. And now pray excuse me for there are innumerable things to be done. Your own suite must be put to rights and the lackeys on my staff are wholly inadequate without my personal supervision. So until later, *monsieur*. Adieu."

"Adieu." Cleve nodded.

De Maupin swept into a low bow, which Cleve decided against attempting to duplicate; and then marched in a sprightly fashion back up the corridor. Cleve stared after him, smiling. But he was completely aware of de Maupin's importance. That little magpie knew more concerning the palace personnel than anyone else, Duke Vincent included.

"At times a man must use the weirdest of allies," he muttered and then bent his attention to Sir Harry's door.

BEFORE HE could rap his knuckles against the paneling, the door swung inward and he was facing a goateed gentleman of fifty, dressed somberly in black and carrying a small leather case beneath one arm. The fellow was startled. He half-closed the door before Cleve extended his foot and jammed the partition with the toe of his boot.

"One moment, m'lad. I've come a long distance to visit Sir

Harry and it is hardly polite to slam his door on my face. Cleve is my name. Lord Richard Cleve at your service, sir."

"Oh."

The gentleman appeared uneasy. He took control of himself with visible effort. "You surprised me, *monsieur.* I am the duke's physician, Doctor Despartes."

"A pleasure to know you, doctor. But of your patient. Capable, I trust, of receiving visitors."

"Er—well, *monsieur.* He is asleep and—"

Sir Harry's baritone echoed from the depths of the chamber. Cleve recognized it immediately—deep, grating and pompous.

"Who is there, by Gad?" Sir Harry wanted to know.

Cleve smiled at Despartes and eased himself gracefully around the physician. "With your permission, doctor. Matter of state, you know."

Despartes nodded. "But of course, *monsieur.* Enter." He seemed to have regained perfect composure. "I have other matters demanding my attention. I bid you good day, *monsieur.*" And nodding again politely, he departed.

Cleve stared after him. "Queer coot," he muttered.

He found Sir Harry propped up in a large bed, a triple layer of pillows beneath him, his splint-fitted leg jutting at an angle from beneath the coverlet. Sir Harry was scowling his surprise. His rugged features wore an expression of incredulity which he strove vainly to suppress.

"Cleve, by Gad!"

The English rakehelly nodded. Despite the importance of this meeting to him, he could not control his old impulse to deflate Sir Harry's pomposity.

"A remarkable deduction, Sir Harry," he commented easily. "Er—for you, that is."

"Hmmph! You haven't changed much. Well, what do you want?"

CLEVE REACHED out and pulled up a chair that appeared

as if it might rightly belong in milady's boudoir. He sat down on it gingerly and regarded his surroundings. The room was square, comfortably large, with scatter rugs on the polished floor, an ornate fireplace in the corner and two doors, closed, facing each other from opposite walls.

"My permit to return home," he admitted quietly. "I've pursued you the full way from Paris to get it."

Sir Harry rubbed his chin. "All the way from Paris, eh? Gad's teeth! Perchance you *have* changed. The Cleve I knew wouldn't have bothered." His veined eyes narrowed. "Why are you in such a rash to return home, m'lord?"

"Well." Cleve tilted back in the chair. "Well, I've become fearfully sick of what the French pass as ale. My tongue has been out for the real brew ever since you escorted me to the docks at Portsmouth. Faith! A man can develop a famous thirst in five years, you know."

Sir Harry stiffened. "By Gad! My first analysis was correct. You are still a wastrel, a roistering rakehelly, with nothing in your head but pleasure. Why I should have troubled to procure your pardon is more than I can conceive. Probably love for your late sire. Your father, m'lord, was a true gentleman and my closest friend and I am happy that he did not live to see the wild, pleasure-bent hellion into which his son has developed!"

"Temper, Sir Harry," Cleve reprimanded.

"Bah! I'll give you your pardon to rid myself of the sight of you. It's in my dispatch case along with many more important papers. Reach under my mattress, Cleve and fetch it out."

"Ah," said Cleve running fingers swiftly into the place mentioned, "secrets, eh? Do you always sleep on your missions, Sir Harry?"

The older man snorted his disgust. "I dislike your inference, puppy. It so happens that my mission concerns business vital to the defense of England—important contracts which Spain would be overjoyed to read. I dare not let them out of my sight. Frankly, I believe those secret contracts are the reason for my broken shank. The wrecking of my coach was intended—" Suddenly he paused and looked uneasy. "What is the trouble?"

CLEVE HAD run eager fingers between the mattress and the base-slats without encountering the precious dispatch case. Now he skirted the foot of the bed and repeated the quest. He ended it at the head of the mattress and straightened.

"There is no dispatch case here," he said.

Sir Harry went white. His gnarled fingers were trembling as he rolled awkwardly on his side to verify the announcement. "By Gad! It must be! I—" He suddenly fell back against the pillows, panting from his efforts, staring in horrified anticipation of the future.

"If a Spanish agent has taken them, Spain will know how pitiably weak our naval defenses are. Venice was to furnish sufficient vessels of war—" He broke off. "Look again, Cleve. The dispatch case *must* be there!"

But it was a futile gesture, although Cleve went through the motions. The dispatch case was gone.

"When did you last see it?" he asked.

Sir Harry seemed stunned. "Last night. Last night I took it out to ascertain its safety. Everything was in order, last night. I—" He reached suddenly upward and clutched Cleve in an iron grip. "You must get it back, lad! If Spain learns how inept our forces are, she might attack immediately to take advantage. England needs that dispatch case! If you cannot bring it—"

"Be easy, friend. Faith! 'Tis not the end of the world, you know. We'll fetch it back." And Cleve grinned. "Damme! That rogue stole my pardon!"

And suddenly Sir Harry realized something he had never seen before. He realized how much Richard Cleve resembled his father. This trick of using a few light words to conceal a deep sincerity of purpose was inherited. The elder Cleve had once ridden the hoofs off a horse to buy a new bonnet in London and also warn King James I of a plot on his life. Now his son was planning to prevent possible war, ostensibly because of a stolen pardon. Sir Harry was faced with the possibility that perhaps he had been misjudging Richard Cleve for years.

CHAPTER XVI

THE SCARLET PONIARD

CLEVE DECIDED LATER that the filching of the case was the work of an amateur. Sir Harry's visitors since last evening could be counted on three fingers. Of course there was Andrews, the valet. But Andrews had been with Sir Harry for forty years. He was beyond suspicion.

Only three visitors: Duke Vincent, who had dropped in to inquire as to his guest's welfare; Jacob, who had visited his master during breakfast; and Doctor Despartes. It was this latter Cleve intended seeing first. Despartes had acted skittish at the door; he had appeared overly anxious to leave once Cleve had entered.

"Despartes!" the English cavalier muttered, pacing down the corridor leading from Sir Harry's suite. "Damme! I'll wager he's been bought. If I can reach him before he turns that dispatch case over to his purchaser, then—"

He allowed the sentence to trail, and increased his stride. He was rounding the corner which joined the hallway with the gallery when he first noticed the squad. He was halfway around the gallery when the squad first noticed him.

It was a routine squad, sent to patrol the corridors—not because they needed it, but because tradition demanded it— and the men were not alert. But the officer in charge was; the moment he saw Cleve, his bared blade swung up in a flourish.

"Halt, Gardier! Halt in the duke's name!"

It was the popinjay of the gate. The same arrogant, mustached officer who had almost incarcerated Cleve the night before. He was wearing a new hat.

"The devil!" Cleve muttered.

Without breaking stride he reversed direction.

Then began the chase. He led them once around the circular gallery. He started to do it again with the intention of descending the grand staircase upon reaching it, but the fact that guardsmen were pouring into the foyer below, attracted by the popinjay's yowls for assistance, deterred him. He paused uncertainly before the corridor that led into the palace's south wing. Then he whirled and sped down it.

"This would have to happen now," he panted.

Behind, guards were streaming into the hallway. The clatter of their side-arms, halbard staffs and running feet threw muffled echoes far ahead of him. One of the doors lining the corridor flew open and a man peered out owlishly.

"Wash to do?" he inquired drunkenly. "Wassa dif'culty? Quiet!"

Of course, Cleve didn't recognize Henri de Casale. He had never before seen Henri's weakly handsome face; but Cleve did recognize the opportunity to prevent himself from running into a cul-de-sac. The corridor apparently ended a few rods further along in a blank wall.

"Mind if I join you, bucko?"

The English rakehelly shouldered open the door and burst past the gaping Henri with desperate agility. He couldn't afford to spend a day in the dungeons with Despartes loose.

HENRI'S APARTMENT was in wild disorder. The table in the center was covered with bottles, plates, half-eaten food and the remnants of two long-stemmed pipes. A rapier lay discarded in the corner.

Near the rapier a fat man lay snoring, his doublet open, his unshod feet on an overturned chair. Two more men were sitting at another table playing at dice. One of them, a swarthy-faced fellow with shirt open to reveal a chest covered with black hair, stood up. His hand shot to a dagger.

"*Por bacco!* Who are you? You dare disturb—"

But Cleve paid little heed. On the far side of the room, a latticed window reaching to the floor attracted his eye. He was headed toward it even as the speaker started to protest.

"Best forget your game, lads," he advised. "In a moment you are going to have visitors." Then he was through the window and crossing the narrow little balcony outside. It had stopped raining. Sunlight was straining to filter the clouds.

He paused a moment, one leg over the balustrade, calculating his chances. The balcony stood a good fifteen feet from the glistening cobbles. But pursuit allowed no alternative and he was forced to flip himself over the side, gripping the balustrade low before releasing hold. He landed limply, but even so the impact nearly jarred the senses from him. One leg felt numb.

"Faith! Trust it still works!"

Then someone on the balcony fired a pistol and he stood up and broke into a run.

A coach was leaving the grounds as he approached one of the side gates. It was a small coach, gilt-trimmed, with only a driver and a footman in charge. They sat stiffly in the seat forward, and he was able to pad up to the slow-rolling vehicle without being observed. Running beside the door, he drew his blade, reached for the knob and climbed swiftly inside. There was a startled gasp.

"Your pardon," he said, pointing his blade in the direction of the gasp. "No outcry, please."

"You!" exclaimed the passenger.

"Eh?"

Kneeling tensely on the floor, eyes cast back through the window, Cleve hadn't time to inspect his hostess. That it was a hostess had registered vaguely upon first entry, but now he turned to survey her more closely. She was slim, dark and beautiful. Her name was Mary de Sarasnac!

"WELL, IF it isn't my old friend the horse-thief." Cleve grinned. "Greetings, *mademoiselle*. Is this coach actually yours, or have you embarked on larger ventures?"

She strove to edge cautiously around the point of his blade that was still resting against her middle. He shifted it to follow her progress.

"Really, *monsieur!*" she exclaimed. "Must you prod that weapon at me?"

He nodded pleasantly. "Until we pass the gate. If I remember correctly you are a tricky one. There are several gentlemen who desire me to remain in the palace as their guest for a hanging."

"Hanging!" Her dark eyes looked startled, and then they swept to the rubied hilt of his rapier. "Oh," she said, suddenly calm. "So you are he? I never suspected it on the road, or I wouldn't have missed with my first shot."

He questioned the statement with his eyes, but his lips were smiling. "Is murder another of your practices?"

"Against such as you—"

"Faith! And just who do you think I am?"

She shrugged. "We are past the gate, *monsieur,*" she said glancing out of the window. "You will be kind enough to remove your sword." She paused. "And yourself, as well."

"Faith! Not the least hospitable, Mary." He laughed and groped behind him for the door handle. "I crave to tarry longer, but there are several pressing affairs to attend to, so I must away." He stepped back through the door, one foot dangling cautiously. "See you anon, my sweet!"

"And I trust from the end of a rope."

Cleve caught a flashing glimpse of a shapely calf, a small satin slipper. He felt the sole of the slipper on his chest; and then he was suddenly sprawling backwards into the street.

THE ENGLISHMAN sat there a moment, legs wide, cursing. The coach rattled on over the cobbles and he heard its door clack emphatically as she jerked it shut. Ignoring the crowd which was collecting, he climbed painfully to his feet, half-tempted to pursue and place her over his knee to administer vengeance;

but then the humor of the situation struck him and he grinned ruefully.

"Score two for you, lass. But mark this, my child, some day we'll have a reckoning."

Brushing the road-dirt carefully from his clothes, he wondered who she really was and why she was in Casale. Another Cordoba, perhaps? A high-born adventuress? Whatever the answer, he was positive of one thing. Mary de Sarasnac meant trouble. Then he shrugged her from his mind and elbowed his way through the curious.

He hadn't the vaguest idea of where to go. To return to the palace and its attendant risks would be both foolish and futile. With the whole garrison on the alert, Cleve's chances of locating Doctor Despartes were very slim indeed. But even without this hazard, he realized that his quarry would not be lingering on the grounds. Despartes would be somewhere delivering his loot.

"Faith! You've mangled the first move of this business beautifully," he told himself. "That dispatch case has arrived at its destination."

A rough bench beside a moss-slimed fountain, which was used as a watering-trough for horses, attracted him. He eased his frame onto it thoughtfully. A peasant, with two foul-smelling steeds in tow, approached and set his charges to guzzling. The horsey odor, combined with a thousand and one flies, soon caused the cavalier to quit the place, still undecided as to his course, but definitely annoyed. A man can't think with the hindquarters of a farm horse looming before his eyes; nor is a coarse swishing tail in his face much of an inducement, either.

"It resolves to but a single point," he told himself at length. "To recover the case, I must needs start from the beginning. To start from the beginning I must find a thread, a definite clue, and since Despartes is for the nonce unavailable, the only alternative is to delve willy-nilly into the intrigues of Montferrat in hope that I come up with something. Faith! 'Twould not be the first time that one conspirator aimed at two targets. Perchance Catherine Cordoba's Baron X is also interested in English affairs."

Of course the idea wasn't as logical as he strove to make it sound. But with the quest for the dispatch case momentarily stalemated, he could think of nothing better to do, and ten minutes later he was pacing in quick strides across the market square toward house number twelve.

THERE WERE four horses standing in front of the door, attended by a soldier of the palace guards. The Englishman frowned slightly.

"Your pardon, my good fellow," he addressed the trooper. "This is the residence of Mademoiselle Cordoba, isn't it?"

The man smoothed the front of his red-edged surcoat and nodded. He owned the sort of face that went with a monosyllabic conversation—toothily blank.

"Uh huh. *Oui,*" he said.

"These mounts belong to your officers?"

"Uh huh."

"Mademoiselle Cordoba is not in trouble, is she?"

"Dunno."

"But surely there is a reason for your presence here?"

"Uh huh."

"Damme. What is it?"

"Orders," said the fellow.

Cleve gave it up. Hitching up his rapier, he strode past the man to the door and when the fellow offered no protest, decided that there was nothing serious afoot after all.

He hadn't read the papers Catherine had given him, but he banged cheerfully on the door anyway. The knock of a loving brother. He grinned. He'd pick up his cues about being Emile as she dropped them. Then the door opened and a swarthy cadet-officer eyed him questioningly.

"Monsieur?"

"I have come to visit Mademoiselle Cordoba," Cleve told him.

"That will be difficult, *monsieur.*"

"Why? Is she ill?

Before the other could reply a basso boomed from the interior of the house. A familiar basso.

"Hola, Brisson. Who is that?"

Cleve made his own answer, recognizing the tones of Colonel de Boussey. He knew that to play Emile Cordoba now was out of the question. "Have your gentleman permit my passage, Colonel," he called. "This is Richard Cleve."

"But of course. Pass him, Brisson."

The doorman stepped aside with a nod and Cleve entered. He did it with a multitude of mental reservations, wondering how she would react when the Colonel introduced him. De Boussey met him in the foyer.

"Corbac! You surely have a nose for trouble, *monsieur.* Whatever led you to suspect murder in this house?"

"A mur—" Cleve hurriedly clapped a smile over his astonishment. "Sorry to disillusion you, Colonel," he said. "I was totally ignorant that murder has been done." He sobered and posed the question gingerly: "Cordoba?"

De Boussey nodded. He led the way into the sitting room and gestured eloquently. The room was a study in violent disorder. Torn draperies, smashed lamps and shattered crystal-ware. A silent trooper was engaged in cleaning it up.

Cleve stepped forward. An overturned chair attracted his attention. It was the dainty Venetian chair in which he had sat the night before. Now it was broken—stained with blood. He looked quickly at the colonel.

"Not very pretty," he said.

"It isn't, *monsieur.*"

DE BOUSSEY pulled aside the chair and revealed a sheet-draped figure on the floor. Cleve didn't need to be told who it was, but de Boussey lifted the covering to reveal the beauty of Catherine's face, now frozen into a death mask of terror. Cleve fought down the clammy revulsion that the sight of death always inspired in him and pushed his wide-brimmed hat to the back of his head.

"Too bad. I wanted to ask her several questions. Wonder what caused it?"

"Passion," returned de Boussey and dropped the sheet. "Brutal, drunken passion!"

Cleve cocked an eyebrow. The colonel's tones had the ring of authority, but knowledge of Catherine's secret activities caused the English gallant to question the statement. He said nothing, but apparently de Boussey sensed his doubt for he added quickly:

"You see, *monsieur,* I am fully aware of the identity of the murderer, and the reasons for his act. As you have mentioned, there were questions you desired to ask Cordoba. When I first arrived this morning, I had a similar mission."

"Then you were here before? Two visits?"

"*Oui.* The first time I discovered the body." De Boussey regarded the Englishman gravely. "This is no ordinary affair, *monsieur.* I discovered Catherine Cordoba with this stiletto in her throat." He gave Cleve a finely worked blade of Italian design, crusted with gems and bearing a family crest on the hilt. Cleve inspected that crest thoughtfully.

"Beside the body of Catherine Cordoba was the owner of that weapon, *monsieur,*" de Boussey continued grimly. "He was insensible from drink. I took him with all dispatch away from here and then returned to tie up what loose ends he might have left."

"You are positive that he committed the deed?"

"*Mon dieu, monsieur.* 'Tis a terrible admission, but in the face of the evidence, what else can I conclude?"

"Nothing, I fear," Cleve replied and handed him back the stiletto.

Shortly thereafter he quit the house. He was frowning. If de Boussey was right, if the news spread, then hell would pour through the streets of Casale. But there was more to it than that. His first lead into the maze of mystery had brought him nowhere. There remained nothing to do but to search for a new one. Antone, for example. But he hadn't taken ten steps down the street when he glimpsed a figure that immediately changed his mind—the person of Doctor Despartes.

CHAPTER XVII

HIS UNHAPPY HIGHNESS

FOR THE FIRST fifteen minutes of waiting, Guy d'Entreville sat quietly in his chair, previewing his interview with the duke; asking questions concerning Antone the Archer, Henri, de Boussey, and even a brief inquiry regarding that little fluff de Maupin. But at length, the game grew tiresome, so he gave it up.

Then he considered Cleve. The Englishman's firm refusal to have anything to do with the affair was discouraging. Guy needed Cleve and he was wise enough to admit it. Montferrat was a great kettle of trouble with dark things simmering beneath its surface, and to fish in it, one must be an expert angler. The Englishman was all that, and more. How to force him to cast a line was a poser. D'Entreville planted elbows on the table and scowled. Finally he cursed and gave it up too.

He inspected the blade of his rapier, resheathed it and arose. He passed solemnly the length of the room, critically surveying the portraits lining its wall and then he paused. A door centered in the rear wall was ajar and the faint muffled murmurings of conversation drifted to him.

Had he been in any other mood, he would have virtuously returned to his former position, well out of earshot. But the fact that he was bored, plus the honest belief that he might learn something, caused him quietly to draw up a chair and then to seat himself with a sort of furtive dignity. The conversation in the adjacent chamber was being carried on by two voices: a man's and a woman's. The woman was speaking.

"—since I've been here, Enrico. I have seen Henri but twice in that time. I fear that my mission to Montferrat is futile."

Guy frowned.

"Ah, but wait, my lady," a man's lower tones returned. "Is the grand-daughter of Charles Emmanuel to surrender thus easily? You were sent to entice the heir of Montferrat into marriage. You must not fail. Savoy needs this duchy. If you are Henri's wife when he comes to power—"

"I understand, Enrico. But so long as Catherine Cordoba holds Henri's heart, I can do nothing."

"You have nothing to fear from her any more. From now on, you shall have Henri for yourself, my lady."

"Enrico!" The faint stirrings of horror edged the woman's tones. In the other room, Guy strained sideways to hear as she continued: "Enrico! What do you mean?"

A pause. "Catherine Cordoba is dead, my lady."

"How do you know?"

"I visited her this morning. She is dead."

"Dios! You didn't—you have not done this thing! I know it was my grandfather's plan to send me here to interest Henri, but violence was not the course. I wish none of your violence, *señor!"*

The man's tones were flat. "Have I admitted thrusting the fatal blade?"

"No. No, Enrico. But I know of your tricks."

"Nevertheless, I have not admitted to the deed. Be easy. I suggest you dismiss the thought from your conscience and plan to see more of your—er—future husband."

"Perchance you are right."

"Naturally. And now, my lady, accept my arm. Let us promenade the wall terrace. The sun is beginning to break through the morning's clouds and the fresh air will be invigorating."

In the audience chamber Guy heard the pad of their footsteps, followed by the soft click of a door closing, and then silence. He sat frowning.

THIS WAS the first inkling that he'd had that the grand-daughter of the Duke of Savoy was in Montferrat. He didn't like it. But then, Richelieu had warned him against the cunning duplicity of Charles Emmanuel.

The French cavalier gnawed his upper-lip thoughtfully. He wondered if this fellow Enrico had murdered Henri's paramour. *Pecaire!* Eavesdropping paid! However, he had little time to ponder. At the end of the room, the doors swung open and Duke Vincent entered. The nobleman hesitated a moment, frowning.

"Monsieur le Comte d'Entreville?" he asked.

Guy stood up and bowed. He found himself liking the older man immediately. There was dignity in Duke Vincent's bearing. He was an erect figure, gray-eyed, crisply bearded and silver-haired—very much the military gentleman of the old school. He nodded a polite return to Guy's bow, took a position at the head of the table, and beckoned Guy closer. He looked tired.

"Isn't Monsieur Cleve with you?" he inquired after Guy had seated himself.

"Somewhere in the palace, *Monsieur le duc.*"

The duke nodded. He appeared strangely restive. It showed in his eyes, his twitching fingers. He strove to control it. He said: "I see," and steepled the fingers to keep them still. "While one of you questions, the other observes. A good policy, *monsieur,* especially in this nest. We are enduring great difficulties in Montferrat. That is why I sent for you." He nodded into the future.

Guy tried to use it as a cue. "So I understand. Last evening *Monsieur le colonel* explained—"

But Vincent wasn't listening. He was staring straight ahead, eyes contemplative, worried. "The robberies are but an instance, *monsieur.* One of many riddles. For example, have you noted the number of idlers in Casale—armed vagabonds, military-appearing men with apparently nothing to do?"

Guy hadn't, but he decided against admitting it. He looked wise and allowed the duke to continue.

"Another peculiarity, *Monsieur le comte*, is the sudden unrest of the populace. Until recently my subjects were contented, almost docile. Now they murmur and band on street corners to listen to rabble-rousing orators. I believe—"

He stood up and fell to pacing in short nervous arcs. Guy bit his lip and eyed Duke Vincent curiously. Something was eating into the man's mind—something other than the subject under discussion. Finally, Vincent continued.

"The people are being stirred up by someone, *monsieur*. A force of evil has invaded my realm. 'Tis strange but only my trusted aides seem in danger. M. de Boussey has thrice been fired upon. Despartes, my physician, has narrowly escaped poisoning. And Henri, my son—" He broke off abruptly and sat down. "My ward informs me that a killer has arrived in the city. A bravo named Mazo Gardier."

Guy nodded. "Cleve and I know of Mazo Gardier, *Monsieur le duc*," he said. "I can assure you that there is nothing to fear from him."

"Really? Well, *monsieur*, perchance you'll be interested to know that last night this very Gardier had the effrontery to attempt an entrance of the palace. I fear any man who possesses such cold nerve. It might carry him further than the daring of an ordinary rogue."

Guy chuckled. "That wasn't Gardier," he said. "The real Gardier is dead—slain before he ever reached Casale."

"Are you positive, *monsieur?* The man last night was carrying a ruby-hilted blade, and my information clearly states that Gardier—"

"Cleve has Gardier's weapon," Guy interposed simply.

DUKE VINCENT paused. "I see." Then he stood up again, crossed to the wall and jerked a bell-cord. "I have not been able to eat, *monsieur*. Perhaps you will be kind enough to dine with me." He returned to his chair, patted Guy lightly on the shoulder. "I am relieved that you and Cleve are here. I have heard of your competence."

Guy frowned. *"Merci."* He hesitated, and then blurted the thing which was on his mind. "You are troubled, *monsieur,* aren't you?"

Vincent's gray eyes hardened swiftly. *"Corbac!* Do not be ridiculous young man. I am—" Then he wilted suddenly. *"Oui,* d'Entreville, you are right. I am troubled—deeply troubled." He paused, moistened his lips thoughtfully and straightened in his chair. He regarded Guy with a fleeting plea for understanding, and then began.

"As a representative of the Crown, *monsieur,* you have a right to this news, for it concerns the future of this duchy. My son, Henri de Casale, heir to the principality of Montferrat, this morning has murdered his mistress!"

Before Guy could reply, the speaker proceeded. "Candidly, *monsieur,* in other times the crime might not mean too much. I am speaking now, of course, as a sovereign—a cold-minded diplomat, *monsieur,* and not as a father."

"I understand."

"Bien. As I have said, in other times the deed would not merit consideration. Henri is a duke's son, above the law. But with the people restless, Henri unpopular, and traitors rampant, his crime might act as the spark to set off civil disturbances which would be disastrous."

Guy was startled by the implications. He leaned forward. "Have things progressed that far, *monsieur?*"

Vincent shrugged. He seemed like a weary, almost hopeless old man. He said: "Maybe. I don't know. With troop morale low and this cursed undercurrent of intrigue washing away the very foundations, it is not possible to predict anything. But I fear the worst."

The French cavalier stood up, still leaning forward. He knew only one answer for revolution. "Troops," he declared. "If what you fear is true, then Montferrat needs troops! A regiment! A whole army if need be. The Cardinal must be notified."

"He has been, *Monsieur le comte*. Accompanying the wage-wagons next week will be three thousand soldiers under Marshal Menehoulde. I have just received word."

"*Bien*. And now, *Monsieur le duc*, perchance we can get down to a few names which may lead the way to—"

A respectful knock upon the door interrupted them. Duke Vincent turned.

It was le Sieur de Maupin, this time garbed in green with a froth of lace cascading his shoulders. "You will pardon this intrusion, Your Highness," he said. "Capitaine de Merion, officer of the watch, desires to inform you that the assassin, Mazo Gardier, has been apprehended. He is now safely chained in a cell, awaiting your pleasure."

The duke regarded Guy askance. "Did you not say that Richard Cleve was wearing Gardier's ruby-hilt, *monsieur?*"

Guy nodded, eyes dancing. Here was his opportunity. "That's right," he chuckled. "*Sangodemi!* And you have arrested him!" Then he began to laugh, pausing only long enough to choke out: "With your permission, *monsieur*, I would care to handle his release."

Vincent nodded, frowning. He couldn't understand why a comrade's imprisonment should cause merriment. "Very well, *monsieur*," he agreed.

CHAPTER XVIII

COME INTO MY DUNGEON

THE KEY GLISTENED like a silvered minnow on the hoop hooked to the jailor's belt. Cleve, staring through his barred window in the depths of the palace dungeon, regarded the symbol of liberty with a covetousness. He thoughtfully

Cleve stared out through the bars of his cell

measured the distance between his door and the jailor's position, reckoning it to be approximately four feet. The jailor was asleep, snoring in deep wheezing gurgles with chin on chest and arms folded.

"Damme! Hold that pose, fatty."

The Englishman stepped back. His prison was small, square and foul-smelling. A mattress of filthy straw lay in one corner, and in the center a crude bench topped by a bottle-based candle served as the only furniture. The candle-flame cast dancing shadows upon the slimed walls, lending a touch of the macabre to the scene.

An iron collar had been bolted to Cleve's neck and then chained to a hook high in the left wall. But moisture had long corroded the hook with the result that he had managed to free himself by gripping the chain and jerking on it convulsively. Even so, his movements were now accompanied by the faint clank of free links dragging. He grinned. Sounded like Hamlet's ghost.

As he removed his sash, tearing it carefully into inch-wide strips, he speculated about Henri's crime. As de Boussey had intended, the crest on the fatal stiletto had told him the identity of Catherine's murderer. The Englishman had been in Montferrat long enough to recognize the escutcheon of the royal house.

Cleve appreciated the discretion with which the colonel had given the information with a common soldier in the room. If the story leaked out there'd be a scandal in Montferrat that might blow the lid off the plot-ridden duchy. Henri was a fool. Cleve dismissed the subject.

Being in this cell was the fault of that over-jealous popinjay at the gate, for Cleve had almost succeeded in talking his way past the new *capitaine* when his nemesis had appeared. Didn't the fellow ever sleep?

He sighed, bundled the straw from the bed into two lengths and lashed them together with strips from his sash. Complete, they formed a wand three feet long. He retrieved his hat and unhooked the brooch holding its white plume.

By tying the brooch to more sash-strips, previously knotted to the end of his straw-wand, he possessed a crude but efficient fishing rod.

The jailor was still asleep. Gingerly Cleve extended the improved pole and began to maneuver to drop the open tongue of the brooch over the fellow's key-ring. It was hard work, and leaning against the door, with his arm straining through the window, soon caused sweat to bead his forehead.

But after ten torturous minutes, his brooch-hook at last settled beneath the upper arch of the large iron key-loop and he discovered that the ring was not hitched to the belt, but lay free on the chair beside the man, propped against his side.

"Come to me, my darling… Easy… E-a-s-y.…"

The straw wand curved and swayed beneath the strain, threatening to buckle. He gave up his attempt to hoist it through the air, surrendering to the slower, safer method of dragging it along the floor. He stepped away from the window to allow greater freedom of movement while lifting the ring perpendicularly. There was no strain now, for he was gripping the straw close to its extremity. Then, with a chuckle of triumph, he pulled the brooch into the room. But that was all—just the brooch. No key-ring.

"By Gad! I've been robbed!"

CLEVE GLARED out of his cell window into the grinning face of Guy d'Entreville. The Frenchman was standing back in the flickering wash of the dungeon torches, half-clad in shadow. He was holding, between gloved fingers, the precious ring; jingling it tantalizingly just out of reach.

Cleve sighed and leaned wearily against the door. The mere fact that it hadn't been opened immediately told him the whole story. Guy was bent on banter and bargain, and there was nothing he could do about it.

"All right, Kitten," he said. "What is it?"

Guy pursed lips and shrugged. "Nothing much. Your promise not to leave Montferrat until we've made certain of its security."

"Uh-huh." The Englishman nodded. He'd expected that. He rested chin on the windowsill and waited.

D'Entreville chuckled, toyed with the keys. The situation was perfect. For the first time in months he had Cleve cornered, and after being at a verbal disadvantage for so long, he meant to enjoy it.

"Come to heel, cheri," he advised. "One word and you go free." He looked sad. "Otherwise, I might decide not to know you. You might be forced to linger as that despicable villain, Mazo Gardier. Perchance you might hang."

"Kitten. I don't know what I'd do without you—but I'd rather!"

Guy laughed and lifted the keys. "Your answer, *mon ami?*"

"Go to the devil. I'll get out of here on my own hook!" Cleve nodded. "And I do mean hook," he said.

"Very well. But of course, I must needs warn the jailor to sleep further away from the door. *Au revoir, Gardier!*"

He turned as if to leave. But Cleve halted him with a single suggestion. "While you are out, Kitten, you might inquire about

Antone's relationship to a certain lady known as Catherine Cordoba."

The Frenchman whirled, his eyes alight with interest. "What do you mean? *Parbleu!* Do you know Catherine Cordoba?"

"Did," the prisoner admitted. "Dead now, you know."

"Eh? *Pecaire!* How did you discover—" Then Guy stopped, realizing better than to ask the question. He stood arms akimbo, scowling. "For a man who desired no part of Montferrat's intrigues," he declared, "you have compiled a remarkable fund of information. Just how much do you know about her? How did you know of her death anyway?"

Cleve grinned and indicated the door. D'Entreville squirmed. Somehow he no longer held the advantage over this conversation that should be his. "You'll not walk free till I have your promise of aid," he decided, reverting to his original course.

"All right," the Englishman surrendered with a chuckle. "Since Sir Harry's dispatch case has been stolen, I might as well step into this mess, if only to get it back."

Guy smiled. "A robbery, eh? How sad, Richard."

Cleve's eyes suddenly narrowed. "By Gad! If you are the man who took it to force me into this business, I'll—"

Guy opened the door and shook his head. "*Corbac!* Judge not others by yourself, *mon ami.* I had no hand in it, although it is a thought. Incidentally, please remember you are my prisoner, subject to my orders."

"I'll try to, Kitten." Cleve grinned.

The French gallant's dark eyes began to glint angrily. His voice carried an edge. "Cleve, I am growing very tired of being called Kitten. Some day I shall become overtired; and then—" He broke off, staring at the iron collar about the other's neck. A slow smile broke over his features. "Fido!" he said.

Cleve fingered the fetters. "Rover is a neater name," he suggested mildly. "There is a key on the ring which will fit this harness."

Guy, muttering his disappointment, found the key. He wished

Cleve had reacted more sensitively to Fido. He didn't bother to awaken the snoring jailor, for it would be inexcusable to take a man from a task which he pursued with such fervor. The French gallant merely dropped Duke Vincent's release into the man's fat lap; and then he and Cleve moved upward, out of the bowels of the palace.

DURING THEIR progress, Cleve roughly outlined his adventures since the evening before, incorporating everything except mention of Mary de Sarasnac. He decided that she was not a fitting subject for Guy's ears at the moment. He even offered his theory concerning Catherine's ultimate aim and speculated as to the possibility of her ambition clashing with that of her unknown confederate, the baron.

"Then you doubt whether Henri murdered his mistress, *mon ami?*" Guy asked upon the Englishman's completion.

Cleve shrugged. "No, not entirely. 'Tis only a hunch that leads me to probe all possibilities. Catherine Cordoba was cold-minded enough to betray her confederate if it were to her advantage."

"Well—"They were passing through a small chamber now, an open ante-room preceding the palace foyer. "I speak not from intuition when I say that I doubt Henri's guilt, Richard."

"Ah. You've been holding out on me, Kitten. What do you mean?"

Guy repeated the dialogue between Margaret of Savoy and her deep-toned henchman, concluding enthusiastically: "Enrico is the slayer, Cleve. Mark me, it fits. Margaret has been sent here by her grandfather to wed Henri so as eventually to annex Montferrat to the House of Savoy, and such an annexation will be hastened if Duke Vincent dies unexpectedly. The only method to assure Vincent's death is to hire someone to kill him. Enrico realizes this. He hires Mazo Gardier for the deed and uses Catherine Cordoba to serve as point of contact with his killer.

"But Catherine grows ambitious, as you say, and decides to

keep Henri for herself, after the duke's demise. Therefore, Enrico kills her and—"

The speaker ceased and scowled. Cleve was shaking his head.

"Corbac! What is wrong?"

"Oh, 'tis pretty enough," Cleve assured him pleasantly, "but why should the trouble come about *before* the duke's death instead of after it? Both parties can do nothing as long as Vincent lives. Circumstance would force them to work together. No, Kitten, it won't—"

"Folderol!" d'Entreville snapped. "Pure *folderol!* Cleve you're a nuisance. If Enrico is not the man, then Henri *must* be guilty."

"It appears that way."

De Maupin was descending the staircase as they entered the grand foyer and upon seeing them hastened forward. He was carrying Cleve's sword.

"Your blade, *monsieur,*" he said presenting it. "I carried it to your suite but upon discovering your absence, decided to return it to the armory rather than allow so valuable a weapon to remain unguarded. *Ma foi!* 'Tis a magnificent sword, *monsieur.*"

"It is," Cleve agreed, sheathing the blade.

DeMaupin continued: "I was desolate to hear of Capitaine de Merion's monstrous mistake, m'Lord."

The Englishman smiled. "So was I. Incidentally, m'lad, where does Doctor Despartes take residence here?"

The fop made a rolling gesture with one limp hand. "Third door to the left, the lower corridor of the north wing, *monsieur.* Only my duties prevent my escorting you to it personally. But now I fear that I must say adieu."

"Adieu," said Cleve.

After de Maupin had disappeared in a mist of perfumery, Guy finger-combed the crispness of his clipped military beard and regarded his companion quizzically.

"Despartes?" he asked.

Cleve had mentioned the loss of Sir Harry's dispatch case,

but not his suspicions concerning the little physician. He saw no necessity to do so now. There would be sufficient time later.

"That's right," he said, and led the way across the foyer.

THEY HAD proceeded down the oak-paneled north corridor for nearly twenty paces and were beginning to follow its sharp bend to the right, when Cleve brought up suddenly.

He had counted the doors lining the left wall, and so far he and Guy had passed but two. The third—the entrance to Despartes' suite—lay just ahead. Emerging from it was the lithe, velvet-gowned figure of Mary de Sarasnac. Her actions were hurried, somehow furtive. Cleve yanked d'Entreville back and clamped tight fingers over the French rakehelly's mouth.

"Quiet!"

Guy said: "Sambodednee! Clebe, leb go!"

Then after a moment the Englishman released his hold. "Did you recognize that girl?"

"Pecaire!" Twas Mary. Mary de Sarasnac. I'll never forget her! What is my angel doing in Montferrat?" Guy suddenly remembered his companion's actions. "Parbleu! And what right have you to interefere with our meeting?"

Cleve didn't hear him. He was peering cautiously around the corner, to catch the flare of her skirts as she disappeared through an archway further down. He straightened.

"Damme! I'd like to know what she is doing here, myself," he said. "One conviction grows. I am certain that she warned Duke Vincent of Gardier. Come along. Let's see what upset her so greatly in Despartes' suite."

"Curse Despartes!" Guy muttered and his lips thinned with determination. *"Mordi!* I am going after her!

"Do that, m'lad, and I leave for England within the hour."

Reluctantly Guy decided not to test that threat. *"Corbac!* You have nothing but ice in your veins, Cleve. I meet the only women who sets my heart on fire and—"

"Come along, Romeo."

They found Despartes sitting before a great mahogany desk—a desk littered with vials and tools of surgery. The man sat quite still, his back to the door, his head bowed as though in deep thought. Guy, who had preceded Cleve, determined to get the interview over with as soon as possible, drew up with a curse. His lips thinned grimly. There wasn't going to be an interview. Doctor Despartes was dead!

"A neat piece of work, too," Cleve muttered later, drawing forth the poignard which had been rammed to the hilt in the physician's back. "He never knew what hit him."

CHAPTER XIX

THE IRON HAND

THEY REGARDED EACH other from opposite sides of the corpse, each considering the same thought—the obvious suspicion; yet not wanting to say it. Finally d'Entreville shook his head.

"*Sandiou!* I'll not credit the thought! She did not do it, Cleve. She is an angel."

The English cavalier smiled grimly. "An angel true enough." He bent to remove a sheet of foolscap from beneath the corpse's left arm. "But whether an angel of death or not remains to be seen."

Then he studied the paper he had picked up. It appeared as a confession. The dead man had been penning it even as his slayer had struck. The document was unfinished. The last word, a proper name beginning with the letters *Cast—*, ended in a long jagged streak.

"A confession turned into a last will and testament," Cleve observed and read:

I, Jacques Despartes, for thirty years an honorable man of medicine have this day disgraced my honor—the ethics of my profession—by becoming a common thief, a skulking robber.

Yet I stand not alone in my crime. My lust for wealth was seized upon by an unscrupulous villain who tempted it with the promise of ten thousand livres of gold. This man bribed me to steal a certain leather case. This I have committed and now he refuses me the monies. He laughs at me and drives my shame deeper into what has always been an honest heart. Therefore, I accuse the man known as Señor Juan Cast—

The Englishman looked up. "And that is all," he concluded. "A neatly-timed slaying, Kitten. A split second later and that name would have been complete." He frowned. "Señor Juan Cast—something or other. Sounds Spanish."

"*Parbleu!* It also sounds familiar," Guy said. He scowled and then snapped his fingers. "I have it! Juan Castro! The Spanish agent who financed Montmorency's rebellion in France last year."

"A guess, but damme, I believe you're right, Kitten. Castro just beat the King's patrols into Savoy by the width of a whisker. Faith! And if he is playing in Montferrat, we—"

"We have a battle on our hands," Guy finished evenly. "Castro is devilishly cunning. A master *intrigant!*"

THE SOUND of men in the hallway attracted them. They turned as the door burst open and Colonel de Boussey and three gentlemen of the court strode in. The huge *Commandant* and another man had bared steel in hand.

"*Corbac!* What is happening in here?" de Boussey demanded.

Cleve smiled and slid the doctor's confession back atop the desk. "Wrong tense, Colonel. It *has* happened."

De Boussey crossed to the body, inspected it and shrugged. "I was told the truth. *Monsieur le Médecin* has been murdered. He is dead."

"Definitely," Cleve assented and walked away.

He found a chair by the window and sat down. He placed his feet on the wide sill. He felt peevish, half-angry. First Cordoba,

and now Despartes. Every grip he had attempted to gain upon
the mystery seemed predestined to failure. He was becoming
tired of being pushed around. How the devil had he become
enmeshed in this business, anyway?

It was obvious, of course, that Castro had bought Despartes
to filch Sir Harry's precious dispatch case. But did the Spaniard's
intriguing end there? It seemed hardly likely. Cleve had heard
of Castro and it did not appear logical that Spain would send so
important a figure to Montferrat just for the purpose of thievery.

Castro was not an apprentice. He was a spinner of webs, a
shaker of nations. Undoubtedly the Venetian contracts were
incidental to the real purpose of his presence in the Duchy.

But was that purpose intertwined with the plot of the late
Catherine Cordoba? Was Castro her mysterious Baron X? Had
he caused her death, or had Henri? Frankly the English gallant
didn't know, so he groaned and gave it up. He was guessing and
he knew it. So far he had been able to gather only a few pieces
to the puzzle and none of them made sense. He swiveled in his
chair.

Despartes' body had been carried into the next room. De
Boussey was reading the man's confession. In the corner one
of the gentlemen who had accompanied him was sitting on
a wall-bench and holding a head that was obviously aching.
Cleve recognized the owlish drunk past whom he had burst
earlier in the day.

Finally, de Boussey folded the dead man's confession into his
gauntlet cuff and frowned. *"Mordi!* His Highness must see this,"
he decided. "Who would have suspected Despartes of duplicity." Then he turned. "Monsieur Orlando. There is small need
for le Comte de Casale to remain. Be so kind as to accompany
him to the south tower."

The man addressed as Orlando nodded. He was a swarthy,
beetle-browed fellow, stocky and of sullen mien. He had been
in the drunk's room when Cleve had pounded through it. Then
Cleve realized that the man must be the same Orlando of whom

de Maupin had spoken—Henri's close companion. A most dangerous person and rumored to have once been a highwayman.

Orlando swaggered over to the gentleman with the headache. "Let us quit this scene, Henri. In the south tower we have a comfortable bed awaiting you."

AFTER THEY had departed, Cleve regarded De Boussey thoughtfully. A startling suspicion was darkening his mind, although he was careful to keep it from his speech. "So that was Henri," he said.

"*Oui.*" The big officer nodded. "He is to be confined to the tower. I was escorting him there when Mlle. de Sarasnac informed me of the doctor's demise."

D'Entreville looked up. He had been shuffling through Despartes' effects in the vain hope of discovering further clues to the man's activities. "*Pecaire!*" he exclaimed in triumph. "The fact that she raised alarm definitely proves her innocence, Cleve. I knew it all along."

The Englishman grinned. "All right, Romeo." He turned to de Boussey again. "Perchance you can tell me just who Mary de Sarasnac is, Colonel."

"*Sandiou!* Ward to the duke, *monsieur.*" The speaker smiled. "Did you suspect that she—"

"But no!" d'Entreville exclaimed. "We are aware of the person behind M. Despartes' death."

The colonel frowned. "Really, *mon ami?*"

"Of a certainty. The rogue's name is practically complete in *Monsieur le Médecin's* confession. Señor Juan Castro!"

"Castro?" De Boussey hesitated a mere instant and then shook his head. "No," he said. "No. I have never before heard the name." His gray eyes narrowed. "But now that you speak of it, it does fit the title which M. Despartes' was striving to complete."

"There are other matters we have discovered concerning Montferrat," Guy continued. "We intend to—"

"We intend to locate Castro at all costs," Cleve interrupted swiftly and signaled the French rakehelly to hold his tongue. He stood up. "You see, Colonel, apparently the man now possesses important documents which I have sworn to return to my friend, Sir Harry Winthrop."

De Boussey nodded. "I understand. *Sandiou!* But it may be dangerous, *monsieur.* Who knows what peril may—"

A thunderous pounding upon the door prevented his completing the sentence. Then the partition burst open and a sergeant entered. The fellow was panting.

"Monsieur le colonel," he gasped. "I crave indulgence for this lack of courtesy, but you are urgently needed at the main gate."

Even as he spoke, de Boussey was moving toward the door, rapier held wide of his swinging stride; hat-plume rippling. *"Corbac!* What's amiss, Sergeant?"

"A mob, *mon commandant.* A yelling, ugly horde that screams for the blood of Monsieur le Comte de Casale."

De Boussey paused. "What?"

"I speak the truth, *monsieur.* A rumor has spread that Henri de Casale has committed murder and the people feel that at last his escapades have gone too far. They demand justice!"

"Sacré nom! Order out fifty horsemen, Sergeant. If they do not disperse—" He shook his head. "No. I had best handle this myself. Come along." And without another word he quit the room.

GUY REGARDED Cleve. "And now, *mon ami,* perhaps you'll explain why you beckoned me to remain silent," he said.

Cleve sighed, crossed to the desk and sat on it. "Faith! Because you talk too much, Kitten. I am not certain that our friend de Boussey merits full confidence."

The Frenchman's eyes widened. *"Sangodemit* He is the *commandant,* isn't he?"

Cleve's eyes were opaque. "What of it?"

Invariably Guy grew short-tongued when Cleve grew cryptic. The present was no exception.

"De Boussey is trusted even by the Cardinal," he snapped. "If he is false, then no one is safe. Not even Duke Vincent!"

Cleve laughed and hooked his knee in the loop of his interlocking fingers. "I have a good reason for my contention, Kitten. Remember how you sought to prove Henri's innocence a while back, by using the escort of Margaret of Savoy as your scapegoat?"

"*Sacré bleu!* Cannot I make a mistake without censor? I was wrong. I admit it. I know now that Henri is guilty."

Cleve leaned back still holding his knee. "I doubt it," he said.

"What? Now mark this, Cleve! I am in no mood to be made the butt of what you pass as humor. I—"

The English rakehelly wagged a reprimanding finger. "Temper. I doubt Henri's guilt because I doubt that he was ever out of the palace last evening. I told you of the chase I led the guards after leaving Sir Harry, didn't I?"

"What has that to do with it?"

Cleve ignored the question. "Escaped by running through a gentleman's rooms and leaping from his balcony," he continued. Then he frowned. "That gentleman, Kitten, was Henri."

"So?"

"I am thinking of his suite, Kitten. The disarray of it bespoke an all night session. A gay carousal. I have seen such chambers before and they do not fall into that condition unless the revelry has enjoyed an exceptionally long life. Do you follow me?"

Guy nodded, frowning. He was pacing thoughtfully and finally turned. "*Oui.* But what has that to do with not trusting *Monsieur le commandant?*"

The Englishman regarded him in mock disgust; then slipped from the desk-top, grasped him firmly by the arm and began to usher him doorward.

"Did you say that you needed four days to solve this affair, Kitten. Or did you say four years? Faith! The latter is likely."

D'Entreville jerked free. *"Ventre saint gris!* No sarcasm. I asked but a simple question!"

" 'Twas simple," Clive agreed and he grinned. Then he became serious. "Mark this, Guy. When I met de Boussey this morning at Catherine Cordoba's house, he told me that he had found Henri lying drunk beside her body. He showed me a stiletto belonging to Henri, which he claimed had done the deed. In brief, he strove to convince me of the Count's guilt. Yet now I have reason to believe that Henri was engaged in an all-night carousal; that he was never near his mistress's home. Faith! Isn't it sufficient cause for distrust?"

Guy nodded slowly. He smoothed his mustache, bit his lower lip and scowled. "It is," he admitted. "But there is a chance your being wrong. Henri may have gone out and returned to his suite."

Cleve brushed an imaginary speck from the sleeve of his doublet. "Possibly. De Boussey claims to have brought him home after discovering him in Cordoba's house." The Englishman grinned. "You brought me home once, Kitten. What was the first thing you did?"

D'Entreville didn't follow the other's shift in thought, but he answered anyway. "Doused you with water and put you to bed," he said.

"Of course," Cleve assented. "Yet when I met our friend Henri, he was fully clothed, out of bed and unattended. Rather strange under the circumstances, don't you think?"

This information seemed to decide the French gallant. "Perchance you have struck upon something, Cleve. It might help if we question le Comte de Casale."

"You do it, Kitten," the other said. "I have a report to deliver to Sir Harry."

And as the door closed on their heels, another partition—which led to an adjoining room in Despartes' suite—opened slowly and a man stepped out. A pale-faced figure—Enrico, the bodyguard of Margaret of Savoy. He was frowning as he crossed the room.

CHAPTER XX

KITTEN IN LOVE

CLEVE WALKED FROM Sir Harry's chambers toward the south tower. He strolled along to the leisurely tempo of his consideration. If nothing else, his talk with the injured man had hardened his determination to regain the Venetian contracts.

Sir Harry was in despair over their sudden disappearance. He had lain abed, eyes staring, while Cleve had attempted a cheerful account of the progress. He had striven to assure the older man that proof of Despartes' guilt was akin to success. It hadn't worked.

Cleve had never been close to his father's friend, but now it moved him to see how the old bulldog was suffering. Surprisedly he realized that he had some respect and even some affection for Sir Harry.

"Damme!" he muttered, strolling along the carpeted foyer gallery. "Damme! I believe I'd go after those documents now if they were nothing but the old fossil's gambling chits."

Still he recognized, as he said it, that Sir Harry's despair only added to the urgency of the dispatch case's recapture. His future, as well as that of the older man's, was tied up in it. Faith! The future of a whole nation might well rest on his success or failure. *England!*

He thought the word and bit his lip. It seemed further away now than when he'd pounded hell-for-leather out of Paris two weeks ago.

His course led him to the elbow of the palace's south wing and past a casement which overlooked the bailey and part of the cobbled outer-fosse at the main gate. He paused.

THE FOSSE was jammed with people. Sullen, staring people. A man more literate than his neighbors had supplied a placard upon which was scrawled: *Down with Henri,* followed by the single plea: *Justice!*

Facing the crowd from behind the iron-laced portcullis was a double rank of breast-plated palace guards, alert and immobile. The sun glinted on the wicked lengths of their red-tasseled partizans. Behind the guards a troop of horsemen were drawn up.

Cleve frowned. The horsemen wore bright green surcoats and gay yellow-plumed hats. They were men of Henri's personal troop—the most hated body of cavalry in Montferrat.

Egad! Surely de Boussey wasn't intending to use them! To turn them loose upon the mob in his present emergency would be like tempting to quench fire with lamp-oil.

But even as these thoughts streamed through the cavalier's mind, de Boussey stepped into the courtyard, waved once, commandingly to the troop and stood back, arms akimbo. The portcullis swung up and the troopers rode forth, a shouting, pounding group with bared steel flashing.

They struck the mob savagely, splitting it apart, scattering it with the flat of their swords. Then someone hurled a stone, and the next instant a hail of missiles rained upon the charging horsemen. From his point of vantage Cleve saw two riders, pygmy-like in perspective, reel drunkenly in their saddles and then slide to the ground. The mob boiled around them, kicking, clubbing, hurling cobbles. It was a signal for the grimmer work to begin and Henri's men were not loath to take advantage.

No longer did they strike with the flat sides of their blades; now they slashed murderously with the cutting edge. Screams began to pierce the distant din, and when finally the crowd broke, scattering wildly like beads from a severed necklace, Cleve counted seven bodies on the fosse—two of them troopers.

" 'Twill teach the scum manners," a harsh voice said beside him.

He turned, unaware of the other's approach. It was Signor Orlando, his white teeth smilingly framed against his swarthy skin.

Cleve resisted the impulse to knock those teeth and their attendant grimace down the man's throat. He lifted a polite eyebrow.

"Or more determination," he averred. Then he dropped the subject. But the deliberate ruthlessness of de Boussey's move both enraged and puzzled him. To use Henri's men had been stupid. What the devil was the matter with de Boussey anyway?

Orlando said: "You are here for a purpose, are you not, *signor?*"

Cleve nodded. "Yes. Is Henri de Casale in a condition to talk?"

The Italian shrugged and shook his head. "But no, *signor*. Unfortunately Henri is being held *incommunicado* under orders of His Highness Duke Vincent. Your comrade Signor d'Entreville was here but an hour ago and I was forced to tell him the same story. Henri is unavailable unless Duke Vincent deems otherwise."

"I see."

No doubt as to Orlando's veracity. To confine Henri during the present trouble was wise. Of consequence, Cleve found little reason to linger. He asked the Italian where Guy had gone, and upon receiving the man's shrug of ignorance, turned and retraced his steps down the corridor.

"A feather to a farthing that our poet is with Mary de Sarasnac," he wagered to himself.

IT WAS an easily won bet. D'Entreville and the love of his life were in the palace library at the head of the foyer staircase. Cleve found this out by asking de Maupin, who had seen Guy and Mary enter the room.

"At the top of the staircase, *monsieur. Ma foi!* 'tis unmistakable. The doors are gilt-paneled."

The doors were also adorned with tiny figurines depicting life in the medieval monastery. Cleve discovered it as he stood outside of them and cheerfully eavesdropped on the French rakehelly's reverent recital of one of the many poems he had composed.

Guy originally penned the verse for a certain lovely named Desirée. But since Desirée had married someone else, the Frenchman was rededicating it now.

> *When I'm with you,*
> *The things that you do,*
> *Make all of my moments divine.*
> *Your soft finger-tips*
> *The thought of your lips,*
> *On mine.*
> *And* ma cherie—

"Oh Lord!" Cleve sighed and opened the door.

They were sitting on a low divan before the window. Guy was eying her earnestly; she was relaxed comfortably in the couch's corner, a far-away expression on her face. But at Cleve's crashing entrance, both of them straightened. He stood on the sill, arms akimbo, grinning.

"Would you two rather be alone?" he asked.

Color rushed to Mary's cheeks. Her dark eyes began to sparkle with indignation. Then she turned to Guy.

"Who is this churl, *monsieur?* I have seen him before."

"That," d'Entreville admitted reluctantly, "is Richard Cleve."

"Some times known as Mazo Gardier," Cleve added and kicked the door closed with the heel of his boot and strode over the carpet. "Am I intruding?"

"Definitely," Guy snapped.

"Ah. 'Tis most kind of you, Kitten. I shall be glad to remain." He stood before them, arms folded, a look of puckish sincerity on his face. "Don't mind me, my friend. Pray continue where you left off."

Mary bit her lip. Cleve found himself admiring the way the

sun-shafts glinted in the froth of her hair. She said to Guy: "Perchance he will go away."

D'Entreville shook his head. "*Non.* You are unacquainted with him. He is every other inch a gentleman, so he'll stay."

She stood up. "Then I shan't."

The Englishman shook his head and sidestepped quickly before her. "Faith now, I hadn't taken you for a coward, Mary."

She bristled at that, her fine eyes snapping. "La! By what right do you address me so intimately, *monsieur?* To you I shall always be Mademoiselle de Sarasnac. Do not forget it." She jerked shreds from her silken kerchief angrily. "Furthermore, I am *not* a coward!"

"Running away, aren't you?"

"No!" She plumped back upon the divan definitely.

D'Entreville arose at the same time. He was quite indignant.

"*Mordi!*" he choked. "Have you no courtesy, Cleve? *Ventre saint gris!* This is not a barracks—"

"Temper, Kitten. No cursing, mind." The speaker nodded to Mary, sitting stiffly, and added in a discreeter tone: "Ladies present."

GUY DIDN'T trust himself to speak. He stood glowering and then sat down. Cleve stood there, regarding both of them benignly.

"Undoubtedly Mary—er—Mademoiselle de Sarasnac was explaining how she discovered the dead man, wasn't she," he said politely.

"She was!" d'Entreville flared.

"Allow me to speak," the girl interposed and looked at Cleve. "I was passing through the hall, *monsieur,* when I saw a strange man hurriedly leaving *Monsieur le Médecin's* rooms. I called to him. He broke into a run and disappeared. I knocked upon the doctor's door, and receiving no reply, I entered." She bit her lip tightly. "He—he was dead. I sought assistance immediately."

"What did the fugitive look like?"

"An ape," she replied quickly. "His arms dangled and his legs were short. A horrible creature, *monsieur.* I shall never forget the way he grunted an answer when called upon to halt." She arose gracefully, defiantly. "Any more questions, *monsieur?*"

Cleve chuckled. Somehow the dark beauty of the girl was a challenge. He didn't know why.

"Several questions," he admitted.

"Well?" She frowned impatiently.

Cleve stared to the depths of her dark eyes and laughed. "Faith! And what are your plans for the evening, m'lass?"

She stiffened. "To stay as far away from *you* as possible, *monsieur!*" Then she turned to Guy. "Will you be kind enough, *Monsieur le comte.* The room seems to have become unbearably stuffy."

With a triumphant grin, d'Entreville proffered his arm. "But of course. Stuffiness invariably follows the English. And one Englishman in particular." He lifted his hand and wiggled the tips of his fingers cheerfully. *"Au revoir, mon ami."*

Cleve returned the wave in the same manner. "Adieu, Cupid. Incidentally, recite the one you wrote to Constance. I like it better than—"

The tinkling crash of glass shattering in the window behind him halted his advice. Something thudded against his shoulder. It caromed past the curve, of his cheek and fell floorward. A rock with a fold of paper tied about it.

"Sandiou!"

Guy's blade swept from its scabbard and he charged across to the broken window. Behind, Mary de Sarasnac bent to pick up the stone. Cleve approached, rubbing his shoulder absently as he extended his free hand. She ignored his wordless request, tore free the string holding the note, and scanned it swiftly.

"Nosey," he said quietly, and waited.

Meanwhile, d'Entreville had jerked open the casement and was glaring into one of the palace's after-court-yards. He glimpsed a fleeting figure; that was all. The man disappeared around the corner. Guy felt the weight of his rapier, looked at it sheepishly and resheathed it. Of what use was his sword, two stories up?

"Come here, Kitten."

He returned to where Cleve and Mary were standing. Cleve was fingering a paper.

Mary had given it up at last.

"Listen to this," the Englishman said. "It was tied to the rock." Then he read: " 'Fear of my life prevents me from speaking to you in the palace, but should you wish to know things concerning the death of *Monsieur le Médecin*, I shall be at the Golden Crowns at seven. The table in the east corner.' "

It was unsigned.

CHAPTER XXI

FRIGHTENED TOWN

TWO HOURS HAD passed and Rue Vincent, leading from the Palace Gate to the center of Casale, was deserted. Purple shadows, growing longer in the twilight, darkened half its length and the stuccoed house-fronts lining its either side were shuttered tight as though night had already descended.

"Damme!" Cleve grunted. "Lively town."

Guy nodded grimly. They had been pacing silently along the narrow thoroughfare, the tenseness of the city heavy upon them. They had arrived at the end of it without encountering a soul. Not a healthy sign. The French rakehelly licked his lips.

"Lively," he accorded.

He jerked his wide hat-brim a trifle more firmly over one eye and glanced back toward the palace. With the sun-glow framing it, the huge citadel was silhouetted in black contrast against the gold of the evening skies. The blackness made it seem sinister.

"The citizens are keeping to their quarters," he said. "Du Boussey has ordered a curfew."

They proceeded. The clock in the market place was striking the quarter hour as they strode across the square. It finished ponderously and returned to its brooding quiet.

Townspeople hurried furtively, like wary mice, along the edges of the mall. From second-floor windows worried faces peered. Casale was akin to a plague-ridden city, held breathless in fear. And yet it was not all fear. Cleve glimpsed the faces of a few men in passing. They were sullen, dangerous.

"Damn de Boussey anyway," he muttered.

Pacing beside him Guy frowned. *"Pardieu!* For what reason?"

"This," Cleve said and indicated the square. "The whole cursed mess is the result of our friend's *astute* use of Henri's troops. Had he used the guards on that mob with orders to maintain order without violence, it would have been an even wager that Casale would be less restive. Men were killed today, Kitten. The local lads aren't soon to forget it."

Guy shrugged. "De Boussey is a soldier," he replied. "He thinks as a soldier. Oft times an iron first rules where kindness is misunderstood for weakness."

"In this instance, an iron fist may well cause revolution," Cleve said quietly.

D'Entreville didn't answer. He recognized the truth of that. For a moment he seemed swept back to the library of Palais de Richelieu, listening as the Cardinal explained the importance of Montferrat to the scheme of French defense.

GUY HAD no illusions concerning his nation's fitness to fend off invasion once her enemies were inside. France was still licking wounds left by nearly sixty years of civil strife. She was not yet strong. She could not face a war on her own territory. If the bastion of Montferrat crumbled because of rats gnawing from inside, then such a war became perilously imminent.

Renewed determination surged through the cavalier. But with his fresh resolve came an attendant feeling of impatience.

Guy was a man of action. Show him a problem that was clear-cut, well defined, and he would proceed to solve it in a flash of the blade. Show him mystery, hazy uncertainties, and he was invariably bewildered and annoyed.

Montferrat was beginning to anger him.

A thousand questions swirled in his mind. Why had Catherine Cordoba been killed? Had Henri been her slayer? If not he, then who? And what was Juan Castro up to? Did not Enrico of Savoy mean anything to the scheme of things? Where did Antone the Archer fit into the picture? Most important of all these queries was this: Just whom were they really fighting? Spain, Savoy, or Austria?

It was Cleve who called his attention to the scuffle that suddenly was heard from behind them. They had been walking slowly up one of the crooked little streets leading from the market place, each intent on his own thoughts.

"Look, Kitten, as uneven a brawl as I've ever seen."

D'Entreville turned and there, twenty paces away, two bravos were attacking a stripling youth with vicious swords. The boy was backing swiftly toward a corner, crying for assistance in a frightened soprano—a soprano which both Cleve and d'Entreville recognized! Their long blades flashed free of leather.

"*Ventre saint gris!*" the Frenchman shouted in amazement. "It is Mary!"

CLEVE MADE no comment. He recognized her the moment her hat went sailing to allow the lustrous ebon of her hair to ripple free. She was garbed in men's clothing—the same costume that she had worn when first they had met. Upon the loss of her hat, her assailants drew back, surprised, and then turned. But not soon enough. The two cavaliers were upon them.

It wasn't much of a battle. In fact as Guy later considered it, the affair wasn't a battle at all. One chance prick of his sword-tip and both bravos lost competitive spirit, deciding sword play not worth the effort when practiced with such earnest efficiency as the rakehellies possessed. They hurled blades earthward and refused to pick them up.

"*Sandiou!*" snorted Guy and shifted his rapier. " 'Tis no time to stop. Mark me. I'll entertain both of you left handed and alone! Go for your steel!"

But the bullies weren't foolish. They refused.

Meantime Cleve handed Mary her hat and regarded her quizzically. "Neatly done, lassy," he commented. "But suppose you explain."

She frowned and donned the hat. "You needn't use your sarcasm on me, *monsieur*. I was following you in an effort to be of assistance."

He studied her gravely, and then his eyebrows cocked up in amusement. He stared thoughtfully at the two bravos whom Guy had now backed against the wall of a nearby house. "Assistance?" he inquired politely.

She bit her lip. There was delight in the way she rammed her dainty court-sword back into its jeweled scabbard before making answer. He had never before met anyone just like her. Feminine and yet boyish, self-assured, proud.

She said acidly: "Those men were following you. But of course, being so all-wise, *monsieur*, you never suspected a trap in that note."

"Faith no," he replied seriously. "The Kitten and I are horribly naive. We carry weapons only because they are decorative. When did our friends begin to stalk us?"

"As you left the mall. They issued from a house and followed even as did I. La! 'Twas only because I trod too close on their heels that they discovered me and turned."

"Oh. And you trailed us the full way from the palace, eh?"

"Seeking to trick me, *monsieur?*" She smiled. "I was waiting for you in the market square."

He chuckled. "Faith. I think I like it."

Uncertainty wrinkled her brow. "You like what, *monsieur?*"

"Your smile, lass. It's the first you've worn for me, you know."

Her lips tightened. She said nothing, and Cleve turned to the prisoners.

"If they can't find their tongues," he advised, "use the blade, Kitten."

"They shall find their tongues," d'Entreville promised. "They shall find them either now—or never!" He nodded to Mary. *"Mademoiselle*, this is hardly the place for beauty."

"Why not?" she wanted to know.

The bluntness baffled the French gallant. Fair damsels had a moonlit niche in his consciousness; a well-defined place of soft music and beauty, far removed from blood and violence. He frowned.

"Why—er," he fumbled. "Why, this may not be pleasant, *mademoiselle.*"

"Faith, she is used to unpleasantries," Cleve interposed blandly. "Horse-stealing, hold ups, kicks in the chest." He turned to the captive bravos. "All right my gallant knights, would you care to reveal why you were so intrigued by the view of our backs?"

THE PRISONERS were sweating. They were roughly dressed men, unshaven—the sort usually found aloiter near pot-houses. They squirmed uneasily against the wall, staring fearfully at the sword beneath their noses. When Cleve's bright blade joined the French cavalier's, they looked at each other and bit their lips.

"Corbac! Speak up, you rats!" Guy barked. "It makes little difference whether we leave corpses or the living."

"Surely, you do not mean that, *Monsieur le comte.* 'Tis unworthy of you." It was Mary speaking from behind them.

Guy hesitated. Her good opinion of him counted. "Well," he temporised. "Well, er, that is—not if you wish otherwise, *ma petite.*"

Cleve shook his head. "No," he groaned to himself. "Please, no!" He closed his eyes. *"Ma petite,"* he murmured to the air and then regarded his comrade sadly. "Look, Kitten. Send *ma petite* home. As long as she remains here, our friends are not going to be made talk."

"I'll not turn my back on murder, *monsieur*," she snapped. "Besides, I am in this affair. I intended to see it to an end."

"There is but one thing to do," Cleve told Guy. "Proceed as before only—" He eyed the hirelings. "We allow our friends to walk in front."

"Mais non!" cried one of the prisoners.

"Silence!" d'Entreville snapped.

And so they marched away—sullen bravos in the van, Cleve and d'Entreville pacing behind with swords glinting, Mary bringing up the rear.

Guy was uneasy. He was beginning to curse precocious women. If there was going to be trouble, the possibility of Mary becoming injured bothered him. He mentioned it to Cleve.

"We shall attend to *ma petite* immediately," the Englishman promised.

They were approaching a well, a moss-edged watering place set in the center of the street with an iron-rimmed bucket on the flagging beside it. Cleve was pleased to discover that the pail was half-full. He called a halt.

"This is where you leave us, lass," he told her.

She smiled stubbornly. "Ah no. La! This affair may prove amusing."

"It will be amusing, true enough," Cleve agreed and hoisted the bucket shoulder-high. "You know, m'lass, I am not in the least loath to do this." Before she could retreat be deliberately deluged her with water.

She gasped. *"Mon dieu!* You—you beast!" she cried. "You crude lout! Look at me. I—I am drenched to the skin."

He nodded cheerfully. "Precisely. Now trot along and change into dry garments."

She was quivering with rage. He decided on second thought

that it might also be chill. She doffed her hat to free its crown of water; then she reached up and with neat accuracy slapped him.

"Take that, you churl, and next time—" her eyes widened. "What are you doing, *monsieur?*"

Cleve had placed the bucket deliberately beside the well and was approaching her, devils lancing in his eyes. "Discipline," he said. "At this point a spanking seems advisable."

But Mary was in full retreat. "I'll go," she said. "I am leaving right now. *Au revoir.*"

They watched her until the gathering murk of evening swallowed her up. Guy regarded Cleve questioningly.

"*Sandiou!* You wouldn't have done it, would you, *mon ami?*"

The Englishman smiled enigmatically. "She believes so," he answered and chuckled. "That is all that is necessary."

CHAPTER XXII

THE ASSASSIN BLADE

IT HAPPENED AT a corner, a half square from the Golden Crowns, where a shade-murked alley joined the street. Cleve and d'Entreville had allowed their prisoners to advance almost ten paces ahead of them, maintaining greater silence with the distance. There was a possibility that the unsigned message was bona fide and the attempted ambush a coincidence. Whatever the situation, both cavaliers were not taking any more risks than necessary.

Their prisoners marched stiffly, fearfully; convinced that the two rakehellies strode immediately behind with hungry steel in their fingers. Then, as the men passed the alley, a trio of sword-bearing figures rushed from the shadows.

"*Corbac.* I understood," Guy exclaimed. "They planned to take us three from the front and two from the rear. *Pecaire.* Cunning playfellows, eh?"

But the ambushers were quick to discover their mistake. The fellow whom Cleve had guarded began yowling, almost instantly, interspersing pleas for his life with deep lunged mention of his name. The three assassins milled uncertainly.

"Hola, mes amis!" Guy cried. "Here we are!" And he grinned happily. This was the thing he craved—fine clean fight. Beside him, Cleve cuffed back his wide-brimmed hat and pinched the tip of his nose lightly.

"Take the three with swords," he directed. "I'll go after our late prisoners."

"Very well Cleve, I—" And then the import struck the French gallant and he stared. "Huh?"

The Englishman laughed. "Faith. Never mind."

A black-bearded giant in a grease-smeared doublet launched a series of murderous lunges at Cleve's throat. The English rake-helly found them easy to parry, but not when a second assailant decided to deal thrusts from the side. A weasel-faced little blackguard with a wispy goatee.

Parrying, *septime,* Cleve made a swift plan of strategy. He waited until the flanker darted in once more; then instead of merely side stepping with a parry as of before, he side stepped and charged—charged toward Black-beard! Black-beard reeled under the vicious counter attack and the weasel-faced hireling, startled, was suddenly at Cleve's left elbow. Before he could recover, the Englishman's free hand had jerked him sideways into the path of Black-beard's savage counter thrust. The man took his friend's steel in his shoulder. He made quite an ado about it. He withdrew, weaponless, cursing with pain.

"One!" Cleve counted. "Now 'tis your turn, Kitten. I do believe I—"

The words died in his throat. One of their late prisoners on the fringe of the fray had selected a loose cobblestone. Cleve saw the rock arching leisurely toward him, but in the instant of perception he found his reflexes strangely rusted. The cobble grew. It loomed close; and then the world exploded in a sheet of dazzling blue light. He crumpled.

The black-beareded giant laughed. His blade lifted to drive the life from the prostrate English cavalier.

"*Por Dios!* Two! and I shall complete the business."

BUT HIS poised sword never landed. D'Entreville's blade seemed to lick obliquely from the left. The dark-eyed rakehelly's sinewy frame lunged forward to put weight behind it. The tip sank deep into the man's side.

But Guy hadn't time to watch. The man with whom he had been engaged was essentially an opportunist. While Guy had been puncturing Black-beard's hopes, the man used the Frenchman's exposed shoulder as an easy target.

Had he been a trifle more accurate, the fellow might have lanced steel into Guy's throat just under the jaw-line. But as it happened, the blade needled the air past d'Entreville's nose to remind him of unfinished business. He pirouetted cat-like, and landed astraddle Cleve's limp form.

"*Mordi!* Bad timing," he snapped. " 'Tis done, so!"

His rapier whipped up and over the assassin's recovering parry, crashing aside the weapon and sinking deep into his opponent's chest. The man staggered away, fingers clutched to the wound.

And that decided the remaining three ambushers. He of the wispy goatee, although wounded had been contemplating re-entering the fracas, but now he decided to retreat. He led the others away, running with the blood from his shoulder seeping down his sleeve to drip unheeded on the cobbles of the street.

Guy stared after them, his sword held aslant across his boots, sweat-dampened hair-ringlets matted to his forehead. He took off his hat and mopped his brow with the back of his gauntlet. At his feet, Cleve stirred slightly and opened his eyes.

"Faith, I have a giant-sized headache and that's a fact," he stated and stared groggily around him. "What happened? Ah yes. A rock! A friendly fellow thought it playful to scull me with

a rock and I misremembered to dodge. Where is the rat? I'll—"
He ran searching fingers gingerly along the side of his head,
found the lump and winced. "Ow!" He glared at d'Entreville.
"Well, help me up, you oaf!"

IT TOOK them several minutes to organize a pursuit. But
finally, after heatedly discussing the move, they set off after the
fugitives.

Cleve wanted to return to the palace. As far as he was
concerned, the affair of the note had yet to begin. The neat trap
into which they had just walked had been but a preliminary skir-
mish and now the problem lay in discovering the man behind it.
That the fellow lived at the palace was logical. Only a few had
known of Despartes' death.

But d'Entreville felt otherwise. "*Sangodemi!* We have a fresh
trail, Cleve, and the only sensible course is to follow it; capture
one of our would-be slayers, and kick the information we desire
out of him. Mark the blood-drops on the cobbles. They point
the way."

But the tiny blots of red became increasingly hard to discern
in the growing darkness. As the Golden Crowns hove into view,
the two rakehellies lost the trail completely. Cleve chuckled.

"At any rate, we shall gain a tankard of ale from this hunt,
Kitten."

"A lantern," Guy returned. "Perchance the inn will—"

A clatter of hoofs interrupted him. He stared as a trio of riders
pounded out of the alleyway next to the tavern. Men's faces were
revealed swiftly in the light of the fresh-lit court torches; and
then they were away, galloping toward the town gate.

"*Sandiou!* Did you see them, Cleve?"

The Englishman nodded. "I'd recognize that goatee
anywhere."

"They came from behind the tavern. Let's to horse and—"

"Behind the tavern!" Cleve suddenly snapped his fingers. He

gripped Guy's arm. "Damme! Hold a moment, Kitten. An idea has just struck me."

Cleve's eyes were dancing. "Egad! I should be ashamed of myself," he said. "Remember our first night in Casale, Kitten? The musket-ball which bid us such a cordial welcome?"

Guy hesitated. *"Oui."*

"It came from the house behind the tavern."

"So."

Cleve sighed. "Egad! Must I map everything for you? Does it not appear very coincidental that our friends on horseback also seem to have emanated from the same house, or at least from behind the Golden Crowns?"

Guy's eyes brightened. *"Pecaire!* It does, Cleve!" Then he hitched up his rapier. "Well, what are we waiting for?"

CHAPTER XXIII

TRAITORS' PARLOR

THE HOUSE BEHIND the Golden Crowns Tavern was a dilapidated structure, weather-whipped, and silent now. The first evening shadows were closing in, and in the translucent purple of early night Cleve felt the sinister challenge of the place. His slim strong fingers curled reassuringly about his swordhilt.

The deserted building was old, the type men built when each house needed also to be a fort. At one time it had apparently faced upon a broad courtyard, but now the tavern was occupying the space, and so the house was well secluded.

The lower windows were high from the ground and deep sunk in then thick walls. Uneven strips of wood boarded them over. A cracked stone terrace lay under the iron-studded gray door, and beyond there stood an unused stable, its doors gaping open.

"It seems too innocent; too deserted, Kitten." Cleve warned softly. "Take no risks. There may be men lurking in the dark."

The sibilant whisper of the French rakehelly's rapier sliding from its sheath answered him, and he grinned. He drew his own blade. Then they stole cautiously into the shadow of the house.

D'Entreville jerked tentatively on one of the boards barring a window. He was forced to stretch his full six feet one to do it. "Solid," he muttered, relaxing. *"Peste!* How are we to enter?"

Using his rapier as a pointer, Cleve indicated a rusted iron trellis on the wall between the terrace and the stable. Above the trellis was a window free of boarding. Guy caught his companion's intent and nodded.

"Bien."

Then, sheathing their blades, they swarmed up with silent agility. Happily the window was unlatched. They pushed it open. Cleve was first to scramble quietly through it.

He found himself in a small room, black, except where lights from the adjacent tavern cut swaths across it. In their dim illumination he found a table with a tinder-box atop.

"When I strike a spark glance quick to see if there are any tapers about," he ordered softly.

From his position on the window-ledge Guy nodded. The Englishman's hands moved and a spit of light brightened the scene.

"Well?"

Guy chuckled and stood up. *"Corbac.* There is a full box of them at your elbow."

In the darkness Cleve cursed sheepishly, fumbled, found and lit one.

THE ROOM proved remarkably habitable for a part of a seemingly deserted house. It contained a bed, two chairs and a table, and a wall-cabinet, open and lined with bottles. Flanking the chambers narrow door was a row of pegs upon which were hung a plumed hat, a Spanish cape, a sword and baldric.

"A poor weapon." Guy adjudged inspecting the blade and rehanging it. *"Sandiou!* I wouldn't carry it."

Standing over their table, Antone said to
Cleve: "My salutations, Gardier"

"Yet it proves a contention, Kitten," Cleve said. "We've walked into somebody's nest." He selected a handful of candles and gave half to d'Entreville. "Interesting, isn't it? Suppose we explore further."

He sneaked open the door and stepped into a lone narrow corridor with Guy creeping after him, fingers clutched to a flame-tipped candle.

Their room was the first of many. Opposite it was a worn staircase leading down to the Stygian regions of the first floor. Cleve eyed the corridor with its many flanking doors; Guy regarded the staircase.

"This way, Kitten."

"Don't be stupid. Our host is downstairs."

"I hope so. I want to investigate this hallway unhampered."

"Sangodemi! A soldier reconnoiters first before acting."

"Very well. You be a good soldier."

"Pecaire! Then we'll split!"

Cleve chuckled. "Some day we are going to view the same thing alike, and I'm going to faint." Then he slapped the other lightly on the shoulder. "Keep your eyes open, Kitten."

Guy nodded.

Cleve moved to the first door down the hall. Blade held ready, with his candle wedged upright in the crossbar of its hilt, he slowly turned the knob.

The chamber was vacant, but it had been used recently, for upon the table were two empty wine-bottles and a few plates. Cleve was preparing to leave when a slip of paper lying on the dirty floor caught his eye. He picked it up.

There wasn't much to it—a cryptic message consisting of three lines:

> *Richelieu's Devils are in Montferrat. D'Entreville has just stopped at the Red Tassel, and Richard Cleve was here at the dawning. You know what to do, my friend.*
> *J.C.*

"He did, true enough," the Englishman murmured. "A musket from the darkness, and then a five-man ambuscade."

He tucked the note into the cuff of his left gauntlet and smiled. At least he knew who the sender was; J.C.—Juan Castro! The mention of the Red Tassel indicated the possibility of the wayside tavern being his headquarters. But more than that, the message proved Cleve's previous deduction correct. Castro was in Montferrat for a darker reason than the mere filching of a dispatch case.

THE ADJOINING room was locked and after a few hurried tests of its door, he proceeded to the next. This door swung easily. He stood on its sill for a moment, candle held high, staring; and then he whistled softly and closed it again.

"Ye Gods!"

He opened the next, muttered: "Shades of Guy Fawkes!" and almost slammed it shut. He stood for a moment frowning, and then turned and crossed to the opposite side of the corridor. He selected a door, opened it, nodded grimly and closed it again.

Thus he visited three more rooms; each with less caution and more haste. The purpose of Castro's presence in the duchy was rapidly growing apparent. Almost every chamber on the hallway was similar in content; crammed to the rafters. Without doubt the Spaniards design was great in scope—great and deadly. But who in the devil was his accomplice?

Cleve was asking himself this question as his hand gripped the knob of the last door. But then his attention shifted. For the past minute his subconscious mind had been aware that the great house was no longer held in a thick stillness. Things were stirring below. And now suddenly there was a crash downstairs, quickly followed by the clash of steel, the sodden thumping of feet, and sharp scraping sounds.

He scowled, and in that instant a voice rang out: *"Hola!* Cleve, I've found our hosts. *A moi!"*

The Englishman grinned. He left the door and started down the corridor. The vague throp of the lump on his hand reminded him of their most recent adventure. As he descended the narrow staircase he sighed. This time he'd remember to duck! A moment later, he paused before an open door through which light poured in a brilliant flow. He lifted his blade.

"Well, here we go again," he muttered and stepped over the sill.

ENTERING THE large high-ceilinged room—it proved to be the building's scullery—he stood a moment on the landing leading down to it.

"Damme," he laughed. "What have we here?"

The view which greeted him was rare. D'Entreville, his dark eyes a-light, was facing four angry gentlemen. The Frenchman was standing beside a flour-bin in the corner, and he held a pewter scuttle in one hand—a sword in the other. Each of his cursing opponents appeared to be frosted. They boiled around him amid white billows of flour. Whenever their four rapiers converged too close to the French rakehelly, the hand-scuttle would dip back into the bin, come out loaded and swish blinding flour-clouds into their faces.

The four gentlemen would then withdraw, coughing, and Guy would press home four nipping thrusts further to dismay them. Two of them were bleeding freely, but they were stubborn fellows. Yet, given sufficient time and enough flour, the Frenchman would soon wear them all down.

"This a shame to break it up," Cleve chuckled.

He took the two steps leading down from the landing in a single stride. As the backs of the four were toward him, he approached unnoticed. A wooden meat-mallet was lying on a thick wall-table, and he picked it up as he passed.

In the meantime, Guy has cast another spray of flour. One of his opponents stumbled away, coughing and cursing and rubbing his eyes. He banged into Cleve; Cleve banged back promptly with the meat-mallet, cracking the fellow neatly on the crown. The man went down.

"One."

Another man began to hurl wild invectives at d'Entreville. He did not consider the French rakehelly's conduct of the battle gentlemanly. Only a churl would fight with flour. Cleve tapped him lightly on the shoulder.

"Four to one is not gentlemanly either," he told him. "I suggest you retire!" And he used the mallet. The objector regarded him with glazed eyes, appeared to nod agreement, and then slid peacefully to the floor.

"Two," said Cleve.

But his next victim was awaiting him. Cleve caught the fellow's murderous lunge, turned it aside and countered in kind. They fenced for a moment, each feeling the other out, cautious and alert. The man was an expert, Cleve decided. He possessed a pretty *sixte* counter and a dazzling *riposte*.

"Damme! I'd like to play, bucko," the English cavalier said. "Yet time presses." Then he stepped back and snapped the heavy mallet in a short arc toward the other's head. It struck alongside the fellow's jaw.

"Three!" Cleve said.

"Four!" added d'Entreville as his blade skewered the last man. *"Corbac!"* Tis done!"

He stood for a second, panting. The slashed sleeve of his maroon doublet was caked to the shoulder with dough. He was perspiring freely. Finally, he bent and picked up the hem of his late opponent's cape. He cleaned his blade and sheathed it with a snap.

"Stumbled upon them after searching the rest of the house," he said by way of explanation. "I doubt that any more are about."

Cleve nodded. Then he commenced to drag one of his victims toward a warped trap-door. "As soon as we have locked our friends below," he said, "we had best quit this place, quickly."

Guy had been attempting to bat flour free of his hat but he stopped. He frowned.

"Why?"

"No reason in particular, Kitten." The Englishman paused, one gloved hand still gripping the spurred heel of his charge. "Except that there is sufficient gun-powder stored in the rooms upstairs to blast this mansion to Hades and back again!"

CHAPTER XXIV

SIGNOR POOH

THE GROG-ROOM OF the Golden Crowns was brisk and loud with revelry. A troop of players, passing south toward Piedmont, had put up at the inn overnight and in lieu of silver were paying with talent.

From their table in the far corner of the low-raftered room, Cleve and d'Entreville observed the proceedings with a pleasant torpor. Between them were the ragged remains of what had once been a succulent leg of mutton. They had repaired to the Golden Crowns for the purpose of conversation, but the savory aroma of cookery had engaged their attention.

Now they strove feebly to shake off their inertia. It was easier to sit, relaxed, with heels aslant on convenient benches. Guy made the first move.

"You mentioned a note," he said.

Cleve pulled the clay pipe the landlord had furnished away from his lips and nodded. He fumbled in his doublet, drew forth Castro's chit and tossed it on the table. "Here it is."

"J.C." Guy muttered after scanning the paper. He cursed. "*Sandiou!* Juan Castro!"

Cleve regarded him obliquely. "Remarkable," he said.

D'Entreville ignored him, frowning. "A house crammed with powder and arms. You did say that there were weapons with the powder-kegs, did you not, Cleve?"

"That's right. One room alone contained fifty halbards."

"But why?"

"Damme. Do you sit there and profess not to know?"

The French gallant flushed. "Revolt?"

"Of course." Cleve straightened. "To my way of thinking, Kitten, we've uncovered a fragment of the thing which ails this duchy. Some group, of which Juan Castro is a part, is seeking to raise a rebellion. They are clever lads too. First they create unrest among the soldiery by stealing their pay; next they unsettle the populace."

Guy's eyes began to glisten. "*Sangodemi!*" he exclaimed. "It is becoming clear. If they seek to demoralize the soldiery, then Catherine Cordoba's mysterious Baron X is behind everything. Undoubtedly he is the man to whom Castro sent this message."

"THINK SO?" Cleve asked and lifted his tankard from the table and stared into it absently. He took a leisurely sip.

"*Corbac!* Don't you? Has not Antone been in Catherine's hire? Have not his men looted the wage-wagons?"

The Englishman returned the ale-mug to the table. He smiled. "We have no proof of Antone's guilt, Kitten."

"But we have! M. de Boussey has definite information that Antone's men have been seen riding from the looted wagons. Besides, we know that Antone was one of Catherine's hirelings and that she, in turn, belonged to the baron. What more logical conclusion can be drawn?"

Cleve thought a moment, staring at the players who were now taking curtain-bows sans curtain, and then shook his head. "It doesn't make sense."

The Frenchman glared. "No?"

Cleve laughed. "No," he replied. "Faith, in the first instance I doubt that the lootings of the wage-wagons have anything to do with Catherine's plot."

"Eh? What leads to that surmise?"

"The conversations I had with her as Mazo Gardier. I learned that the lady rather fancied herself as the future Duchess of Montferrat, and to gain the desire she and Baron X were proposing to murder Duke Vincent. She admitted as much and Baron X had hired Gardier for the business."

"You have explained that before," Guy snapped.

The English cavalier rambled on unheeding. "Upon Vincent's death, Catherine was to coerce Henri into marriage. She would thus become the Duchess of Montferrat, and of course her comrade Baron X would be on hand to share in the profits."

D'Entreville snorted. "*Sandiou.* I find nothing in your remarks to eliminate Baron X as being the instigator of a rebellion."

"Don't you, Kitten?" Cleve grinned, then sobered. "Well, let us consider the affair we have just uncovered. The house behind this tavern—charged with powder. Damme! If Catherine and the baron wanted to grasp the reins of power then civil strife, insurrection, unrest, would be the last thing she would play for. A new crown must be set peacefully if it is to remain solid. And yet we have reason to believe that the lads who own that houseful of munitions are planning to the contrary. Rebellion."

The Englishman shrugged and relaxed against the wall. "Mark me, Kitten, we are facing two distinct conspiracies and have been wasting most of our attention on the lesser."

D'Entreville frowned. "I doubt it," he stated. *"Mais oui,* I doubt it very much."

"Your privilege," Cleve said and yelled for more ale. While it was being brought, he added: "Castro is our culprit, Guy."

The Frenchman shook his head. *"Non.* He is but an attendant figure. His main purpose has been to filch the papers which Sir Harry was bearing and nothing more."

CLEVE WAITED until their tankards were refilled, and then chuckled. "Explain the reason for his note being discovered where we found it?" he challenged.

"I said that he was an attendant figure," Guy reiterated sharply. "I did not eliminate him. Undoubtedly he has a part in the plot—but only a small one. Your convictions to the contrary, I still believe that if we ferret out Baron X, we ferret out everything."

"Uh-huh." Cleve nodded wisely.

"Parbleu! You needn't appear so cursed superior. I have good reason for my contention. The importance of Antone the Archer in this affair seems to have entirely escaped you. He *is* an important factor, *mon ami!* It is his relationship to Catherine and Catherine's relationship to the baron that exposes the complete conspiracy. True, she may have plotted Vincent's death, but behind her was the baron who plots complete domination of this duchy. With Catherine in power, his task would be easier."

"In brief, you doubt that the intrigue ends with her ascending the throne."

"Precisely."

"How do you explain her death?"

Guy frowned. *"Corbac!* How do you explain it?"

Cleve wagged a chiding finger. "Ah now, I asked first."

The other pursed his lips and took a deep breath, frowning. "Henri!" he snapped and glowered. "Well?"

Cleve eyed his finger-tips thoughtfully. Finally he shook his head. "I don't know," he admitted, then grinned. "But I'll wager ten livres that it wasn't Henri, m'lad. Ten livres, even!"

D'Entreville's fist crashed upon the table. "Taken!" he snapped.

They finished their ales. Preparing to leave, Cleve suddenly noticed a high-crowned hat appearing between the shoulders of a cluster of departing guests. He gripped Guy's arm and pulled the French cavalier back upon the bench opposite him.

"Hold a moment, Guy. We have a visitor."

THE PROPHECY proved accurate. The wearer of the hat wiggled free, threaded his way rapidly toward their corner. He was a small man with a swarthy face, youngish in cast. He approached with a bandy-legged stride. He wore an exceptionally long dark cape beneath which bulged an object which Cleve knew immediately to be a quiver full of arrows. It was Antone, his swarthy face still holding the same fixed grin; his button eyes hard.

"My salutations, Gardier," he said easily and slid onto a stool at the end of the table. He regarded Guy briefly. "I would speak alone with you."

Cleve ignored Guy's questioning glance. He collared a house lackey, ordered another round of ales and turned to the little bandit.

"You may speak freely, bucko," he said easily. "This is a henchman of mine, Anastasias Pooh by name."

"Eh?" frowned the archer. "Anastasias who?"

"Pooh," corrected Cleve calmly. Guy squirmed. He'd settle with Cleve later for this.

"A ridiculous name, I think," Antone said.

The English rakehelly nodded, straight-faced. "He is. But entirely trustworthy. Anastasias, Nasty as I call him, is one of the most notorious poisoners in Europe." He turned. "Aren't you, Nasty?"

Guy glowered. "There is one whom I would enjoy to poison right now," he muttered.

"You see," Cleve said with a nod.

Antone shrugged. "Well, if you vouch for him…." Then his voice flattened. "I learned of Signorina Cordoba's death this evening, hence I risked coming here. Tell me, Gardier, who did it?"

Cleve shrugged. "They say, Henri—"

The little bandit nodded. "Then the rumor is true." His beady eyes glittered. "I have an arrow for him."

"An arrow?" Guy started. He eyed Antone with sudden recognition. "Is this the famous Archer of Montferrat—er—Gardier?" he asked Cleve.

The Englishman inclined his head. "That's right."

"*Mordi!*"

Antone regarded him sharply. "*Sapristi*, is my person so offensive, Nasty, that you must—"

Guy winced at the name but hurriedly interposed a quick disavowal. "It was because I felt surprised that you dare appear in Casale, *monsieur*," he finished lamely.

THEN THE lackey appeared with three foam-capped tankards. The brew did much to ease the situation, although Antone's smiling insistence that he and d'Entreville exchange tankards before drinking caused merriment almost to strangle Cleve. One thing was certain, the small bandit's rascality was exceeded by a deeply suspicious nature.

Greedily gulping his ale, the Archer abruptly stated: "I have sent word to the baron concerning the murder of Signorina Cordoba, Gardier. You will meet him when he arrives."

The Englishman's expression did not alter. "Good enough," he assented and stared thoughtfully. "Where?"

"My headquarters. The Old River Chalet."

D'Entreville wanted to know where it was. Antone ignored him, speaking to Cleve. "Ask any peasant," he told him. "The Old River Chalet is well known. It is supposed to be haunted, and of course it is. *Sapristi!* Haunted by the men of Antone the Archer." He laughed shortly.

"I see." Cleve nodded. "Clever, m'lad. Guarded by a reputation. Faith! Small wonder that the soldiery has never found you." He smiled faintly and swished the ale of his tankard into a foam. "At what time will the baron arrive, Antone?"

"Ah. Who knows? Perchance at high noon, but more likely later. Certainly before dusk." And here the bandit shrugged. "Choose your own time, Gardier. I but offer you the facts. I arrange this meeting only because she would have me do it, and for no other reason. The intrigues of the gentry are not my concern. You and the baron need not fear my ears or my tongue." He paused. "Understand?"

Cleve nodded. He understood completely now. Without a doubt Antone knew very little concerning the plot. He was but a tool—Catherine's slave. Apparently he had obeyed her unquestioningly, almost fanatically, in all things.

On the other side of the table, d'Entreville shifted. One question had been burning in his mind and now he blurted it out: "Just who is this baron, *mon ami?*"

Antone's dark eyes narrowed on him for an instant and then shifted to Cleve. "I deem your friend overly curious, Gardier."

Cleve's gaze pinned Guy with mild censure; and then he smiled. "Not necessarily, Antone. I have hired Nasty in this enterprise. Naturally he is interested in knowing the identity of his true employer."

It was weak and the bandit seemed to sense it. "I dislike people with long snouts. If your friend desires the Baron's name, you speak it, Gardier. Nasty is your responsibility." Then he stood up. "I have loitered in this place long enough. Who knows, the guardsmen may be already on their way. Good evening, until tomorrow."

They watched him until he had disappeared; and then Guy faced about. "*Sangodemi!*" he said. "A careful rogue, isn't he?"

Cleve smiled abstractedly. "Careful is understatement, Kitten." He lifted his mug. "Sheer understatement."

CHAPTER XXV

TWO ROUTES TO PERIL

THE FOLLOWING DAY came too soon. Lying face down against the pleasant softness of his bed, Richard Cleve dimly recognized its arrival, yet he fought stubbornly to remain in the luxury of warm oblivion. The twenty odd tankards of ale abetted him somewhat, but even they were insufficient to protect him from the clamor of voices, the hand which shook him. He rolled over.

"Noisiest damned place I've ever slept in," he complained. "Damme! Quiet!"

D'Entreville was standing over him, fully dressed. His beard had been freshly trimmed. Behind him a dumpy individual who wore the apron of a barber, stood with laver in hand, a look of estimation in his eyes.

"Arise, Cleve. The duke's barber is here to shave you."

The Englishman allowed the weighted fuzz on his eyelids to pull them closed. He took a deep breath. "I am growing a beard," he announced and snuggled deeper into the bedclothes. He yawned slightly and added: "Beginning now."

"Oh no you don't, *mon ami. Parbleu!* We have much to accomplish this day. In half the hour we shall be a-horse."

Cleve felt the coverlet whisked from him and a rush of cold air.

"Up, *mon ami. Sandiou!* Have you forgotten that this day we learn the identity of Baron X and arrest him?"

With a leisurely stretch the English cavalier threw his legs over the side of the bed. He massaged his face vigorously and it seemed to help. Their room in the ducal palace assumed normal portions. There was a warm blaze dancing in the hearth, and with a grunt of satisfaction Cleve walked over to it and pulled up a chair.

"Faith. What is the hour, Kitten? From the nip in the air it must be dawn."

"Half past the hour of eight," the Frenchman informed him. "I deem it necessary that we ride immediately to the Old River Chalet."

The barber approached and unfurled an embroidered linen sheet. Cleve allowed him to tuck it firmly about his neck and accepted the crescent-shaped laver submissively. The fire crackled.

"Why the haste, Kitten? The baron will not arrive until later."

"I plan a trap," Guy replied. "I shall take a troop of guards and surround the locale. When the baron arrives he shall be arrested immediately." He snapped his fingers while pacing cheerfully with one hand held to his rapier. "As simple as that! *Corbac!* Our visit to the Golden Crowns was filled with fortune last evening."

CLEVE INCLINED his cheek to allow the industrious barber full leeway. "Of course Antone will await docilely as you gallop up to his nest with fifty troopers behind you," he chuckled.

Guy smiled. He was in excellent spirits. "Hah!" he exclaimed. "I have attended that problem, my wise friend. I have been astir for over an hour and while you were still snoring, held council with M. de Boussey. *Monsieur le colonel* will dispatch a troop of horse from Casale promptly at high noon. They shall secrete themselves near the Old River Chalet to await my signal. Upon receiving it, they shall close in. *Pecaire!* That is all there is to it."

"Why not allow the men to close in without our presence?" Cleve asked. "Faith! We know that Antone and the baron will be there. Let the troopers take them. We can interrogate those two when they are brought to the palace."

D'Entreville looked shocked. He stared incredulously at his friend. *"Mordi!* Are you serious?"

"Surely, I'm serious. Why waste time riding to them when they can be brought to us?"

Guy shook his head as though recovering from a blow. "I don't understand it," he told himself. *"Sandiou!* It is beyond comprehension! We engage in a problem; labor desperately upon it; finally contrive its solution; and when the end is in sight, we withdraw to allow others to complete it! *Sangodemi,* Cleve! What manner of man are you?"

"Damme, a nice enough fellow," Cleve replied between strokes of the barber's razor. "Kindly disposed toward old women, children, dogs—I like you too, Kitten. And—"

"Never mind." The French rakehelly's dark eyes narrowed with a sudden thought. Whenever Cleve acted this way, there was usually a good reason for it. He frowned slightly and stepped resolutely between the English cavalier and the fire. "All right, *mon ami,*" he said, "what is your motive for such a lazy suggestion?"

Cleve waited while the barber put the finishing touches to his face before answering. He handed the laver to the man and sat back chuckling.

"I have more than one motive," he admitted. "It seems foolish to waste our time with minor concerns when the real puzzle still needs solution. For another reason, I don't think my pose as Gardier will—"

D'Entreville interrupted him with a sweet venom. "And pray, what is the *real* concern, *mon ami?*"

Cleve regarded him mockingly. "A visit to the Red Tassel might uncover it," he said.

D'ENTREVILLE SAW his point and discarded it immediately. He had lain awake half the night wrestling with the Castro question, only to arrive at the point where he'd begun. Juan Castro was unimportant. Guy was positive of it. He gestured impatiently.

"Castro!" he snorted. "Bah! We have no proof that he is anywhere near the inn."

"It's worth the try," Cleve said.

Guy grew irritable. *"Parbleu!* I told you last evening that Juan Castro is not so important as is the baron. I do not propose losing the main *intrigant* to gain one of his henchmen. We can locate Castro later. *Peste!* The only reason that you are so intent upon his capture is because of Sir Harry's papers and your pardon. Why don't you admit it?"

Cleve shrugged, crossed the room and began to dress. During the night somebody had polished his boots, brushed his black doublet and laundered a fresh collar for him. He thought of de Maupin and mentally thanked the diminutive steward. Then he looked at Guy.

"All right, I admit it," he said. "But mark me, there is more behind Castro than the mere robbery of English documents. He may lead us to the figure behind this filthy business—the man who has been having the wage-wagons looted and powder-stores collected."

"Pecaire! Must I repeat for ever that Baron X is that man?"

"No," Cleve denied slowly. He pulled on his high Cordovan boots and stood up. "Look, Kitten, there is no need for us to race immediately to the Old River Chalet."

Guy's chin jutted out stubbornly. He had enthusiastically planned today's business and Cleve's airy dismissal of its importance angered him.

"I say there is. We must arrive in advance of the baron and pump as much information from Antone as possible."

"You'll find that little rogue dry pumping, Kitten. Besides, the Baron knows the real Gardier. I've tried to make that point before. Once he sees me, the jig will be up. He'll know me for an imposter and undoubtedly have Antone's men murder us on the spot. Also consider Catherine's death. We know Antone is searching for her slayer and so it can be no one in the baron's plot. I'm sure she was murdered for a reason, Kitten, and perhaps I can find it at the Red Tassel."

But Guy wasn't in the mood for logic any more. "All right," he snapped. "Go on your futile errand, Cleve. Henri is the man who slew Cordoba and Castro is unimportant. Waste your time. I'm leaving for the Old River Chalet immediately!"

The Englishman shrugged. When Guy developed one of these stubborn streaks he knew better than to cross him. "Very well, Kitten." He slapped the Frenchman lightly on the shoulder. "Good luck. If nothing comes of my jaunt to the Red Tassel, I'll join you with fifty of the palace guards. Tell Antone that I was unavoidably delayed and that I sent you in my place."

An hour later he cantered his horse through the main gate of Casale. He didn't follow the ragged yellow road which stretched to the west, but galloped north for almost five minutes before veering gradually into an invisible parallel with the thorough-fare.

He was wearing a new white plume in his hat. The rubies in his rapier-hilt flashed crimson at his thigh. As he rode, he mentally summed up his knowledge of Montferrat's mysteries. That Castro had had Despartes put out of the way was obvious, as was the fact that the fat Spanish spy had something to do with the duchy's threatening rebellion. But who was his accomplice?

Cleve scowled into the wind. By Gad! The man *had* to have an accomplice. The precision of the wage-train lootings, the note cast through the library window—these were evidence enough.

Last night's ambush was definitely Castro's work. Baron X wouldn't be interested in slaying Mazo Gardier, and to all extents and purposes Cleve *was* Gardier. Therefore, it had been Castro, or his fellow conspirator. The English rakehelly's eyes narrowed. Faith! Here was a man everyone had overlooked. A man whose government would be as interested in Montferrat's fall as Juan Castro's. The unobtrusive companion of Margaret of Savoy. The elusive man named Enrico!

"Could be so," the cavalier muttered and reined up.

He approached the Red Tassel from the rear. The place was strangely silent. There were horses in its afteryard; and although most of them were saddled, not a grooms-boy or a stableman was in sight. The rear door was closed.

Cleve slid from his steed and tethered it loosely to a nearby sapling in a clump of round-leafed bushes. He stood amid them frowning. Suddenly his gloved fingers dove for his hilt. From the quiet of the tavern came a scream! A woman's scream! What the devil did it mean?

CHAPTER XXVI

BARON X

THREE LEAGUES AWAY, Guy d'Entreville sat his saddle atop a craggy hillock and shook his head. After wandering aimlessly for thirty minutes in a brambly forest of gnarled trees and vined underbrush, he had been exasperated to find the object of his search at a point he had previously passed. He cuffed back his plumed hat and mopped his brow. Then he regarded the setting again.

Below him, the Old River Chalet lay decaying amid the ruin of its garden. It faced the River Po from behind a serried rank of rotting stumps. It carried with it the melancholy aspect of a haunted place—bleak gray walls supporting a roof which in part had been chewed bare by the weather; vacant eye-like windows; and a sagging, vine-webbed chimney. Small wonder that the peasant who had directed him here had spoken with a superstitious tremor.

Staring at it, the French gallant dropped his hand to the hilt of his blade. He glanced back up the road toward Casale and wished for a fleeting moment that he had the comforting companionship of Richard Cleve. The road was deserted. It was little more than a cowpath anyway, trailing away from the main highway at a point two leagues distant. He was alone.

Then with a curse, the cavalier put spurs to his mount and descended the hillock. He reached its base without mishap and was preparing to canter toward the distant edifice when two men stepped from behind trees.

"Hold, *signor!*"

D'Entreville reined up. The men had horse-pistols and they were trained unswervingly upon him. He was careful to keep his hands exposed, folded on the pommel and away from his swordhilt.

"Your master is expecting me," he said.

"Antone expects Mazo Gardier," the taller of his captors stated. He shook his head. "I have seen Signor Gardier, and you are not he."

"That's right," d'Entreville accorded. "My name is—" And he bit his lip angrily. "My name is Pooh, *monsieur.* Anastasias Pooh!"

The man frowned. He was a grizzled ruffian wearing a green bandanna in lieu of a hat, a leather jerkin and a knife-laden sash. "Pooh?" he queried.

His smaller companion suddenly nodded. *"Sapristi,* Luigi, I remember now. Our chief mentioned the name to me last night. This man with the funny name is Gardier's friend. He is all right."

But the other was a cautious fellow. He waved his pistol commandingly. "Dismount. Attempt any tricks and I shall blow your brains out." And as Guy obeyed, he turned to the smaller guard. "Back to your post, my friend. I'll take this bravo in."

ANTONE THE Archer was not surprised to see d'Entreville. In fact, he seemed rather pleased. The little bandit was seated at a bottle-littered table before the fire-place in the chalet's main hall.

"Por Bacco! I am sorry to hear of Signor Gardier's illness," he exclaimed after Guy had laid Cleve's non-appearance to an

attack of stomach trouble. "It is probably caused by that rancid brew which the Golden Crowns serves as ale. I have had the pains myself. You drank much after I left?"

Guy dropped into a chair opposite the speaker. He nodded. "Twenty tankards," he admitted and stole a quick glance around.

The room was bare-walled and carpetless, its only furniture consisting of some rickety chairs and the long table at which they sat. Six of the Archer's men were in evidence. Guy wondered how many more of them there were. Then he resumed the conversation.

"Of course Mazo might recover sufficiently to ride here," he said. "He is anxious to receive his orders. Yet if he does not appear, then I am to speak with the baron and relay that gentleman's commands."

There was a strange hard light in Antone's beady eyes although the smile beneath them remained the same. He reached across the table and selected a bottle.

"I'd like to propose a toast, *signor,*" he said, filling two goblets. "A toast to which I am sure you will agree." Then he handed one to Guy and stood up. "To the slow death of the man who murdered Signorina Cordoba."

Guy arose slowly with the slender stem of the goblet between his fingers. He held the glass eye-level. He felt obliged to embellish the toast.

"To Henri de Casale," he said; and then froze with his eyes glued to the goblet's mirroring surface.

The wine which Antone had poured was a crude vintage, and its murkiness formed a perfect basis for reflection. D'Entreville found himself staring at the face of Baron Friedrich Carl Von Erla!

"No, Signor Kitten. To you!" said Antone, his voice suddenly vicious.

But Guy didn't hear him. He was too busy attempting to judge the distance between himself and his old enemy. The face drew nearer. Guy wasted no more time—dashing the glass and its contents over his shoulder. The wine sprayed into the Austrian's face.

Guy spun to see him stagger back, and then the French gallant had his rapier in hand. He accepted the murderous lunge of the saturnine man who had accompanied Von Erla. Guy beat aside the tip of a blade jabbing in from the side, then returned his first opponent's with a deadliness that left the fellow gasping out his life's blood on the floor. A man hurdled the body, Guy served him in turn—a sword in the belly.

The French cavalier tried to retreat. A comforting wall was needed at his back, but the long table denied passage. He reversed; tried to go forward; tried to sword-whip his way through the press. No good! Then the uneven match was ended abruptly. A wine-bottle in the hands of Antone did it.

Having been caught immobile by the unexpectedness of d'Entreville's sudden action, the swarthy little archer was quick to recover. Sweeping up a long-necked flask from the litter on the table, he waited until the rakehelly was comparatively stationary; and then he reached out and struck with shattering violence.

Guy's hat-crown, plus the rippling thickness of his dark hair, saved him his life but not his senses. The room spun crazily in a spark-splashed maelstrom. A clap of thunder seemed to re-echo in his brain. His muscles became liquid. He staggered, dropped to his knees; and then slid slowly forward on his face. Oblivion.

WHEN THE lucidity of reason returned, he was still on the floor in the same position in which he had fallen. He could not have been senseless very long. He was listening as Von Erla said:

"*Gott!* I knew he was a devil, but not such fierce one. To call him the Kitten is a jest. He is a veritable tiger. Two deaths in a wink of the eye!"

"*Por Bacco!* Had I not struck with the bottle, Signor Baron, who knows how many we might have lost?"

That was Antone's voice. Guy slowly opened his eyes. The world was confined to that section of the flooring immediately in front of his nose. He attempted to roll over. He found himself incapable of the effort. He did not move. The shock of the blow was still gripping his reflexes, numbing them.

"He still lives, fortunately," came the baron's voice. "We shall see that he is made to pay for many things!" There was the jarring shock of a boot-toe against Guy's side. "The swine shall answer for the ruin that he and his English friend have made of my plans. I vow to slay them both before aught else. Fetch water, Antone. Revive him."

It was peculiar. Guy knew that he was destined for torture if he did not immediately manage to escape, for the vicious edge to the baron's voice was warning enough. Yet the Frenchman couldn't move. He lay paralyzed, listening with all the indifferent detachment of an incurious eavesdropper and feeling only slight surprise that Von Erla should turn up as Baron X. It seemed so simple and logical now.

Then rough hands seized him, jerking him upright. He closed his eyes. An icy cascade deluged him and he opened them again. He was being supported on either side by a pair of garlic-smelling ruffians in greasy surcoats. For the first time he discovered that his wrists had been bound behind his back.

The room came into focus. Before him, like judges at a trial, sat Von Erla and Antone with several of the robber band standing behind. Von Erla was smiling with all the amiability of a wolf.

Guy stared. Gradually his strength was coming back. His head began to throb in thick bulging aches. The side which Von Erla had booted commenced to grow tender. He shook his head to clear it. He was sopping wet. A full bucket of water had been sloshed over him.

Von Erla crossed travel-grimed boots and relaxed easily against the back of his chair. "So we meet once more, Kitten," he said softly. "The fortunes of war and intrigue are sometimes just, are they not? Where once you held me prisoner, now I hold you. Only this time you shall embark upon a longer voyage than did I." He nodded pleasantly. "No return."

Guy bit his lip and glared. He did not say a word, waiting tensely.

"It was a mistake for you and your playful comrade to mix again in my affairs, d'Entreville," the baron continued. "But perchance it might interest you to know that all your work is for naught. Upon disposing of you and the Englishman, I personally shall proceed where my assistant failed."

"Assistant? Do you mean Gardier, or Cordoba?" Guy asked.

The baron's pale eyes narrowed. "It was clever of you to dispose of Gardier, my friend. But it was a mistake to murder La Cordoba."

Beside him Antone cursed, his beady eye fanatical with hate. "A bad mistake, *signor*," he whispered. "You will soon learn that when I start on you!"

LITTLE CLUSTERS of muscle bulged at the corners of the Frenchman's jaw. "Neither Cleve nor I slew Mademoiselle Cordoba!" he said.

The baron smiled with his lips, but his eyes grew harder. "Come now, d'Entreville, I am not a fool. I'll admit that when I received word of her death last night, I believed Henri de Casale to be guilty. But that belief vanished when Herr Antone here offered me a description of the men whom he believed to be Mazo Gardier and Anastasias Pooh. Then I knew the devils who had mangled my coup—Cleve and d'Entreville!"

Guy frowned. "You haven't just arrived in Montferrat?"

"No." The speaker shrugged. "Night is an excellent mask for one who is obliged to ride unrecognized through French territory. I reached this hovel in the gray of dawn after an all-night gallop from Turin." He laughed grimly. "In time to set the trap."

"Pecaire! You have not yet trapped Cleve!"

The baron sobered. He nodded thoughtfully, a frown creasing his narrow forehead. "Not yet," he admitted. *"Himmel!* Why has he not arrived?"

"Sapristi!" Antone exclaimed. "Perchance he has learned your full title and fears recognition."

Von Erla shook his head and stood up. "No. If that were the case, he would not have permitted this French pig to ride into this nest. The English rogue is cunning. There must be another reason."

He snapped his fingers. "But of course! Cleve realizes that I would know the real Gardier even if I were not Von Erla, so he sends d'Entreville, a supposed henchman of Gardier's to learn what he might. *Ja!* And I know what to do about it. We shall send a message in your name, Antone, stating that the baron has left and that d'Entreville has had an accident. *Ach!* That will fetch him to us quickly enough."

The speaker gestured to the men holding Guy. "Lock him in the cellar!" Then he turned to the Archer. "Patience in this game will prove a virtue. When Cleve appears to inquire as to d'Entreville—" He shrugged. " 'Twill be easier to work upon two birds instead of one. After we have disposed of them, my friend, then I shall begin to work upon Duke Vincent and his son in order that Margaret of Savoy—"

But Guy heard no more. His guards had jerked him through the chamber's door and out of earshot. *"Parbleu!* A nice pot of trouble I've brewed for myself," he muttered as they led him away.

CHAPTER XXVII

SOMEWHERE A SPY

LIKE THE SUDDEN turning of a string-peg on a lute, the scream from the depths of the Red Tassel jerked Richard Cleve's nerves to a vibrant tension. He crouched behind his screen of bushes, staring at the building. Nothing stirred.

The pall of silence had once more settled upon the place. He wondered vaguely whether he had actually heard that sharp, faintly indignant outcry, or whether fancy had played his ears a trick.

Then he shook his head, muttered: "Damme! I heard it true enough," and started forward.

He drew his rapier and used the blade to part bushes in his path, moving toward the stable with silent grace.

The interior of the inn's stable only increased his perplexity. Entering through a half-door cut in its side, he immediately discovered that instead of being deserted, it continued a full complement of horses. Every stall was occupied. He frowned and counted the mounts therein. There were twenty of them. A goodly number indeed for a tavern which outwardly appeared unpatronized.

His lips curved into a reckless smile. Something big was afoot and it was an odds-on wager that he'd meet trouble before finishing. With this consideration in mind, he stripped for action, divesting himself of his swirling cape, his sword scabbard and baldric, his spurs.

From his berth behind the last stall, he started down the central aisle, but quickly retreated. Framed in the portals of the stable-entrance was a man. A guard apparently, for he carried a heavy-stocked Spanish musket cradled in his arm. Cleve eyed him narrowly.

"Interesting," he murmured. "A tavern with an armed sentry." Then he started to steal forward. "Well m'lad, it remains for me to make your acquaintance—but without your making mine first."

He advanced, stall to stall, on silent cat-feet. The guard turned. With a start the Englishman slid out of sight. The horse into whose stall he darted stamped the turf restlessly and snorted. The man at the door continued to stare back into the stable.

Pressing breathless against the rough planking of his concealment, Cleve cursed the uneasy mount and waited. Then things
became quiet again and the guard relaxed.

There was a broken wheel-spoke at the cavalier's feet, half-
buried in the straw. He picked it up, felt the neat balance of it
with a crooked smile. He loathed using steel upon an unsuspecting man. Yet wisdom told him that he was not engaging in
an adventure which would permit the niceties of open warfare.

HE RESUMED his journey up the straw-padded center aisle.
The guard did not turn again. He didn't receive the opportunity, for upon reaching him Cleve used the wheel-spoke with
neatness and dispatch. There was a satisfying *thwock* and the
guard dropped.

Ten minutes later, the Englishman swung lithely through
an open casement on the second floor of the inn. His reasons
for thus entering were obvious. All of the tavern's lower rear
windows were shuttered; its kitchen door bolted. To risk forcing them would be to invite discovery. Therefore, Cleve had
thrust his improvised club into his sash and, gripping his rapier
buccaneer-fashion between his teeth, had cautiously ascended
the thick-stemmed ivy dressing the tavern's northern corner.

Blade held tense, he crossed to the room's single door and
eased it open a crack. The tramp of feet rewarded the effort and
he started to close the door again. He paused. The slitted view
showed him a portion of a red-rugged corridor and doors along
the opposite wall. Stepping into his line of vision appeared a pair
of hard-faced gentlemen carrying bared blades aslant on their
shoulders. Cleve paid them scant heed. His eye was focussed
upon the two prisoners. A man and a woman.

His gauntleted fingers flexed on his hilt. His heart did a peculiar little squirm. The man was le Sieur de Maupin, his froth of
lace askew at his throat, a trickle of blood seeping from a wound
in his sword arm. The woman was Mary de Sarasnac!

Cleve shifted. The hard-faced gentlemen stopped before a
door and opened it. The taller of the two ushered the captives

inside and reappeared a moment later with a key in his hand. He locked the door and nodded to his companion.

"I'll stand the first guard, Leon. Return for my relief within the hour."

Leon left quietly and silence fell over the corridor again. From his concealment Cleve measured the possibilities of jumping the remaining guard unexpectedly, but saw immediately that they were dismally slim. Ten paces separated him from the man. He'd not get two steps without being seen. Then suddenly he grinned and loosened the wheel-spoke in his sash.

Directly opposite his position beside the door stood a small corner table, a squat glass vase atop it. Shifting the rapier to his left hand, Cleve tapped the vase lightly with its tip. A melodious little chime rang through the stillness.

OUTSIDE, THE guard frowned curiously, so Cleve tapped the vase once more. This time, the lilting ring definitely interested the fellow. He left his post in front of Mary's door and approached. He was more curious than suspicious. Again the Englishman's blade struck the bowl.

Slowly the door opened. Cleve shrank against the wall and slid free his improvised baton. The guard's hatted head poked into the room.

"Won't you step into my parlor, lad?" Cleve asked and whipped the spoke in a sharp descending arc against the base of the fellow's scull. He caught the body in the crook of his left arm as it slumped forward.

Cords from the window drapes made admirable bonds, a discarded kerchief served as a gag. Upon completing the trussing of his victim, Cleve quickly located the key, flipped it cheerfully in his palm; and with a wave to the senseless man he quit the room.

It didn't take him long to break into Mary's improvised cell. A twist of the key and he was stepping smilingly into her presence. Her back was to him. Le Sieur de Maupin was sitting in a chair, suffering her administration to his wounded arm. The little fop's face was grey with pain. He was first to see Cleve and his mouth gaped in an astounded O.

The girl leaped up. The crude bandage she had been trying to apply to de Maupin's wound spiraled from her fingers.

"M. Cleve! What are you doing here?"

The English cavalier grinned cheerfully. "I could ask the same question of you, *mademoiselle*," he said. "In fact, I shall ask it. What are you and our diminutive friend doing at the Red Tassel?"

De Maupin answered tor her. His brilliant purple doublet had been torn at the shoulder so that Mary could attend the wound. It was a clean wound, not dangerous.

"*Ma foi!*" he chirped. "As you see, *monsieur*, we are being held against our wishes—that is what we are doing in this cursed place!"

THEY BOTH ignored him. Mary looked at the Englishman's naked blade and the hope which had first gleamed in her dark eyes faded away.

"You are alone, *monsieur*. The furtive manner in which you have come to us, the rapier which you hold so tensely tells me that—"

"Faith!" he interrupted. "You underrate me, Mary." He cocked an eyebrow and chuckled. "You are addressing Lord Cleve, your dashing rescuer; the hero of more tavern-brawls than you can shake a finger at; the knight who cares not for odds if only to serve your beauty." He nodded. "And you are most beautiful, you know." Then he bit his lower lip uncertainly. "Incidentally, how many rogues are there?"

"Nearly thirty," she replied.

"And a murderer," added de Maupin from his chair. "Remember, *mademoiselle*, it was after a murderer that we came to this miserable tavern."

Cleve eyed him sharply; and then turned to her. "What is he babbling about?"

Mary's face quickly tightened then. "Monsieur le Sieur de Maupin speaks of *Monsieur le docteur's* assassin," she said. "The brute whom I witnessed leaving the physician's chambers at the palace."

"I remember you spoke of him." Cleve nodded. "A large fellow with apelike arms. Is he in this place?"

"*Oui.* While M. de Maupin and I were engaged in our morning canter along the river bank early in the day, we chanced upon this churl. He was watering his mount, but when I called for him to stay, he bolted into his saddle and raced away.

"Knowing that the duke wanted to interrogate him, I urged Monsieur de Maupin to accompany me in a pursuit. We trailed the fugitive to this tavern, *monsieur,* and I foolishly insisted upon entering it."

"MAIS NON," protested de Maupin from the corner. "I very foolishly agreed. I knew that we should have sent for the soldiery! *Sacré nom,* Monsieur Cleve! We entered into a company of cutthroats and villains who laughed at *mademoiselle* when she requested their assistance to arrest the assassin. Nor would they permit us to leave. One of the ruffians laughingly seized *mademoiselle,* saying that she was a pretty wench and foully pawed her. Being a chevalier of France, *monsieur,* and her protector, I drew my blade."

Cleve stared at the wound in the speaker's arm and nodded. "And he drew his blade, eh?"

Mary bit her lip. "I screamed; and then a large fat man entered the grog-room. 'Twas his servant, Beppo, who murdered *Monsieur le docteur.* He admitted as much before sending us under guard to this room." She shook her head puzzledly. "What does it all mean, *monsieur?*"

Cleve flicked the tip of his rapier thoughtfully. "It means, my sweet, that your willfulness has dropped you willy-nilly into the center of a major conspiracy against your God-father, Duke Vincent, and France. The reason that I am at this tavern is because I suspected it as a meeting place for the plotters. From what you have told me, I was apparently right. That fat man you saw was undoubtedly Juan Castro, a Spanish agent."

Outside a hoarse shout of alarm stopped his words. Cleve stepped quickly to the window. He noted absently as he peered through it that it was barred with thick iron rods. Then he whirled. Three men had dashed past on the ground below. They were headed toward the stable.

"Quitting this place is the wisest advice in the world right now," he said. "If I am not mistaken, they have just discovered the bucko I left slumbering in the manger. Come on!"

CHAPTER XXVIII

MADEMOISELLE CANNONBALL

HE LED THE way down the dim, door-flanked corridor. The quiet of the Red Tassel was abruptly shattered now. Men called. There were shouted commands, and below the thud of many boots resounded. The discovery of the guard in the stable had acted upon the building like a stick in a bee-hive. Cleve licked his lips and smiled reassuringly over his shoulder at his charges.

Suddenly the door to his right burst open. A man, fuzzy-eyed with sleep, stepped out of it. He stared in frank disbelief at Cleve and the Englishman recognized his goateed ambusher of the night before.

Though wounded, the fellow went for a slim poniard at his belt. He began to yowl for assistance and Cleve remembered at the same moment that he still carried the wheel-spoke from the stable. He used it—used it neatly with the swift fluid grace of experience. The yowler went back to sleep and Cleve gave de Maupin the fellow's knife.

Then, gripping Mary by the arm, he started forward again. He hoped that there would be a small rear-staircase at the end of the hall—a stair which would lead down into the scullery, or some unfrequented section of the tavern's ground floor. But the yowler had given them away; and as they reached the end of the corridor to discover the staircase for which Cleve had prayed, they were met by a quartet of bravos swarming up it, sword in hand.

"La!" gasped Mary. "What next?"

Cleve didn't answer for he needed his breath. Lifting her nearly off her feet, he doubled back, racing toward the carved newel of the Inn's main staircase. Behind them, men bayed like a hunting pack. The staircase was wide. It led down to the main hall and upward to a balustraded landing at which there was a door, apparently opening into the tavern's garret. Cleve was noting this when Mary cried out in dismay.

"Richard! They've taken de Maupin!"

IT WAS true. In trying to duplicate Cleve's agile about-face, de Maupin had become hopelessly tangled in his tracks and he'd crashed forward with a yelp. As the English rakehelly turned, the four bravos were jerking him to his feet. And one of them struck the little steward in the mouth.

"Cease your squirming, little pig!"

It looked pretty hopeless. Cleve whirled again to start down the stairs, and cursed. Pounding up them from the door below came a wedge of yelling men. There were six, seven—maybe more. He hadn't the time to count.

As the first of them hit the top step, the cavalier's long blade darted out like a glinting snake's tongue and the man toggled back, a ribbon of blood streaking his chest. Cleve struck again, desperately. Another went down. Then Mary's voice, alarmed, swung him about.

"*Mon dieu!* Behind you, Richard!"

By Jupiter. They were surrounding him. She had warned in time. Three of the four bravos who had chased them were now striking for his back. Something burned a wound in his left bicep. His blade licked out in a feint, he bounded back atop the first step of the staircase. Men closed in.

"Ye gods! A one-man army!"

*In the gunpowder
room, while
the attackers
thundered at the
door, Cleve took
Mary in his arms*

His brain ceased attempting to follow his movements and he fought from pure instinct. Ten blades were knitting a pattern of steel before his eyes, and he could only sweep his own sword furiously before him. His sword-arm was beginning to grow numb, leaden.

But gradually, he realized that only five blades were danger-ous. The base of the stairs was six feet wide. The swords which licked from around its corner and over its lower bannister constituted mere threat. Thereafter, he paid no heed to them, crouching out of reach with boots planted one above the other.

"Mary! Haste! Unlatch the garret door. We're retreating!"

He heard the clack of her slippered heels as she hurried upstairs. He began to give ground slowly. The glinting tips followed. He had the weary satisfaction of taking one of his more daring adversaries in the throat before hostilities miracu-lously ceased. A deep basso thundered a heavy command.

Quite suddenly, Cleve was standing alone on the stairway, his red-tipped rapier slanting tiredly, his lungs sobbing in great gulps of dusty air. His recent enemies had withdrawn to the foot of the stairs. Somehow they reminded him of surly hounds called off just before the kill. Then a veritable paunch of a man, olive-skinned, piggy-eyed, elbowed his way between them. It was Juan Castro.

"**WELL FOUGHT,** Señor Lord Cleve," Castro said. "I bow to your excellent swordsmanship, but now I suggest that you surrender!"

A grim smile lifted the corners of the rakehelly's mouth. "Faith! And miss the fun? Don't be silly, m'lad. I am but warm-ing to my task."

The oily amiability of the other didn't alter. Yet his words were harsh, uncompromising. He said: "Had you come last night, *señor,* I might have indulged you. But now it is inconvenient. There are many things to be accomplished in Montferrat this day and I cannot waste the time."

Cleve's eyes brightened. Many things to be accomplished, eh?

Faith! And that sounded as if Castro and his unknown accomplice were getting ready to strike. He shifted his position a trifle.

"Another murder perhaps?" he hinted.

Castro inclined his head. "Perhaps," he said and gestured briefly to the stocky individual who had white-faced de Maupin by the scruff of the neck. The little fop's arms were folded tightly across his chest and he did not change their position as his brutish captor yanked him into the clearing beside the Spanish agent.

"Either you surrender your sword, Señor Cleve", Castro continued smoothly, "or your friend here surrenders his life!"

Cleve didn't doubt the sincerity of that threat. What the devil was he to answer? He glanced up at Mary standing tensely on the garret landing with her slim fingers gripped tight to the bannister. No help there. It was his decision! He turned again to Castro—that obese hog in brown and green.

"Damme! 'Tis a hard bargain you offer me, you fat louse! Perchance I consider my life more valuable to me than his."

The Spaniard conceded the point quickly. "We shall not kill any of you, señor. You shall be my guests for let us say, three days."

Cleve's mind was racing. Without doubt Castro expected his plans to be accomplished in three days. It probably meant that Montferrat would be a Spanish protectorate.

He bit his lip. Compromise! Gad's teeth! He had never compromised a decision in his life! And he had decided to help Guy keep this duchy French. Yet with the situation so hopeless, what else was there to do?

And then little de Maupin decided the business. His thickset captor had relaxed vigilance a trifle and the fop made use of it. His folded arms suddenly flew apart. In the fist of one, glittered the poniard Cleve had given him. De Maupin had craftily kept it hidden until now.

It flashed in a murderous arc, plunging deep into the muscular neck of his captor. The man tried to scream and the bubbly sound of it was ghastly. De Maupin wrenched free of the dying fingers; scurried through the center of the swordsmen like a frightened rabbit. He bounded down the stairs.

"Hold them, *monsieur!*" he shrilled. "I fly for *le colonel* and aid! Stand your ground!"

FOR A moment the men in the corridor below seemed frozen into a tableau of astonishment and incredulity. It was Cleve who broke the spell. The decision had been made! He heard the slam of the door as de Maupin raced through the tavern's front, then the fading pound of horses hoofs. New vigor poured into him and he laughed.

"Shall we continue, Castro?"

Castro hesitated a moment; and then his basso boomed two commands. He pointed down the staircase toward the inn's main hall and roared: "After him! Those who remain, cut that fool on the stairs to ribbons!" Then with a curse he walked away.

Men boiled up the staircase. Cleve set his blade to take them, but a bouncing clatter on the steps behind caused him to dart a glance over his shoulder. There, thundering down the stairs with increasing momentum, came a large gray-black cannonball!

Cleve scrambled aside. The thing bounded past his booted ankle, cracking the stair-board in passing, and took off chest-high. It crashed into the center of his advancing attackers. A swath was cut through them. Then above the howls of rage and dismay, Mary's clear voice rang out.

"Retreat quickly, Richard! I have three more prepared!"

"My faith! What a girl!"

He reached her side and toed one of the cannonballs she had set on the ledge of the landing. It started its thumping, crashing descent.

But the men on the staircase had taken warning. They were ready for this one and veered to permit its careening passage. While thus watching it thunder by, they were struck by the ball which Mary had released a split-second after Cleve's.

Chaos! Men went down like ten-pins, tumbling over one another, yelling and groaning with pain. A fourth ball was not necessary. The staircase leading to the garret was clear of enemy.

"A neat game of bowls, Mary," Cleve panted.

The girl didn't smile. Her fine features were suddenly drawn; she stood beside him for a moment, staring; and then with a choked sob she buried her face in his shoulder.

The cavalier felt the trembling of her close in his arms and shook his head in wonderment.

"Come now, m'darling. 'Tis no way for a heroine to behave."

Her voice came muffled to his ear. "That last ball killed a man. I'm certain it killed him. I—I have never killed anyone before. It's horrible."

Then from the corridor below came a smart report and a shower of splinters burst from the railing. With an oath Cleve thrust her behind him, for he knew what it meant. Muskets! A glance down the stairs verified the assumption. Three men were standing safely to one side of the newel, aiming their cumbersome pieces. Cleve heard the vicious slap of another ball striking the wall behind him.

"Damme! There'll be no more bowling today, lass."

He pushed her through the iron-studded oaken door. As he rammed home the three door-bolts from the inside, he heard the pound of boots charging up the staircase. He wiped the sweat from his forehead and tried to shake his fatigue.

"It will hold them for a while," he said with an eye to the door's solidness. "Long enough for de Maupin to return with aid."

"If you place this rack of cannonballs against it," Mary suggested from beside him, "it should better reïnforce it. La! With all of the kegs and boxes I see about, we could build a veritable fort."

Cleve turned. What the girl said was true. The garret of the Red Tassel was crammed with kegs, rough wooden chests and crates. He whistled. Behind him the door began to throb under the blows of shoulders. He ignored it. This great unfinished chamber with its sloped walls and naked roof-beams demanded a complete inspection. As in the case of the house behind the Golden Crowns, it was a secret arsenal.

CHAPTER XXIX

SEÑOR SPY

"**DAMME, LASS! A** cozy nest, isn't it?" he said. He glanced over his shoulder to grin at her.

"What do you mean, *monsieur?*"

Cleve selected a small keg, kicked in its head and scooped a handful of gunpowder out of it. He poured it into her cupped palms. Mary trickled the black grains through her fingers and stared at him. The door shivered under shocks as more shoulders were brought into play.

"Musket powder, Richard! *Mon dieu!* There is sufficient here to supply an army."

"I believe that is the reason for it." He nodded and looked around.

Because the Red Tassel was built upon the principle of a thick-based U, its attic followed a similar pattern. There were no partitions in it. He could see both ends of its case-packed ells. The thudding oaken door through which they had just passed was the chamber's only entrance. A series of gables along each wing furnished light, and dimly revealed the rough brick of two great chimney shafts. Cleve shook his head. Mary's voice came to him.

"And is its purpose to supply an army, Richard?"

"I think so. Either that, or to arm the peasantry. Come to consider it, the peasantry seems more likely." He placed his rapier thoughtfully on a chest of muskets. "Castro and another person are brewing a big pot of trouble."

"But who is the Spaniard's confederate?"

He chuckled. "If I could tell you that, I would not have bothered coming here."

Then he eyed the ball-rack beside the door. He knew better than to attempt moving it while the weight of thirty cannonballs lined its grooved shelves, so he began to take the balls down.

Mary bent to help him. She struggled to lower a particularly large ball from the rack. He took it from her as the door vibrated anew beneath the slam of musket-butts.

"Damme," he chuckled. "That is typical of you. Ever attempting something beyond your strength."

"You think so, *monsieur?*" she snapped stiffly.

He nodded and pushed the heavy rack in front of the door. "I think so." He fell to replacing the cannonballs he had removed. "I don't know what you were doing on the road to Jussey, m'lass, but whatever it was, it had run a trifle beyond your control, hadn't it? There was a charming fellow chasing you with intent to kill!"

Her eyes widened. "How did you know that?"

Again the door shuddered from a concerted attack, but held. Cleve paid no heed to it.

"Because he mistook you for me. Not very complimentary to either of us, I'd say. I had a bit of trouble with him which finally resulted in his giving his sword to me and his soul to God."

"So that is how you came into possession of that rubied rapier, Richard?"

Cleve slipped the last ball into position and nodded. He began to roll powder-kegs in front of the rack. "I'm more interested in learning how you came into possession of the knowledge that Mazo Gardier was going to assassinate Duke Vincent," he said.

The door rattled against the heavy ball-rack as the men outside hurled themselves at it *en masse*. She eyed the door nervously. "It is too long a tale for the present, Richard."

THE CAVALIER stepped back a pace and viewed his work.

With the heavy cannonball rack solidly in front of the door and a line of powder-kegs beginning to brace it, the buttress was assuming encouraging proportions.

"Faith, we have little else to do. The door will hold sufficiently long for you to tell the story. Frankly I'm curious about our highway meeting. In fact, I'm curious about many things. What were you doing in Paris when the Kitten first saw you?"

"Delivering a message from my god-father to *Monseigneur le Cardinal*," she told him and attempted to aid as he began to roll more powder-kegs into position.

He took her firmly by the elbows and sat her upon a thick bundle of halbard shafts. "I'll attend to the fortification," he declared. "You sit and talk."

"La! But this is so weird, Richard. We are trapped in a garret which has great stores of musket powder. Outside men are athirst for our lives. Yet you want me to recite past history."

"You were delivering a message from Vincent to Richelieu," he reminded her. "Why weren't the duke's couriers used?"

She shrugged. "I should think you would have deduced the reason, *mon ami*. My god-father could no longer trust anyone. So alive with unseen treason had Montferrat become, that the usual couriers were out of the question."

"Therefore, you were entrusted with the mission, eh? Faith! It must have been very important for Vincent to risk so beautiful a messenger."

She laughed at that. "Very important *monsieur*. A request for the services of you and Monsieur le Comte d'Entreville. Your fame had reached the duke's notice and he decided that if any two men could root out Montferrat's traitors, you were the ones."

Cleve grunted beneath the weight of a box of grape-shot. "Faith! A dubious compliment. Places the Kitten and myself in the category of snoopers."

THE ASSAULT on the door was diminishing, but neither of them noticed it. Cleve continued to pile kegs and cases while she talked. Finally he asked: "What of Mazo Gardier?"

She shrugged. "I put up at the same tavern in which he was staying. It was upon my return journey. Speed was essential. I was garbed in men's clothing and rode a fast horse rather than a coach. Old Gaston, Duke Vincent's faithful valet, was my companion and protector." She bit her lip tightly. "Gardier killed Gaston while I made my escape."

"Now hold a moment, my lady. Escape?"

Mary nodded. "I overheard Mazo Gardier bragging to another man that he had been hired to assassinate Duke Vincent. It was quite accidental. Gardier was drunk and I chanced to overhear his remark as Old Gaston was escorting me down the darkened corridor to my quarters. The door to his room was slightly ajar and curiosity prompted us to eavesdrop."

"And you were caught?"

"Mais oui. Gaston sneezed. The door flew open and we turned and fled blindly. Gaston was not as swift as I." She hesitated for a moment, reliving the scene; and then shrugged. "Gaston told me to go on. 'Warn His Highness, Mary. Warn His Highness!'

"I ran as I have never run before, Richard." She smiled. "And with your help I escaped."

Cleve grinned, then swung suddenly to the iron-studded door. The battering had ceased. Uneasy silence had set in.

With a frown he picked up his blade and drew near. Even with the door barricaded by a weighty rack of cannonballs, a heavy case of muskets and fifteen or sixteen powder-kegs, he somehow felt less secure now than when the men had been hammering against its outer panels.

He stood there, tense, listening before finally relaxing with a shrug. "Those lads are up to something," he stated.

She replied with attempted flippancy. "La! Don't be ridiculous. Monsieur Castro has undoubtedly resigned himself to capture. M. de Maupin and the forces of the duke should soon arrive, and Castro is probably downstairs in chamber preparing a plea for leniency."

He smiled at her, wishing it were true. There was something

about the way she kept self-contained in the face of imminent peril which appealed to him.

"I believe I'll make a tour about this nest," he said abruptly. "Will you be kind enough to inform me if we have callers?"

She stood up and made a curtsey. *"Oui,* m'Lord," she agreed. "Delighted."

He was aware, as he returned her gesture with a grave bow, that the sight of her standing there with her dark hair in disarray and her red lips smiling sent a curious pain through him. By Gad! The girl was dangerous!

As he threaded his way through the stacked munitions of the garreet's north-west arm, the Englishman found himself pondering the possibilities of a low rambling country house in Wykeham and a lithe, dark eyed wife to go with it. He grinned wryly at himself. Faith! That would be taking roots with a vengeance!

HE BENT to peer through the dirty pane of a window in the inner gable-niche of the wing. The sight of five heavy drays in the courtyard creased a frown in his brow. Five peasants, under the direction of a cape-swirling gentleman, were loading powder-kegs into one of them. They were covering the loaded kegs with straw.

Castro, apparently, was about to bring his plot to a climax.

Cleve completed inspection of each window. Although he hadn't mentioned it to Mary, he had been worried over the possibility of Juan Castro using long ladders to storm the garret. But the rest of the area outside the building was deserted and he felt better. Four ladders canted up to the garret from four sides, with armed men climbing simultaneously, would be a devilish problem to combat.

He started to return to Mary and their barricade, but the dull glint of two squat little carronades nestling beside the brick of a sooty chimney shaft deterred him. The wide-mouthed cannon would make weighty additions to the barricade, further insuring security. He bent to inspect them and in the doing accidentally banged the heavy hilt of his rapier against the chimney. A slab of brittle stone shattered itself on the breech of one of the carronades. Cleve stared at the wide chimney thoughtfully.

The heat of many fires had cracked gaping seams in it. The English gallant forgot about the carronades and began to tap lightly against the lip of the largest seam as Mary approached.

"Richard," she said tensely, "Castro is outside and he has an ultimatum. You had best speak with him."

Cleve stood up. He pointed to the crack. "See how much mortar you can gouge out of it, m'dear. It may mean our lives. I'll interview friend Castro and see what he wants."

CHAPTER XXX

SURRENDER OR DIE

CLEVE PAUSED BEFORE the pile of powder-kegs. He could see that she had been attempting to abet his improvised buttress by managing to work a box of grape-shot into the uppermost vacant shelf of the ball-rack. He grinned. And then he sobered. From the other side of the door came the scrape of feet, the murmurings of voices.

He went to one side; pressed an ear to the door-jamb below the heavy upper hinges. Juan Castro was talking.

"He's taken the lives of two already and the wench with her cannon-ball has crippled three more. No, Brisson, that English rakehelly has the sting of death in his sword-tip and I do not propose to lose more men on it. Not unless absolutely necessary. We'll talk first; and then, if he is stubborn—"

Cleve tapped lightly with his swordhilt. Even as he did so, his brain was fumbling to place that name. Brisson. Where had he heard it before? Then he said: "Start talking, Castro. You have no idea how stubborn I can be."

There was a pause from the other side of the door; and then

the Spaniard spoke smoothly. "I have little to say to you, Señor Lord Cleve. You have tried my patience severely, but we can forgive that if you become sensible now."

The Englishman eased one foot atop a keg of musket-powder and rested his blade across his knee. He smiled.

"Damned nice of you, fatty. And of what does becoming sensible consist of?"

"Of immediate surrender, *señor. Por Dios!* I admire you, Richard Cleve, thus I am offering you the life of the duke's ward and your own."

Cleve laughed. "Damme! I admire you, too, in a horrified sort of way. But I fear we are fast arriving nowhere, Castro. I have this door well barricaded and in but a short time the duke's men will arrive. Faith! The shoe is really on the other foot. I believe Mademoiselle de Sarasnac and I will give you ten minutes to disarm your men."

"Dios arriba! What impudence!"

Cleve chuckled and finger-combed his chestnut hair with his free hand. A stiffening pain in his arm reminded him of the wound in his bicep.

"On second consideration," he said, "I think we'll make that five minutes. The little messenger whom you allowed to escape should be in Casale by now. The soldiery may be well on its way."

Choked gasps rewarded this announcement. His voice husky with restrained hilarity, Castro finally said: "Ah. So that is the reason for your complacence, *señor?* The little man who rode away to the palace!" His voice rolled in a deep chuckle. "The little man who was going to fetch the aid of Colonel de Boussey. *Por Dios!* You will pardon my unseemly laughter, Señor Cleve. It is very comical."

CLEVE'S FOOT came down from its keg-rest with a thud. He didn't like the sound of that. There must be a sinister significance to Castro's amusement—a dangerous significance. But he kept his voice even.

"Very comical from my point of view," he accorded. "Your

arrest and the imprisonment of your hirelings should prove funny. Well, what is your decision?"

He could hear the harsh jarring laughter of the other men outside on the landing. Howls of merriment and exclamations. He bit his lip uncertainly. Finally, the hilarity subsided and Castro's voice came to him.

"Santa Maria! Who do you think has been looting the wage-wagons from France these many weeks, *señor?*"

Cleve suddenly had a terrible sinking suspicion, but he hopefully answered: "You of course, my fine fat rascal."

"Ah no, *señor.* 'Tis true I have directed the raids, but I did not do so without first receiving orders. I assure you that I am not the true leader of the intrigue. I am but a partner in it—a silent partner, working in the interests of His Majesty, Philip of Spain.

"Consider a moment, *amigo.* Could I have known when the gold shipments of France were due; where they would enter the duchy? Of course not. But Colonel de Boussey could know, couldn't he?"

And then Cleve really felt sick. He leaned against the wall and cursed himself for a fool. How could he have been so utterly, so completely blind! The big blond colonel had had both the position and opportunity for this treason.

"*Si, señor!* Colonel de Boussey! He is the leader of this clever enterprise, not I! For weeks he has been laying the foundation for a successful *coup d'état. Monseigneur le Cardinal* made a large mistake when he sent the colonel to Montferrat. De Boussey did not like having to leave Paris and the many opportunities of court life. He is very ambitious, *señor.*

"So, with Spain's help through me, he is about to realize his ambition. He will be a duke within the next two weeks." Here the speaker roared with laughter. "And you were depending upon him for aid. *Por Dios!* It is like sending to Satan for absolution!"

Cleve shook his head as though recovering from a blow. But he didn't give up. De Maupin might, on a slim chance, first communicate with Vincent. "Your prisoner did get away, didn't he, fatty?"

"*Si.* He escaped. But what good will it do? For De Boussey will take care of him when he arrives at the palace. With this day to start the culmination of our weeks of preparation, the colonel will be unusually alert." Once more Castro's heavy mirth jarred against the Englishman's ears. "Ah, *señor*—basing your hopes upon Colonel de Boussey! What a delicious jest!"

IT WAS funny, true enough! Tragically funny! Cleve found the bitter taste of humiliation in his throat as his mind slowly picked up the past and revealed to him its now painfully obvious secrets. He should have guessed the connection between de Boussey and the conspiracy long ago. The very first night should have put him more firmly on guard.

The question of how the colonel had learned that he and Guy were in Casale when no one else knew was now perfectly clear. That note of Castro's, found in the house behind the Golden Crowns, explained everything. De Boussey had received that message; he had sent that musket ball into their room. Without doubt, one of his henchmen had trailed Cleve earlier and had arranged for those troopers in the square to attempt riding him down.

On the other side of the door Castro continued his revelations with apparent relish. The spy seemed to be enjoying it.

"We have brought this duchy to a pretty boil, the Colonel and I. Garrison desertions, heavy taxes, an unsettled populace. *Si!* A pretty boil indeed. Why do you suppose, *señor,* that we have planted hatred of Henri in the minds of the people?"

Cleve took a deep breath. The more Castro talked, the more lucid everything became. So they had deliberately arranged for Henri's unpopularity, eh? He saw now why de Boussey had committed the apparently mad act of sending the riders of Henri's personal guard into the mob outside the palace gates. Naturally the people hadn't blamed de Boussey. They had blamed Henri. And Catherine's murder! By Gad! That had been a ruthless master-stroke.

He lifted his voice. "Damme, while we are on the subject, fatty, suppose you tell me which one of you murdered Mademoiselle Cordoba?"

The spy's oily chuckle rumbled through the partition. "Ah, you are very clever, Cleve. The colonel himself did that. It was part of the policy. First he caused Henri to drink himself senseless at a secret party; and then—"

Cleve interrupted him. "I know the rest of it. A neat set of rogues, aren't you? But why was it necessary?"

"To instill hatred in the minds of Henri's future subjects, of course. *Dios!* Do you not yet see the point of these stratagems, *señor?*"

"I'm beginning to," the English cavalier admitted. "The colonel intends to put Duke Vincent out of the way, of course," he added.

From the other side of the door Castro laughed. "Ah. Again you prove your astuteness, *señor*. This very afternoon he shall arrange so that the Duke of Montferrat unfortunately dies. It will be poison of course, but he shall see that it is called heart-failure.

"Henri will then be installed as the new duke. But as you have undoubtedly guessed, *señor*, Henri will not reign long. The people hate him too much. There will be a spontaneous rebellion—a rebellion led by Señor de Boussey in person. That is why we have collected these stores of munitions. Even now our men are carting them to various points for distribution."

"IN OTHER words, the colonel plans to usurp the throne of Montferrat with money looted from the wage-wagons sent from France," Cleve said coldly.

"*Si*, Señor Cleve. Precisely. A rebellion against the French, bought with money from the French! But it grows even more comical when I tell you that these munitions have been bought from the Spanish in Piedmont. Santa Maria! I can picture

Richelieu tearing out his hair by the fistful when he learns of the true facts."

"So can I," Cleve admitted. "After de Boussey is in the saddle, your government will recognize him as the legal Duke of Montferrat, eh Castro?"

"*Si*. You have a ready grasp of political affairs, Señor Cleve. My king is not yet ready for an open rupture with the French. Therefore, Spain has no official knowledge of what Colonel de Boussey is accomplishing."

De Boussey was truly the sole author of the intrigue, acting of course with tacit Spanish endorsement. First the colonel had raided the wage-wagons to gain a war-chest; then he had purchased arms from the Spanish in Piedmont—no legal cause for war; and next he had weakened Montferrat by use of hired rabble-rousers and saboteurs. It was simple. It was perfect.

The other threads of the plot were equally clear now. Montferrat was easier to defend than to attack, and with Spanish aid it would be impregnable. As for last night's ambush against d'Entreville and himself, the English rakehelly knew now its author. Undoubtedly de Boussey had become uneasy because of their deductions regarding the Despartes murder. Here Castro's rumbling tones interrupted Cleve's train of thought.

"And now, *señor*, you have complete knowledge of the scope of this affair. Frankly, it is only to impress you with the hopelessness of your position that I have wasted this time in its explanation. Let us be realistic about it. I do not desire to lose any more of my men. You do not desire to lose your life, or the life of your charming companion, Mademoiselle de Sarasnac."

CLEVE SHIFTED. He recognized a certain amount of logic in that. Castro, after all, was essentially interested in procuring the powder stores in the garret, for if Duke Vincent was to be poisoned this afternoon, the arms were going to be needed.

"What if I decide to fight it out anyway, Castro?"

The other's voice came flatly: "I shan't quibble any longer, *señor*. Either you surrender, or I shall have my men batter down the door with the tree-trunk which has just been brought up from outside. And then for your stupid resistance, both you and Mademoiselle de Sarasnac shall be put to the sword! I am in deadly seriousness, Cleve."

There could be no doubt of that. Catherine Cordoba's murder proved the cold inhumanity of these men. But the Englishman needed time and decided to gamble for it on bluff.

"Very well, fatty. Batter away! But before you commence using that tree-trunk, I believe you should know one thing. I have twenty-odd open kegs of powder stacked against the door and atop them I have placed a lighted candle. The first jar from the outside will cause the candle to topple into an open keg. We'll all go up in a blast of glory, m'lad! Now tell your men to start the business."

Breathless silence greeted this announcement. Cleve bent forward tensely to learn how his bold-faced lie was affecting them. Finally Castro laughed.

"My friend, I don't believe you. But being a paragon of patience, I shall give you fifteen minutes to think it over. Fifteen minutes, Lord Cleve, to consider saving your life and the life of your lady."

Cleve sighed relievedly and turned away.

CHAPTER XXXI

THE MALEVOLENT MUTE

MARY WAS WAITING by the chimney. Her face was very white, her fingers grimy with soot and powdered mortar. She had been scraping at the crack in the chimney-front with a metal-edged quoin from one of the carronades and the seam was nearly a half-inch wide now, zig-zagging across the rough stone facade. Cleve picked up a heavy-handled demi-pike from a litter of arms on the floor and bent beside her.

"Did you hear friend Castro's conversation, lass?"

She nodded, lips pale. "*Oui.* Everything. It is incredible, yet you did right in refusing to surrender. I much prefer to be blown to bits if I can partially destroy their plots. That monster de Boussey—"

Here he interrupted her. It was a crazy thing to do. He was never completely able to describe the impulse prompting it. Suddenly he turned her face to his and kissed her full on the lips.

How long it lasted wasn't important. But the fact that she returned it was. He could feel the eagerness of her soft lips and of her arms about his neck. At last they parted, surprised, shaken by emotion. His gloved fingers pressed tight to her shoulders.

"We are not going to be blown to bits, Mary. We are not going to die!"

She regarded him, uncomprehending. He unfolded the mad plan which had been looming in his mind since first noticing the crumbly condition of the chimney. Mad! But it had to work now!

"We'll knock a hole in this," he explained, indicating the shaft. "It should lead down to some open hearth below, and God willing we might be able to escape."

"*Mais oui,* Richard." Her eyes were beginning to sparkle with renewed hope. "But will we have time?"

He nodded. "Think so. The chimney stones are very loose in their beds. It shouldn't take longer than five minutes. Faith! And if we work clear, Mary," he smiled suddenly, "remind me to speak of a certain rambling country-house in Wykeham, England."

His estimate was uncannily accurate. Well within five minutes. The heavy demi-pike in Cleve's strong grip worked miracles. He used it as a lever in the cracks she had cleaned; prying free obstinate slabs of mortar-crusted stone. Mary pushed aside the rubble.

The chimney was old, brittle and heat-cracked. In very little time Cleve had jerked, pried and hammered a gaping hole in it large enough for them to climb through.

Mary fetched a rope from the base of one of the carronades.

He looped it quickly about a jutting roof-beam, and then with its length trailing into the black maw of the chimney-shaft, he turned to her.

"I'll need your prayers, lass." And then he held her close. "Frightened?"

She essayed a white smile. "La! I have been petrified with fear since arriving here. A little soot will not lessen or increase it. But, Richard—" She bit her lip to keep it steady. "Richard, do be careful. I—I desire to hear more about that rambling country-house in England. Much more."

He kissed her for that.

THE CHIMNEY shaft was very wide, very black, very dirty. Cleve lowered himself cautiously, biting his lip against the pain in his left arm. He must have re-opened the wound in it. He could feel the warmth of fresh blood in his sleeve.

Then he looked down. The dimly lit shaft furnished two wide hearths, back to back. He reached the wall-top separating them and paused to take stock.

The hearth below on the left carried the feathering smoke-wisps of a dying fire. His rope was trailing in it. Resting his shoulder against the side of the sooty shaft, he quickly hoisted the charred hemp and dropped it down the cold shaft to his right. Then he kicked free of his perch and descended.

He landed quickly and crouched low in order to see into the room he had thus entered. It was a question who was the more astonished: Cleve, or the bald-pated worthy into whose face he gaped. The fellow was standing alone in the center of a lavishly furnished chamber, a cleaning rag poised over a great mahogany desk, an expression of complete incredulity widening his eyes. They were mud-colored eyes, dull, lacking intelligence.

Cleve acted first. He scrambled out of the ashy hearth and straightened. Soot-grimed, with his sweat-streaked doublet torn and with blood crusting its shoulder, the English rakehelly presented a wild appearance. He grinned uncertainly and said the first thing that entered his head.

"Just dropped in to wish you a very good day, sir. Alone, I trust."

Then the other dropped his cleaning rag and went for his poniard. He made gurgly animal noises as he did so. He was a mute. The murderous looking blade glinted free of its sheath and action picked up immediately.

Cleve evaded the first rush by more good fortune than good management. The mute came at him with a sudden grimace, slashing savagely. Cleve dodged it by leaping sideways. He felt a little sick. Of all times to grow absent-minded, this was the most inconvenient! He had left his rapier lying on the garret-floor beside the ragged aperture in the chimney-shaft.

"Hold a moment, bucko!" he gasped. "Let's talk this over."

It was apparently the wrong thing to say. His enemy must have been sensitive about being mute, for he charged again with increased ferocity. The poniard drove toward the cavalier's stomach. Cleve gave a choked gasp and tried to leap sideways again. But this time his boot-heels caught in the rumpled hearth-rug and he pitched heavily to the floor.

"Ugh!" grunted the mute triumphantly and swooped over him.

The prostrate gallant drew up his knees. Suddenly he felt the cold knob of one of the hearth's heavy andirons beneath the fingers of one outstretched hand. He swung it desperately at the mute's shining pate. There was an ugly sound like a hammer crushing through a rotten melon and the mute toppled across his body.

SLOWLY CLEVE eased the fellow away. He just lay there for a moment, entirely lacking the energy to stand. All of the frenzied action of the past two hours seemed suddenly to weight his body with fatigue. His shoulder ached; his legs felt leaden; his brain felt incapable of any more thought.

There was a decanter of wine on the great mahogany desk. With a groan the Englishman staggered to his feet and crossed to it. He gulped half its contents before lowering the gaudy flask to inspect his surrounding. The wine had the kick of an over-loaded musket and it shocked his senses alive again.

The mute was dead. The andiron had crushed his skull like an egg-shell. Cleve rolled the corpse to one side and jerked lightly on the rope leading upward into the chimney. It was the signal he had arranged with Mary for her descent. Then he crossed lightly to the large double-doors on the far side of the chamber and locked them. He stood there, listening to the shuffle of feet outside in the corridor while he finished the rest of the wine.

He started to cross to the sun-framed bay-window opposite the desk but paused suddenly. Something in the leathern trash-hamper beside it attracted his attention. Atop the balled conglomeration of discarded papers were two short lengths of gold-edged ribbon. He picked them up with a soft curse and fingered them thoughtfully. He had seen their counterparts many times before in the somber confines of Whitehall. They were used by the diplomatic servants of the English Crown to bind the official decrees and dispatches of the king's ambassadors abroad. Finding them here could only mean one thing—Sir Harry Winthrop's dispatch case.

"Damme," the rakehelly exclaimed. "I do believe I have stumbled into Castro's private quarters!"

Then he went to work. The first drawer he opened contained a number of unintelligible documents couched in Spanish, but in the second he found the case. It lay amid a clutter of papers, half-hidden, with the embossed crest of England smiling invitingly up at him. Cleve yanked open the top of his doublet and stuffed the flexible leather case inside.

A whispered noise behind caused Cleve to turn. It was Mary, her velvet dress smudged with soot, her dark eyes smiling at him in relief. The Englishman chuckled. With a black streak across the bridge of her piquant nose, her dark hair unbraided, her hands filthy, she looked little like the grand lady he had seen at the palace. Yet she was adorable. With ludicrous ingenuity she had thrust his rapier like a great pin through her skirt near the hip. Now she drew it forth and extended it.

"You forgot this, Richard."

He accepted the blade gravely and thrust it through his sash.

"We haven't much time, Richard. I overheard—" And then she saw the body beside the hearth and recoiled with a gasp.

"Tripped while we were playing," Cleve told her. "What kept you so long, m'sweet? I was becoming worried."

Mary pulled her gaze from the dead man with difficulty. Her voice was shaky. "That man. He is Castro's servant, Richard. He is the man who killed *monsieur le médecin*."

"Then I've saved Montferrat the price of a hanging," he said and led her quickly away.

CHAPTER XXXII

THE VANISHING INN

CLEVE MADE HER sit on the window-seat while he went in search of something with which to make a rope. As he lifted his arms to jerk down the heavy velvet drapes across one of the windows, she called to him softly.

"A rope won't be necessary, Richard. There is a wagon piled with hay directly below me and I can see no men about."

He left the drapes and approached. The wagon was there, true enough, squatting on the rough gray gravel of the little alleyway leading to the stables. Apparently its contents had been partially used to furnish camouflage for the powder-bearing drays in the front court. Cleve opened the wide casement and stared back along the length of the alley. It was deserted. But what pleased him most was the sight of four horses hitched to a temporary rack near the rear corner of the building.

"Faith! A soft landing to you, Mary," he said as he lifted her. "And let us hope that there is nothing in that hay to do us injury."

Then they stood on the windowsill for a moment, gripping each other's hand, steeling themselves for the leap. Cleve squeezed her fingers reassuringly. He held his sword away from his body to prevent its breaking when they landed.

"Ready?"

The girl nodded silently. They leaped and struck the hay a second later, piling waist-deep into its crackling yellow strands. Mary was first to recover.

"Ma foi! It was fun, Richard. La! Fear and fun oft-times go together, don't they?"

He didn't answer. The hay's dry smell had tickled his nostrils and he was forced to clamp hurried fingers over his nose to prevent sneezing.

They scrambled down from the wagon, standing behind it for a moment to listen. No shout of discovery shattered the stillness and they both breathed again.

"Wait here in the wagon's concealment," he ordered quietly. "I'll return with a horse."

It wasn't much of a trick to steal furtively along the side of the tavern, bent low to avoid being seen from the inn's lower windows. But Cleve found his nerves singing under the strain. The sound of conversation and activity seeped through the wall beside his ear to warn him of the number of men astir inside. He gripped his rapier and hurried on.

Then he was at the corner, untying the nearest horse with deft fingers. As the reins finally slid free of the hitching-rack, Cleve darted a glance over the horse's back, half-expecting to see men pouring around the corner.

But the alleyway was still empty. Cleve was able to mount; then to canter cautiously to the haycart and swing Mary de Sarasnac across the pommel of his saddle before two men suddenly issued from around the front corner of the building. They stared incredulously. And then a shout went up. But Cleve and Mary were already dashing past; galloping madly toward the main highway and freedom.

UPSTAIRS, JUAN CASTRO heard the shout but he paid no heed to it. He was intent upon the garret door and the heavy tree-trunk which his men were lifting. There was not much room on the landing, and the fat Spanish spy was forced to stand close to the wall.

He looked thoughtfully at the iron-laced partition and bit his lip. The grace of fifteen minutes he had granted was up. Now it was time for action.

"Señor Lord Cleve!" he shouted. "Señor Cleve! Do you surrender, or do you die?"

Silence answered him. Castro's small eyes began to glitter. Below he heard the slam of the front door and the sound of somebody racing up the stairs. He repeated the question again before signaling his men to begin their work.

"Excellency," one protested weakly. "The man inside spoke of a candle atop a powder-keg. If we jar it, we shall all be killed."

Somebody below was yelling up to Castro. But the Spaniard ignored it.

"Madre de Dios!" he snapped. "The English are not the sort to commit suicide. Now obey! Crash in that door!"

More frightened than assured, the men tightened their grip on the heavy timber. They lifted its butt and swung it without much enthusiasm. A tiny crack appeared in the door and Castro frowned. He opened his mouth to curse them—and then it happened. The whole world seemed to explode.

The blast lifted the roof of the Red Tassel. It blew out its sides. It flattened its floors. It all but wiped the great tavern from the face of the earth. With it went the life of Señor Juan Enrico Luis Maria Castro.

And from their position atop a small hill a half-mile distant, Cleve and Mary heard the sullen rumbling roar of the great explosion and turned, startled. Cleve pulled the horse to a stop.

"Now what in the devil caused that?" he wanted to know as he stared incredulously at the Red Tassel now partially obscured by billows of flame-pierced smoke that spiralled high into the sky. "Who set that off?"

For a moment, too, Mary was held silent by the grim spectacle of flaming wreckage; then she placed her head against his shoulder.

"The candle, of course," she replied. "You forgot to set it atop the kegs. I was forced to attend to it. *Ma foi,* Richard, you are becoming most forgetful. First your rapier and then the powder-trap." She snuggled closer. "And now that it is over, I feel suddenly faint. Keep your support on me, please."

But Cleve could only gulp and continue to stare back at the settling fiery ruin of what had once been the Red Tassel Tavern. The threat he had made to Castro had been pure bluff and he had never considered the possibility of her not knowing it.

Ye Gods! What if the Spaniard had not waited the promised fifteen minutes? What if the candle she had planted had melted sideways? What if it had dropped a spark?

"Damme, Mary," he said. "I'll flip you a coin to see which of us faints first."

IT WAS well past high noon. Guy d'Entreville stood on an empty wine cask, staring through the barred arch of the cellar window, and frowned. From the shadows on the Old River Chalet's ruined garden he knew that almost three hours had elapsed since he had been cast into this musty prison.

With a puzzled curse the French rakehelly stepped down from his perch. Where was Colonel de Boussey and his raiding party? What had gone amiss? He stood staring.

The cellar had once been a combination store-room and wine-cellar. Half of it was lined with rotting casks and bottle-shelves. It was the sight of these that again caused Guy to smile briefly.

Antone possessed more animal cunning than thinking intelligence. He had thrown a bound man into a unused wine-cellar— a cellar littered with broken bottles. It had taken Guy precisely twenty minutes to cut free of the ropes on his ankles and wrists.

But he was still a prisoner. The door to the cellar was made of stout wood. A guard was posted on its other side, so Guy had worked for nearly two hours on the corroded iron bars of the cellar's crescent-shaped window. Hours of wasted effort. The bars were solidly set in stone. Guy had been forced to quit his attack on them. It was no use. He stood for a moment, the sweat of his labor streaming down his back between his skin and his shirt, while he sought other means. And then a rattle from the door warned that he was about to have a visitor.

The Frenchman scooped up a bottle he had previously selected. He went quickly to where the remnants of his bonds were coiled, by the foot of the stairs, and managed to wrap them loosely around his ankles before the door opened.

His caller was a big man and alone. One of the two who had cast the cavalier into the cellar. He came stumping down the steps with a leer on his bearded countenance and his dirty thumbs hooked in his weapon-loaded sash. Guy regarded him.

"Well my fine bird," the man said, "you have rested long enough. The leader has invented a new game for you to play and I have been sent to fetch you. A moment and I'll loose the ropes about your ankles. You are too heavy to carry."

The speaker laughed and bent down. Guy straightened. He had been lying on his back with his hands behind him, clutched to the bottle. Then the heavy-based wine-flask flashed briefly and it was no trick at all to handle the bravo after it landed.

The Frenchman took the knife and the two great horse-pistols which he found in the man's ragged sash and stood for a moment, listening. One thing he had learned from his stay in the wine-cellar was the fact that Antone's band was not nearly as large as de Boussey or local reports would have him believe. *Sandiou!* Not more than ten men. Ten men with four of them posted in the forest surrounding the house made the odds against him a trifle less serious. Besides he would have the advantage of surprise and two horse-pistols.

"*Ventre saint gris!*" he muttered. "I believe I shall invent a new game for them to play, myself!"

CHAPTER XXXIII

MESSIEURS MAGNIFICENT

LE VICOMTE DE BOUSSEY was in excellent spirits. He paced grandly over to the gold framed mirror on the rear wall of the duke's private reception chamber and smiled at himself. He even posed a little, assuming various attitudes that might befit the future ruler of Montferrat. He was waiting for Duke Vincent to join him.

There was good reason for his high humor. His intrigue was completed. It remained for him to spring the trap which would topple a kingdom into his hands. But more than that, he had received news not an hour past that Castro had cornered Richard Cleve in the garret of the Red Tassel. *Corbac!* It was fine!

De Maupin had brought the information. De Boussey had expressed appreciation by having Orlando cast the little fop into a cell, out of harm's way and out of Duke Vincent's hearing.

"And with Guy d'Entreville vainly waiting for my aid amid Antone's cutthroats," the colonel chuckled, "I do believe that the danger from those two has at last been eliminated."

The Venetian clock on the mantel chimed two softly. Time was wasting. The huge blond *commandant* fished briefly in the cuff of his gray military gauntlet and produced a small colorless vial of poison.

He walked to the mahogany buffet at the far side of the room and unstoppered the gold-laced decanter of wine sitting thereon. He paused, quickly visualizing his forthcoming actions. A brief conversation with Vincent—the suggestion that perhaps Henri de Casale be freed—and then a toast in the duke's favorite wine to seal the meeting. The plan was so simple as to be amusing.

But somehow the colonel never quite managed to dose the decanter. There were three doors in the chamber. He was able to see two of them, ignoring the third because it was rarely used. He should have been more alert, for as his gloved fingers held the vial poised against the decanter's lip, an amiable voice interrupted him. The voice came from behind—from the direction of that third door.

"Uh-uh, bucko. Naughty, naughty!"

DE BOUSSEY whirled, the poison spilling from his fingers. His ruddy face was twisted with incredulity, astonishment, and fear. "You!" he gasped.

Richard Cleve was standing with his back to the far wall. A disheveled, cloth-torn Cleve, who smiled brightly despite the soot smearing his face. He was holding a rapier carelessly across his thighs.

"Good wine should never be adultered," he said. "Faith! I thought you knew that."

De Boussey's big hand flashed for his swordhilt. His eyes were glinting with the dangerous light of a trapped animal.

"You—you shouldn't have come alone," he whispered. "You shouldn't have come alone, Cleve!"

The Englishman chuckled. "Faith! I didn't, laddie. Look behind you!"

De Boussey swung around to find the doors wide and a full squad of musketeers crammed between the portals with their weapons leveled.

"*Sacré nom!*"

He turned to the next door. It too was open and standing amid a cluster of halbardiers stood Duke Vincent, his aristocratic features grim, accusing. The colonel whirled back to Cleve.

"I'll make you pay for this, you filthy English swine! I'll make you pay with your life!"

But Cleve merely shook his head. "Damme, I'm too cursed weary for more fighting, old man. Been at it all morning, you know." Then he pulled open the door beside him. "However, if you are bent upon exercise, here are some more lads to oblige you."

The door was full of musketeers. Colonel le Vicomte de Boussey suddenly realized the hopelessness of his position. Surrounded! The sight of Orlando standing bound and guarded in the center of these latest guards, seemed to end his resistance.

He stood staring at Cleve with dull, beaten eyes. His plans, his ambitions—swept from under him in a flash!

DE MERION, *capitaine* of the guard, pushed his way through the press and formally relieved de Boussey of his sword. The Colonel stared. He was like a sleepwalker, numbed by incredulity. A moment ago he had had a duchy in his grasp. Now, he was a prisoner.

The colonel shrugged. There was nothing. He appeared incapable of making a move, but to play safe two guards bound his hands behind him. Then, as de Merion gave the command for the escorting musketeers to fall in, there came a sudden clamor of curses from the direction of the hall.

The guards at the main door parted and two men with hands firmly lashed, stumbled into the chamber to sprawl on their knees. They were followed by a third who carried glinting pistols in hand and waved them commandingly at the nearest halbardiers.

"Pick the prisoners up, *mes amis*. Let everyone have a look at them!"

It was d'Entreville, his hat gone, his face dirty and his doublet torn.

"Kitten!" Cleve laughs. "By Gad! Kitten!"

Guy grinned. He accorded Vincent a bow and turned once more to the captives, now being held upright between two guards.

"Monsieur le duc," he said. "May I present two conspirators against the throne of Montferrat, Baron Carl Von Erla of Austria, a notorious agent, and Antone the Archer, one of Montferrat's infamous bandits,"

He paused and cast an oblique look of triumph in Cleve's direction. "Baron Von Erla is the mysterious Baron X, whom Monsieur Cleve and I have been after since arriving in Casale. He is the man whom hired Mazo Gardier and plotted against your life. As for the other, Antone, I shall not enumerate his crimes other than to state that he was Von Erla's accomplice."

DUKE VINCENT was astounded. He had heard of Von Erla vaguely from his correspondence with Richelieu warning him to be on the alert for the man—but Antone was a different matter. Vincent had by attempting for years to lay hands on the ruthless little robber, and now Guy had done it singlehanded where troops of soldiers had failed.

"But *Monsieur le comte,* how did you do this?" he exclaimed. "You required no troops from me. You must have accomplished this miracle alone!"

Guy crossed his arms so that the two pistols angled upward from either elbow and nodded. He was enjoying the moment intensely.

"I *was* alone, *Monsieur le duc,*" he said. "For a while I considered my life at an end. Von Erla and his henchman had captured me and were preparing my death. However I managed to cut my bonds and when they sent one of their band to escort me to the scene of my execution, I overpowered the fellow and took his arms." He waved the pistols. "These weapons, *monsieur.*"

"And then, *monsieur,*" Vincent pressed eagerly.

"And then I confronted the robber-band with the pistols, monsieur. They were collected in one of the rooms of their headquarters. First I made all of them discard their weapons; then I ordered them to bind Baron Von Erla and their leader. They were cowardly louts, *monsieur,* and obeyed, pleading for me not to shoot them."

Guy continued: "Then I forced the robbers at pistol-point to fetch three horses and to scatter the rest. I wanted no pursuit, *monsieur.*"

Vincent nodded understandingly.

"It was very simple after that," Guy concluded. "I forced my prisoners to ride on my either side and held my weapons on them constantly. We passed the robber outposts in the forest easily; I told Antone that I would shoot him if he did not command the men to step aside." He paused smiling grimly. "The men did, *monsieur,* and we arrived at the palace without incident. Truly, a simple feat, *monsieur le duc!*"

"*Mais non!* It was magnificent. Almost as brilliant as the feat of your comrade Lord Cleve, *monsieur!*"

"**ALMOST AS** magnificent?" Guy's eyes widened in surprise. "*Almost?*" he repeated and turned to his comrade. "*Sandiou!* And what have you been about to top that performance, my fine friend?"

Cleve laughed and pointed to de Boussey. Then he told the story with as much brevity as possible. Guy grinned sheepishly when he had heard all.

"*Pecaire,* Richard," he said. "Then, I was wrong concerning the Red Tassel. Perchance it is—"

"Nonsense, Kitten," Cleve interrupted. "Mark this. It's a fact that no one can deny. Between us we have cleaned intrigue from Montferrat and neither of us could have accomplished the business alone. 'Twas you who insisted that we follow those ambushers to that house behind the Golden Crowns. Had I been alone I would have returned to the palace." He grinned. "As a matter of fact, I would never have returned anywhere. I'd have been dead."

D'Entreville saw the point and chuckled. "*Corbac!* As Richelieu has said, one without the other worthless—It seems to bear—"

But the entrance of Mary de Sarasnac interrupted him. Mary had changed her dress, but her face still bore evidence of chimney-soot. She reached Cleve's side and nodded brightly to d'Entreville.

"Ah, *Monsieur le comte.* I see that you have returned in time to join in our triumph. La! 'Tis too bad that you went riding instead of accompanying Richard to the Red Tassel Tavern. Have they told you the incredible plot we discovered there?"

Guy was gaping. "Richard?" he muttered. "We? Our? *Sango-demi!* What has happened between you two?"

Cleve chuckled. "Tell you later, Kitten!" he said. "But right now I believe I shall visit Sir Harry with the return of his dispatch case."

He turned to go, but Mary caught his arm. "Ah no, Richard. Not without me. You asked to be reminded about a rambling country-house in England when this affair was over. La! And now you can speak to me of it while we walk to your friend's suite."

And when they had left, arm in arm, Guy d'Entreville turned to Duke Vincent. The Frenchman knew what had happened well enough.

"Why the dirty double-betraying lout," he roared. And then he broke into a laugh. *"Corbac!* What have I to regret, monsieur? As my wife your ward would have probably been a damned nuisance anyway!"

ABOUT THE AUTHOR

THOSE RAKEHELLIES CLEVE and d'Entreville cover a lot of ground; but in comparison to their creator they're a couple of old mossbacks. Murray Montgomery has been so many places and tried his hand at so many things that he sounds slightly confused by it all.

Maybe that's because he was born in Winnipeg, Canada, on the day Great Britain declared war on Imperial Germany. He says, a little wonderingly, "It was a case of enter Montgomery and commence firing!" During adolescence in New York and on Long Island, he tells us, "I developed a six-foot-one frame; a distaste for polo—the result of a lack of compromise between myself and the horse; and a positive lust for yachting.

"Books had always interested me, so I read prodigiously and after consuming such teen-age tomes as Nietzsche's *On the Genealogy of Morality,* Kant's *Critique of Pure Reason,* Plato's *Republic,* etc., etc., I decided to write something of equal importance. I gave my all to the literary world—and the literary world promptly gave it all back. I decided to become an artist."

At this point the record becomes a little breathless. From ten easy lessons in art he proceeded to trap-drumming "in a snappy little aggregation known as Kings of Rhythm." This particular brand of royalty appears to have been out of fashion at the time, for Murray quickly makes his second appearance as a writer (selling two stories out of twenty), then decides to become an actor.

Follow closely now. He gets a part in a play—and the play closes after a brisk two-day run. He becomes a salesman for the Royal typewriter company. Then he decides to write a play, but first becomes an actor again (the part he gets is in another turkey); takes a fling at producing for the Flushing Summer Theater; and goes barnstorming with a road company of "Let Freedom Ring."

"I lost ten pounds," he comments ruefully, "and a lot of enthusiasm. Returning to New York, I wrote my play. Because the Broadway producers seemed to regret that very much, I got a job as a reporter until the thing blew over."

Still with us? We're almost through. Watching corpses dragged out of the river wasn't quite to Murray's taste, so he gave up police-reporting and went to work for the scenario department of Twentieth Century-Fox.

"They had gotten hold of the play I had written and felt obliged to pay hush-money," he blushes. "Even so, I felt encouraged, so I tried my hand at writing again—and wonder of wonders, sold everything I wrote, with the result that I am still writing."

We like happy endings, and we like Mr. Montgomery and all his works—so there remains only to add a few hearty cheers and the statement that the Rakehellies' papa is now a full-fledged American citizen, resident in Great Neck, Long Island. No puns, please.

THE ARGOSY LIBRARY ™

SERIES 7 INCLUDES:

* BRAND * TUTTLE * BECHDOLT *

HORN * MCCULLEY * ROSCOE *

* HALL & FLINT *

* BEYER * MCCALL *

* MONTGOMERY *

THE BEST FICTION
FROM THE FRANK
A. MUNSEY LINE

www.ingramcontent.com/pod-product-compliance
Lightning Source LLC
Chambersburg PA
CBHW022004010726
47494CB00003B/884